The Prince
of
Almond Manor

By

Gregory Jonathan Scott

DEDICATION

To Scott, as always, I love you and will never, ever hide that I do.

To our beautiful baby boy, Dylan, who inspired Chadwick's
character. Love him so much.
He will always be our little puppy.

To our baby girl, Abigail, a real sweetheart of a kitty cat,
who has a set of beautiful wings in heaven now, and I guarantee,
a halo too.

I cannot forget my comical and caring father William (Willy), who
is my true number one fan and has been ever since I can
remember. His enthusiasm and support with everything I'd set
out to do and accomplished has been cherished and will always
be held dear.
I hear you bragging about me from where I stand, even to the
people you just met. I love that about you and it tells me you
really care.
Thank you for letting me be me, Pop. I love you for that, more
than you know.

The Prince of Almond Manor
Previously published as The Plantation Affair. This book has been revised and expanded considerably from its original version to alter both characters and plot events to enhance the reader's enjoyment.

e Edition November, 2019

Paperback ISBN-13: 9780991467488

Also available in Hardcover ISBN-13: 9798778511446

Published by Gregory Jonathan Scott LLC

gregoryjonathanscott.com

Facebook.com/gregoryjonathanscottauthor

Twitter.com/GregoryJonScott

instagram.com/gregjmeier/

amazon.com/Gregory-Jonathan-Scott/e/B00IGXP82S

ACKNOWLEDGEMENTS

To all those who have a difficult time understanding me, us, him, her and them.

A special acknowledgement goes to Conrad Sutherland-Dunn. Your valuable input was sincerely appreciated.

To Sue Allen Milkovich, an amazing person with heart and soul. Your continued support is totally appreciated.

Chapter 1

A yawn. A stretch. A groan. The wakeup ritual had begun as early as the sun burned over the horizon well before Oakland thought it should have—its unyielding luster boring straight through the window pane, drawing him from his restful sleep.

"Be gone, sun," the grittiness of his groaning had cut through the peaceful morning like an angry axe chopping down a tree. "Six in the morning is way too early for your eye piercing rays. Go. Away."

There hadn't been anything predominantly notable about that morning, nor had Oakland expected it to have been different from any other. He'd followed through with his usual routine—eyelids erratically flickering mere moments following the rooster's daybreak welcome.

There he lay. Slowly coming to life in the upper loft of the small carriage house out behind the large South Georgian Manor where he labored at day after day, along with other servants like him.

3

Squinting to the outside through the bright blazing window, he'd taken hold of the clear skies promise. It was a beautiful morning, however if anything like the days before, knew the sunny welcome would quickly diminish as soon as the dismal shadows of associate Manor staff challenged his attempt at happiness. Every day, he tolerated the direct hostility that seemed personal, unable to understand why the color of his skin had been a key part of the helps ridiculing. Since the year had recently rolled into eighteen eighty-three, it was unclear to him why there should have been a division between people with differences, and seemed skin tone shouldn't have been a motive for violence anymore. Those days of old should have been long gone, curbing the white folk's thoughts regarding cracking a whip if the black family hadn't obeyed a direct order that had no longer stood any grounds. Some people apparently couldn't let that go, would always find blackness deserving of poor treatment.

How much longer would that despicable nonsense go on? People are people.

That glorious morning, Oakland had two choices. Either get out of bed straightaway, or lie prone and expect the ruthless kitchen constable to pound a fist against the door as he'd done so many times before, practically breaking it from the hinges. The less conflict between any staff member and him, the better, and to avoid friction, he forced himself to rise and shine with the hungry hens.

By way of his mother, it was the order of the cards dealt that had placed him at the Manor. At the time, his direct family had been small, only his mother and him. Oakland's father, who he'd never remembered, had been hunted by the organized supremacies back in the day when black skin was considered a lower life form than anything else on earth. Even the grass that had been walked on received more respect.

From what his mother had told him, his father had gone to battle a few years after Oakland was born and had never come home. It was at a time following eradication of slavery where black men had been sent off to war as front linesmen in a fight for freedom. It hadn't quite panned out as making much sense, 'We set you free to fight a battle so _we_ can be free'.

Oakland's mother mentioned a notice had never been received that his father had gone missing, or died in battle, or had been taken away by the enemy. There wasn't any final understanding as to what had happened to him, only guessing he'd been killed during the war and had gone to share a table with the Lord, forever placed to watch over his family from above.

Later during Oakland's teenaged years, his mother had also become a saddened memory, that of which included an incident that had taken place while employed at the Manor. Street bystanders in town reported she'd been trampled by a runaway horse carriage startled by a bandit who had stolen food from a corner merchant. At the time it happened, she had been crossing the street after that morning's trip to the fruit market — understood she never saw the carriage coming. Within that split second after the thief had run by, the horse and buggy knocked her to the ground and dragged her along the cobblestone roadway to her place of death.

That day was dreadful, drastically changing Oakland's life, as would have anybody's. Someone else's selfish act had taken his mother away, and it had taken weeks before Oakland recovered from the loss. He couldn't understand why both his parents had been taken at such a young age, but felt perhaps the reason would become clearer as he moved along with life.

Oakland had never once been ungrateful to the Royal family for keeping him on staff after his mother's sudden passing, but as any child would have done, he still wished for a life that included both his mother and father. Surviving his parents seemed worse to him than anything, with omission to a secret he had of his own that he'd never shared with a living soul.

Even though Oakland's mother had skin as white as snow and it was rare for Caucasian's to work as servants, the Royal's still employed her to work the kitchen. The banquets she prepared were health hardy, and Oakland's sturdy form was proof of a properly fed child who developed into a strapping man.

Oakland's mother had always told him he was as striking as his father, blessed with the same chiseled jawline and full rose-colored lips that exposed teeth as white as pearls when he smiled. Apart from sharing the skin tone of a black father and a white mother, his hazel-gray eyes that shimmered when graced by a hint of light had certainly been inherited from her.

His parents had come to know each other during their short time of employment at the Manor. His father managed the grounds while his mother kept the family fed. The two never married, and in those times couldn't—there were laws, and they might have been stoned in the street if they had. In regards to discovering an unwedded existence with an illegitimate child between them, most people would have cast Oakland aside, or petitioned him for hanging.

Mister and Missus Royal thought a bit differently than most people had, couldn't find much wrong with a fair skinned black boy with gray eyes born to an unwedded couple, much less parents from opposite sides of the color spectrum. People were people as far as they'd mentioned, everybody deserved a pleasant life as much as the next person had, no matter what difficulties life had drawn for them. They had also taught the same human values to their son.

As it turned out, the Almond Manor was the primary place for a couple like Oakland's parents. The property was spacious and secluded, which helped veil the interracial family from bad influences here and there. The world could be a cruel and dangerous place when people hadn't understood what they weren't familiar with. Some turned away in disgust on sight, and many crucified without question because they hadn't been educated to do any different.

Fracturing Oakland's peaceful morning like thunder and lightning had struck, the expected knock on the door had come without suspension, including that nasty tempered kitchen servant hollering for the long awaited breakfast elements.

Oakland rose with a clatter, wearing the same cinder tarnished clothing he had on the day before. He splashed his face with cool water from the tin basin on the cabinet next to his bed and headed over to the wooden plank that brought him to the ground level.

Sleeping in the carriage house behind the Manor with the animals wasn't because Oakland had no other choice, but because he actually liked to. He enjoyed the chickens and goats that shared his home. They never hollered bad words, talked back, or judged him for who he was.

The human race could learn a lot from animals. Truth be told.

The pets Oakland shared a space with hadn't cared he was a man of two shades, or that he was different from other gentlemen. The interests other men found stimulating, he had not. He'd taken admiration for what many other men seemed uninterested in, making him believe he was the only person like himself in the whole entire world. His mother had always told him he was very unique, never to trade his individuality for anything, no matter what. Without any doubt, Oakland held onto that testimonial as if she'd known how deep his distinctive soul had gone.

The sudden thumping at the door caused the chickens underfoot to squabble as if acting out a determined stampede to get away.

"Hush your noise," Oakland shushed, hopping backward onto the sloping platform to give the birds a chance to scatter for safety they seemed to have been in search for.

Encouraged with optimism, Oakland cheerfully whistled in step toward the backside of the carriage house where he retrieved a sack of grain he'd feed the flightless birds. Following him and acting out of line as though impatient, Oakland was rump rammed a few times by goats. He hollered, "Hang on fellas. You're next. Wheat and oats are coming up."

After letting the cows out to pasture, he collected hen laid eggs and carried them to the kitchen along with large buckets of wheat flour he refined a day earlier with the grinding stones. Before he had the chance to tap his toe against the kitchen door to announce he was there, it'd burst open and a big fat woman whose name he'd never taken the time to know pushed through and yelled at him for being thirty seconds late.

He apologized as he always had and carried what he brought to the massive stone counter along the backside of the room.

The moment Oakland spun round, buckets of food scraps had been tossed at him. Waste swirled inside, sloshing across the front of his shirt and down his trousers. Greasy stench and day old egg ignited his septum, triggering a gagging cough he couldn't quit. He'd known the scum dump was purposely done, knew it was coming, but never seemed to have been prepared for the daily assault.

On the way out the door, he'd felt a foot to the rear that propelled him outside. He stumbled, following through with a face plant into spilled slop and spoiling meat parts that sloshed from the buckets. He lay there a moment while servants laughed from the open doorway behind him. He wouldn't look back—refused to give them the satisfaction of his grub covered humiliation.

Standing up with a smile on his face, Oakland thought of how much more the animals were going to enjoy his homecoming dressed in slop.

"Silly brown fool," somebody cackled as the door slammed shut, followed by the sound of the horizontal lock bar dropping into place. The only words missing were, "…and stay out!"

Oakland scooped as much of the slop back into the buckets and carried both to the field near the rear of the carriage house where he met the jubilant pigs who'd run toward him—those pink speechless friends endlessly displayed joy whenever he'd come around. The snorts and grunts of hungry pigs had shown gratitude unlike any single minded human being Oakland had known ever had.

He liked the animals and the home they shared, enjoyed the privacy it provided. During the time Oakland lived outside the manor, he abstained from leering into open windows or doorways, finding it disrespectful as well as meddlesome. His own privacy was important to him, kept his distance when it involved human interaction, and in exchange, respected others who might also prefer the same. That thought made him wonder how many people at the Manor had known he was there next door?

Chapter 2

The Manor towered darkly in the night, appearing ghostly as though it were left to mysterious lifeforms—a few sporadic windows were lit by burning lanterns, only.

Inside and from the catwalk balcony above that overlooked the ground level below, Dante quietly commented to his queen standing beside him. "Look at your child, Priscilla."

Their one and only son solemnly wandered from one end of the grand hall to the other. His hands clasped behind his back, watching his own feet shuffle over the floor.

"He does seem somewhat engaged," Priscilla whispered while looking down on Deklan.

Dante responded, "Does he seem lonely to you?"

She uttered no words, only pursed her lips and tugged at the string of jewels around her narrow neck.

"He needs a companion, somebody to share this business with when the time comes to hand it over, which I'd like to happen sooner than later. I wouldn't mind retiring, or at least cutting back on the amount of work I do. Take up fishing, perhaps. Paint a picture. I don't know," Dante uttered. "It's time he learned more about the almond production process, prepare to take over the business."

"I agree," Miz Priscilla shortly replied. She pressed her poofy skirt with her hands before bringing them together at the front of her jeweled waist.

As though she hadn't known, Dante reminded Priscilla of Deklan's twenty-sixth birthday coming soon, suggested introducing a young lady to him by way of an assembly of the town's people on his birthday.

"A nice idea," She bleeped like a lamb, once again keeping her answer brief.

"Okay then. It's decided. I'm certain we'll find him someone to marry during the celebration." Dante turned to a nearby servant and requested he fetch their son and tell him to meet in the dining hall library on the first floor.

Resembling a nervous weasel about to have been eaten by a hawk, the servant scurried away to convey the request to Deklan.

CS   EO

The dimly lit library was dustier than it should have been, encouraging both Dante and Priscilla to stand without touching anything until the place was properly cleaned.

Deklan entered the large room alone and quietly closed the double wooden doors behind him. Dust billowed from the trim above, floating down around him like snowflakes during wintertime. If it had been Christmas, the experience would have been a wonderland.

"It's time to swipe a dust broom over this place don't you think, father?" Deklan suggested, placing a hand above his head, blocking dusty flakes showering down around him. Stepping closer to his parents, he asked what the unscheduled appointment was all about.

As usual, his father had spoken while his mother stood

quietly nearby.

"My son," – his father begun – "it's time you settled down and involved yourself more in the family business. Almonds are your life and will be your fortune. That's how your mother and I had gotten started, and what better way to learn how to nurture a seedling than in the almond field with the help of a charming wife?"

"What are you saying, father?" Deklan replied, not even hearing the mention of a lady suitress. "Are you going somewhere soon? Is your health all right?"

Miz Priscilla stepped forward. "No my dear, Deklan. We simply want you to be prepared when the time comes for us to hand the business over to you. Have you thought much about a companion?"

"You mean marriage? Well, I… well," he stuttered. "Unh, no… Not really." It seemed a bit soon for making a sudden decision like that and the question of marriage had come at him much too quickly. He wasn't prepared for that, nor had he given much thought about it. He'd dismissed the idea mostly, since the companion he would prefer might not be considered a suitable match for what his parents had in mind to represent the leader of the company. His face changed from red to white in a matter of seconds, and the space between his eyebrows had come together into a tightly twisted knot, muddling his handsome features with fear.

Priscilla glanced at Dante with a concerned expression and then gazed back at Deklan for a better answer.

Interrupting the uncomfortable silence, Deklan's father had spoken on the verge of a whisper, "Son. It is only a matter of time when we'll need to pass this company over to you, our only child. It's important that you're ready to take over the responsibilities as a leader and that you have someone at your side to assist and enjoy it with."

"I'm sorry father, but I'm not ready," Deklan proclaimed. "I don't even know anybody that I find suitable. I'm sorry. I'm not ready for marriage, nor do I even want to get married." His anger increased the more he'd spoken.

"You don't have to make up your mind at this moment," his

father added. "Your birthday is in a few days, so your time will come then. Our thoughts were to arrange a formal event on that night and invite town's people to celebrate with us. Perhaps, during this affair you'll come across a suitable bride, or at least become acquainted with someone you might find suitable to join you in holy matrimony."

Carrying on with aggression, Deklan raised his voice, "Father, please. I don't want a bride or a companion or a, whatever you want to call it right now. I have plenty of time to find a sidekick, but now isn't good."

"Deklan, please," his mother stepped in, holding out her hand as if to comfort her agitated child.

His father rattled, "What do you know about when a good time is? We are wiser, and this is the right time."

Deklan rushed to the libraries exit, turning back with his hand gripping one iron handle. "Do what you must. Order me a Princess, but I cannot promise this engagement will be what you plan or expect." He swung the heavy door open and stormed away.

"That went well," Dante commented, scratching his head. "We'll proceed as planned. He'll come round, I'm sure of it. We know what's best for him. Don't we?" He pounded a pointy finger on the table next to him, then looked at his dust coated fingertip. "This place a filthy sty, it needs a good cleaning. Whose job is that?"

Cষ ৪০

With disregard to the conversation Deklan had with his parents, he stomped down the corridor and out to the horse stables. His heart beating to the point his blood had boiled, feeling the pressure building behind his eyes and turning his ears beet red. He hopped on his favorite steed and rode Chadwick into the woods at lightning speed — the wind blowing his hair back, snapping in sync with the horses mane. He needed to get away — to think on his own.

Deklan felt more alone than he ever had before, and wanted

time to himself to figure a way out of the dreadful heartache producing situation. He rode until he reached an open field overcrowded with cloves. There, he brought Chadwick to a stop and hopped off. The scent of the pungent weeds had relaxed him.

His eye lids had become heavy as he quietly lay next to Chadwick on the ground. He dozed while tussling with wayward thoughts of marriage to a mystery bride he knew for sure he wasn't going to be compatible with.

How was he going to make it through a marriage to a lady if a connection didn't feel the least bit natural to him?

Chapter 3

As though ten lanterns had been shining in his face that evening, insomnia had put a wedge between Oakland and sleep. He lay restless in bed with the farm cat crouched above his head — its sharp tongue grooming the hair on his head synchronized with the rumble of the cat's purring. The rough strokes of the cat's tongue felt incredible until the same spot had been lapped at and started stinging.

The smell of chimney soot on Oakland's body stemmed a stronger odor than it normally had, and to relieve the pungent scent, he'd taken to the outdoors for fresher air.

Dusk had its pleasant moments and the sickle-moon above helped Oakland find his way through the darkness a little bit easier than if the large orbiting satellite hadn't been there at all. Its slim crescent sliver cast just enough light to enable visibility a few steps in front of him, helping with navigation along the sparse trail that felt dry beneath his feet.

The breeze shifted once he'd left the woods and had come upon the open field he favored—the cool zephyr caressing his face. The scent of clover everywhere. The widespread field abundant for acres yet never seemed to have flourished a stem with leaves of four. Good luck had been granted, not.

Hiking eastward, Oakland detected movement in the field ahead of him. Darkness prohibited clear vision, and his imagination illustrated a wild animal might have been nearby. He stood frozen, organizing an escape.

It moved again.

"God, be with me." He held his breath.

Taking the same steps that had brought him to where he'd been standing, Oakland stepped backward. There was no doubt the end of him was closing in, he was on the verge of being ravaged, taken out in the dead of night.

"Tonight's not my night," his whispered tone, unsteady. He quietly stepped back, forestalling the moment the animal pounced. As soon as total desperation overpowered any reason to stick around, he heard a cluck. Had there been that four leafed clover he'd been looking for or had God answered his plea? To his relief, there might have been both.

"Damned bird," he grumbled, immediately trying to corral the hen with open arms. After giving him a fright like she had, he really wanted to choke the chicken, but instead said, "Shouldn't you be in your coop laying eggs for tomorrow's breakfast?"

She stared at him.

"Did you hear me, Betty Lu?" he whispered—his raspy tone on the verge of a holler. "You shouldn't be out here. Now scram." Oakland swung his arms, hopeful she'd scare back home where she belonged. He shifted from side to side, blocking the bird from running in the wrong direction, his own bare feet stung from stepping on dry weeds and sticks.

The chicken had taken off and so had he. If there had been anybody nearby, he surely would have appeared absurd while chasing her down the hill with clapping hands and vocal cries.

Behind him up the hill, Oakland heard thundering footfalls, heavy galloping like that of a large horse. Its pounding hooves amplified. He reacted in time, leaping to the side as the horse raced by.

"Betty Lu," he hollered. "Get out of the way!"

The galloping horse whinnied on meeting the feather flapping bird, stopping sharp as if a wall had been erected. The horse reared up, dumping its rider backward to the ground. Its large image eerily silhouetted by the back drop of the moon. The sight frightening, striking characteristics of a haunted night where the dead had returned to earth. Was that possible?

Forgetting the spooky myth, protective male instincts had kicked in and Oakland dove to pull the rider from under the horses stomping hooves. He held the man tightly in a steely embrace, arms around him like those of a mother bear.

Instantly, gravity had taken over and down the hillside they rolled. Together. Under and over each other.

The chicken fled and the horse had too.

When the force of gravity had given out, the tumbling abruptly stopped. Midway down the hill, they lay face to face, Oakland under the man on top, whose dangling hair concealed his identity in a darkened shadow.

Who was the man that caused a charge so quickly between Oakland's legs, the erect evidence pressing against his hip bone? He lay still for several moments until the man looking down on him shifted, possibly dazed before realizing what had just happened.

Oakland observed the look on the man's face had shone somber, signifying he might have been a little bit stunned from the fall. The silence lingered, and Oakland could feel the man's warm breath sweeping across his cheek and ear. Then, the horseman budged ever so slightly before snapping out of his apparent daze. Shuddering as if startled, the horse rider quickly lifted himself off of Oakland, favoring one leg once he stood.

He sounded frazzled at first. "That... well... Um. Excuse me and my wild horse. I do apologize. Damned chicken should be on a plate next to buttered potatoes and a cob of corn," he stuffily said, flicking clovers from the hair on his chest where his shirt had broken open.

Oakland stared, forgetting to breathe.

A mention of moonbeam had fallen just right across the man's face and Oakland slowly inhaled when he recognized who he was — it was Deklan from the Manor he worked at. Oakland's stomach tightened as if feeling ill. Instantly, he pulled his sealed gaze away, forcing himself to stop staring at the regal man.

While Deklan pounded away the soil clinging to his clothing, he mentioned, "It might not be a good idea to be roaming out in these fields all alone so late at night, you know." His deep crisp voice seemed truly concerned.

Oakland stood, trying not to look Deklan square in the eyes, keeping himself as unrecognizable as possible. He replied, "Yes, kind sir." Even though what Oakland had done on his own time was outside of Deklan's business, he still had gone into detail why he was out in the field all alone in the first place. "I was chasing my chicken, sir." He smirked after realizing the phrase had sounded comical.

Deklan snickered too, covering his mouth with his hand that hid his grin. "Did you see where your chicken ran off to?"

Like a shy child, Oakland tucked his thumbs behind his suspenders, "No sir, but I believe she took off into the woods, heading back home, I'm sure."

Lowering a brow, Deklan mentioned, "Please call me Deklan. Addressing me as sir is too formal and it's strange to be called that by somebody who might be my own age."

Oakland nodded and lowered his head as if Deklan was actually royalty, and duty called to respect his title with a bow. The way Deklan looked back, Oakland sensed he might not know the Manor employed him, and he found it strange he hadn't known.

While Deklan switched his gaze to the moon above, Oakland snuck in a glance and could see the man was focused on something other than what he was doing at the moment, almost as if his thoughts were someplace else, or he was troubled. Deklan's blank stare into space had given clue of that.

"Are you okay?" Oakland asked Deklan, concerned he might have been injured from the tumble off the horse.

Deklan looked himself over, shook out his arms and stamped his feet. "I'm good. Thanks for asking." He smiled. "Are you good?"

"I'm fine." Oakland smiled back, catching Deklan glancing up and down his bare chest right before looking into his eyes.

"It's pretty dark out here. You going to find your way home okay?" Deklan kindly asked, once again sounding concerned.

Oakland repeated he was alright and mentioned he was confident the chicken would lead the way.

Deklan laughed. "Okay. Have a good night, then." He walked over to his grazing horse and mounted it like a champion rider. The horse trotted away, leaving Oakland in the field alone.

On his way back to the carriage house, Oakland mused over how polite Deklan had been. It actually surprised as well as delighted him to find the Prince of the Manor was so kind. Since his family was wealthy and established, Oakland had expected a different attitude and tone from him.

Oakland caught up to Betty Lu, found her hen-pecking the ground in the woods where she'd run off to. When he picked her up to carry her, the silly bird seemed irritated, clucked and squabbled in his arms, possibly out of anger for being off the ground where she felt most comfortable. After some time, Betty Lu had become content and had given in to Oakland's handling at carrying her home.

Chapter 4

Back at the big house, Sir Wattsworth buttled the Manor, organizing Senior Dante's celebration requests in Deklan's honor.

Wattsworth retrieved the Almond business registration stored on a dusty shelf in the Manors library. He started there, identifying the town's most influential people who would most likely attend if invited, as well as ordered note postings to place around the village.

The list of admirable companions Wattsworth put together consisted of many different sorts — from the wealthy to the poorest paupers. All those of whom were able to marry Deklan, slightly older as well as younger.

The following morning had come and the demands of the day rested heavily on Wattsworth's shoulders. Orders to release the invitations to the delivery messengers on standby had been announced. Distributions had to have been then or never.

The chaotic commotion around the messenger wagons

outside the Manor had captured Oakland's attention, motivating him to stop what he'd been doing. He inquisitively watched. At first he thought it was excess trash being removed from the premises, but wondered why he wasn't involved with its removal or why it wasn't being tossed over his head as usual. He stood quietly with the goats and chickens while emptying the kernels of dry corn and weedy wheat stalks into their feeding cribs.

It appeared the place had settled down once the wagons started pulling into the lane, taking the sacks to wherever they had been order to go off to.

Making the decision to mind his own business, Oakland finished filling the animals' breakfast before retrieving what the royal family needed for that morning's meal.

With arms loaded, Oakland stood waiting at the kitchen entrance. He stumbled back a few steps when the big wooden door burst open right before a grasp on his elbow pulled him inside, followed by a shove of a hand between his shoulder blades that thrust him to the back of the kitchen.

To avoid a kick to the britches, Oakland propelled himself out the doorway only to clumsily catch his toe on the threshold under foot. Without the help from anybody else, he tripped down the steps to the ground. Coming from behind, he heard laughing as he'd fallen face first into dirt and spilled slop.

Unlike previous times he'd tumbled at the forceful hand of a servant, a parchment note that might have come from a bucket of garbage had found a place against Oakland's cheek. On standing, the paper piece peeled away and feather floated to the ground, landing with the penmanship clearly within view. He hadn't planned on reading what wasn't meant for him, but he couldn't seem to take his gaze away from those written words.

The letter referred to a birthday event scheduled in the upcoming days, and from what he could tell, the gathering was for Deklan. A specific time hadn't been mentioned, only that everybody was welcome to begin arriving at dusk.

Oakland was pretty certain he wasn't invited, as they—the help—never would have been asked. Dates set aside for celebrations were reserved for the servants to work, hired to serve the family and guests, followed by clean up once the event had ended.

Oakland casually picked up the waste that had spilled over the ground, reaching lastly for the small note that had peeled away from his cheek. As he stretched out an arm, a big-footed boot had come in contact with his rear end.

What the heck and why the need to be so cruel?

Angst-like hollering had come with the foot as Oakland belly glided forward across the ground a few feet. His arms flung forward to catch his fall. Slowly, he looked over his shoulder, finding a tall thin black man reaching for the letter on the ground.

"This doesn't belong to you, little bug," the skinny man resembling a skeleton screeched. "As if there was any chance somebody like you would be invited to a special event like this one. You don't mix with those people any more than we do, and you never will. Now get back to work before I send the hounds after you." The man picked up the letter, glanced at it and folded it into his apron pocket before turning away.

Dirty from the fall, Oakland stood and brushed himself off, gathered the garbage from the ground and headed back to the swine shed to feed the pigs—his real friends.

Oakland musically hummed, keeping his mood from turning mad or sad, and at the same time, thought how pleasant it would have been if he was asked to join the birthday party for, Prince Deklan. He dismissed the thought since those fancy people probably hadn't taken the time to get to know his name, or that he lived in the carriage house behind the Manor.

He proceeded to feed the animals, followed by expiring to the river for a morning bath. The water felt more refreshing than it had any other day—maybe because he was covered with hot dirt that time or perhaps because his head was boiling with anger toward the people who had kicked him down every chance they could get.

Oakland wallowed face up in the water a while longer than he usually had, giving in to the rivers tranquil caressing, allowing it to wash away the bottled up anxiety that had brewed like fire inside his soul. It wasn't common for Oakland to hang out like that, but felt it was the perfect time to take advantage of a good thing, solitude away from those who disliked him for no reason, with hopes of washing it all away.

While floating, he watched two birds above him twittering from one tree to another. They appeared happy, pairing off as a playful couple. He thought about how he'd been alone for so long, and wondered if he'd find that same friendly company one day.

Oakland found comfort floating in the river alone, so much so that he'd lost track of time.

Following only moments of sweet serenity, there had come an obnoxious vocal blow that snapped him out of his perfect daze. The voice familiar. Screeching in the distance like a brass soprano bugle horn.

Splashing to a stance, arms chopping water, Oakland trudged to the riverbank.

Back on track in his wet dirty clothes, he sprinted to the barnyard, hastily gathering the final crops needed for the entire day's food menu.

Dashing to the kitchen, barefoot-fast and smelling like morning dew, he squeezed by the fat black woman yelling at him in the doorway. Her enormous stomach grew bigger as she breathed, and Oakland bounced off the great big orb, shooting him to the back of the room like a fired cannon ball, chuckling with laughter as he ricocheted off her spongy stomach.

On his way out, Oakland paused outside the door, expecting somebody to come after him with additional orders. While standing idle, he checked the order basket under the kitchen window. Nothing there. He moved on.

Whistling a made up song, Oakland wandered back to the carriage house to continue with his already scheduled duties — the same chores he'd taken care of day after day.

While he busied himself at getting his work done, he thought about the celebration and imagined being invited by Deklan. It was a long shot for thinking that, but he dreamt it anyway. Looking to the sky, Oakland wished, "Star light, star bright..."

Oakland wasn't the only one who'd gone into a fantasy trance. Once word had gotten out about Deklan becoming eligible for marriage, young ladies all around turned wickedly giddy.

Their radical behavior was a certain sign at how competitive the maidens were at becoming the chosen Princess of The Royal Manor, to inherit immediate wealth and luxury living.

Heirloom Jewels had been treated with polish. Facial paint was heavily applied to disguise the unsightly blemishes that might deflect the decision of being the chosen one. Dusty hairpieces towered as high as they could go and fastened into place. Curly locks pulled down over the cheekbones to unveil more slimming facial features.

Chaos had broken out in the town square as the hysterical ladies shopped for the most exquisite merchandise that would highlight their assets to the son of the royal empire. Gold and silver brocades, shimmering silks and other fabrics of discriminating taste had been purchased like never before. It was outrageous, as if they'd all gone mad, escalating to girl on girl brawls in the streets. Arguments between consumers occurred at the merchant's counters, fighting to the point of mussing hair and tearing silks in two.

All the rivalry had broken loose as if Deklan was planning to choose his prize by appearance alone. A night to remember was certainly in the making.

Chapter 5

Deklan's event was the first major affair Oakland ever had the privilege of preparing for since he'd been employed by the Manor. He was thrilled about having been assigned to such an occasion, however, the day of gathering turned out to be labor intensive since he was the sole person assigned to stock the kitchen for the big bash. It was a hefty chore—tedious and field trip repetitive.

As far as he knew, the staff had enough elements on hand to build a king sized cake and feed a guest list of one hundred, plus. Understanding he was free to go, he thought about a private trip someplace away from the Manor. If anything more was needed, he still had the morning of the event to finish the necessary delivery.

He'd worked up an appetite from the food runs, and for some reason, had a craving for apples and pears. With the required duties finalized, he'd taken off for the clover field, the place where wafting fragrances of wildflowers, various fruits and cloves had always soothed his body, mind and soul. It was a getaway of all getaways for him.

The slivered moon was thicker than the night before, giving off the right amount of light to illuminate a pathway. The slight breeze coming over the hillside felt good against his bare chest and helped blow the day's heat and humidity away.

Oakland climbed the pear tree and sat comfortably on a sturdy branch, biting into the freshly picked fruit. As expected, the sweet sensation had fulfilled his desire. It was crunchy, and with each bite, he hummed a throaty tune of extreme delight.

He turned, leaning back against the trunk of the tree, straddling the branch, his legs dangling limply down each side. His gaze traveled out across the clover field while enjoying the peacefulness he'd been looking for. Night time bugs and chirping crickets had slowly come to life. All that background noise was the same as if a quartet had been playing.

All too soon and like an interruption of a thunder cloud, his heart sped up when he spotted a figure on horseback trotting over the hill. "Not again," he'd spoken to himself. "Who's coming now?" He wanted isolation, not a party.

His heart beat even faster.

"Wait. It's him. My Prince. I mean THE Prince. Deklan?" Oakland tossed away the pear and finger poked his hair as if combing it out. "Oh Lord, he's coming closer." He checked his chest. All good. Abdomen rippling, too. Better yet.

Out of all the trees in the great big field, Deklan had chosen to pause his horse under the one Oakland had been sitting in.

Oakland stopped chewing, fearing Deklan might hear him. He sat motionless on the branch while watching Deklan quietly dismount his horse and lead the huge animal further under the pear tree.

It was either the breeze or his trivial shifting that caused a few pears to fall from the tree and hit the ground next to the hoof of the horse. *"Oh, sweet surrender,"* he slowly breathed, sitting even more motionless.

Deklan looked down, glancing at the fruit where it landed.

Oakland's heart pounded harder, feeling every thump at the core of his ears. The booming so loud, he was certain Deklan had heard it too.

Bending, Deklan picked up the fallen fruit, polished it on the front of his shirt and had taken a bite, humming from what must have been due to the savory flavor.

Could it have been Oakland's dark skin that had kept him secretly hidden? He was certain it helped, as well as keeping his pearly whites and bright eyes closed—a dead giveaway for a black man under a moonlit sky at nighttime.

Before Deklan had finished his pear, he mounted the horse and trotted out from under the tree.

Discouraged Deklan was leaving, yet somewhat relieved, Oakland released a lung filled breath.

Then, the horse turned around and faced the tree.

Oakland froze.

The expression on Deklan's face and the tipping of his head seemed to have indicated he knew Oakland was there.

"Holy black bollocks!" Oakland ranted. There was no use trying to get out of the predicament he put himself in. He'd been caught.

"Who goes there?" Deklan shouted. His horse recoiled from the sudden outburst, stomping his hooves. Deklan reached to his side as if he was going for a weapon. A dagger perhaps. A flint-locked musket, even.

Oakland sat extremely still. He couldn't move. "Bollocks!" he griped again.

"Come out, would you please," Deklan insisted, grabbing hold of the blade attached to his belt.

Without wavering, Oakland climbed down and stood in the shadows of the pear tree. "Hello again," he meekly muttered without giving his name or letting Deklan see his face. He stepped forward into the moonlight and held his hands in plain sight—his way of making it known he had no weapons.

Deklan removed his hand from the blade and looked down at Oakland. "I had my suspicions it was you in that tree. Why is it that you're always running around at night time? Are you hiding from someone?"

Out of habit, Oakland placed his thumbs behind his suspenders and pushed his broad bare chest forward. "I could ask you the same thing."

"Yes, however I asked the question first." Deklan's horse seemed antsy to get an answer as well.

"Nightfall is the only time I have to myself, plus it's peaceful, and... it's much cooler than during the daytime. I comfortably unwind out here at this time." Oakland was distracted by the sound of a cricket at his feet, prompting him to look down. "Your turn. What about you?" he asked.

Deklan answered briefly, "The same. What you said, except I was expecting to be alone."

"As was I," Oakland replied, intriguingly staring at the huge horse in front of him. He'd seen him before, but never that close. He stepped up to the horse and held out a hand. "May I?" he asked.

Deklan nodded. "I see you found the best fruit tree in the field? This one's my favorite. I mean, pears in general are my favorite. But the tree? This one I like best."

"It's a good one. My preference as well. The tree. The pears. Both actually." Oakland stroked the end of the horse's rubbery nose, and by the beast's reaction, seemed to enjoy Oakland's touch. The horse made snorting noises and bobbed his head up and down as if praising Oakland's generous petting. He must have sensed Oakland's kindness. In return, his big nose nudged Oakland's shoulder as if begging him not to stop.

"No shoes or shirt?" Deklan scanned the front of Oakland. "Do you have a home or do you live out here in these woods?"

Oakland laughed. "These woods? That's funny. No. I have a home. Speaking of which, I should get back before I'm missed."

"Missed?" Deklan seemed curious. "You have a companion? A family?"

"No, no. Just the farm animals. They will miss me if I'm gone too long." Oakland fidgeted nervously with his suspenders.

"I see. You need a ride?" Deklan asked, pulling the reigns to one side. The Clydesdale marched a complete circle, starting and ending with his nose toward Oakland. It's extremely long mane swished Oakland's chest.

Hesitating at first, Oakland replied, "Uh, sure. If there's room up there for two?" He stepped back to allow the massive Clydesdale to move aside.

Deklan reached down and grabbed hold of Oakland's hand. With a hefty tug, lifted him up and over the horse's rump where he landed in the saddle seat behind Deklan. The rear saddle rise forced Oakland forward, his bare chest pressing tightly against Deklan's back.

"Wow. You're a solid man, aren't you? Like a stone." Deklan commented when Oakland bumped against him.

Oakland inhaled, taking in Deklan's scent, smelling sharp wood smoked spices and soothing lavender. It was an interesting combination for a grown man, however, Oakland found that specific fragrance suitable for a person like him.

"Ready? Hang on." Deklan turned the horse around and headed up the hill.

The sudden commotion jostled Oakland's balance and he responded by wrapping his arms securely around Deklan's waist, locking his fingers over the buckle on his belt. "Whoa," he said. "Sorry." Oakland loosened his grip.

"Whoa?" Deklan laughed and quickly placed his hand over Oakland's to hold them in place. "Don't be sorry. I told you to hang on. Chadwick can ride a bit rough, but if he feels you shift, he'll lean to keep you upright. He's smart like that."

Oakland inhaled, followed by a quick exhale, leaving his hands right where he'd first placed them.

"Omigawd, his hair smells fine." The light brown wisps of Deklan's shoulder length hair snapped in the wind, brushing like feathers over Oakland's cheeks.

Deklan gently cracked the reigns. "Where to, my kind sir?"

"You're headed in the right direction. Continue on," Oakland replied.

It had taken about five minutes before the Manor had come into view up ahead. Oakland stayed quiet the entire time and found it strange that Deklan hadn't asked his name or anything about him. Not to go against what he himself was thinking, but he hadn't asked Deklan any questions either.

Deklan slowed the Clydesdale with a tug at the reigns. "Hey," he spoke to Oakland. "The Manor is just ahead. Where do I let you off?"

Oakland acted like he wasn't paying attention. "Oh!" he perked up. "You can let me go here. I can walk the rest of the way."

"Don't be slight. Where to?" Deklan insisted.

"Right here is good with me." Oakland unlocked his fingers from Deklan's waist, slowly pulling his hands loose.

"Really? Here?" Deklan stammered.

"Yes Really. You can drop me off right here." Oakland was about to hop off while the horse was still moving, but before he had a chance, Deklan tugged Chadwick to a stop.

"Oh-kaay," Deklan's voice had gone singsong as he twisted in the saddle. "Then this is your stop." He cross reached for Oakland's hand, helping him down, the grip tight and lasted longer than it probably needed to. Oakland noticed the man's touch was warm and could tell his heart might have been too.

Deklan corralled the horse around until he was facing Oakland on the ground. He squinted as if trying to memorize Oakland's face.

Shyly, Oakland looked away. His gaze hadn't focused on anything, he just wasn't content with letting Deklan know who he was, or that he maintained the kitchen that served meals to him and his family.

Oakland raised a saluting hand toward Deklan. "I suppose I'll see you around? Maybe under a pear tree?" His thumbs met his suspenders at his chest before sliding to his waist.

Deklan smiled down on Oakland, eyes directly on his caramel colored chest as it projected forward with labored strength. Deklan nodded and then squeezed Chadwick's ribs with the heels of his boots. He cracked his cheek a few times, prompting the horse to get moving.

Oakland had a silly-happy-feeling going on inside the pit of his stomach as he watched Deklan leave on horseback. It was good and a first for him. The Prince's long dark hair flipped softly in the breeze when he twisted in his saddle one more time to have a look.

On the way back to the carriage house, Oakland felt struck by jubilance, whistling joyful tunes as one would do if infatuated.

When he opened the door to his place, a goat scornfully bleeped at him as if he'd been gone for days, and Oakland was sure he'd heard, "Baaaaahd, daaaaaahd."

Chapter 6

The day that followed was lively at the Manor, every servant seemed frazzled as if they'd never hosted a party before. Oakland had a laugh at that while he watched from the window of his tiny cabin. Wagons delivering what appeared to have consisted of party effects were coming and going. By the way the staff scrambled inside and outside the mansion, looking like nervous ants milling for food, he could tell the evening was going to remain active until dawn.

Erected in the expansive backyard were two gigantic canvas rooftop covers. One placed on each side of the lengthy pool running from the rear of the house to the furthest point of the property. The pool was enormous and Oakland wondered why anybody would need one that large. He figured the tents were meant for shade as well as cover for the food on the menu.

Visually counting workers on the grounds, Oakland might have been the only employee who hadn't been invited to help put the party together. He recognized most of the staff from the kitchen, and a few he'd seen from time to time around the manor. He presumed the skinny black man who kicked dirt in his eye and revoked the invitation the other day was correct—he didn't belong with those people and probably never would.

That wasn't a big deal to Oakland. He'd been content with the life he'd been handed, and most of the time, was happy just being left alone. People bothered him, and the ones he'd been acquainted with, kicked him when he was down and pushed him around when he was up. He was a loner mostly because of that, had everything at his disposal in order to survive, and probably more than most other people had.

Oakland continued wondering what it would have been like if he had been invited to the birthday celebration and what would have happened if he'd run into Deklan while there. The fantasy Prince seemed kind during the past few times they'd communicated, and Oakland could easily see them as mates. The idea of that had Oakland's stomach tossing in a good way. He knew how he himself felt, but wasn't sure if Deklan was feeling the same way. The horseback ride the night before had certainly introduced questions he had about Deklan. The clasping of hands and the eye contact had given a slight indication what Deklan might have been interested in. The thought of what could come of the two of them had left Oakland smiling, which then turned into a full blown grin the more he wondered about what could transpire once meeting up again.

Without actually having been invited to the Manor's celebration, on the upside, Oakland would have been close enough at the carriage house to have seen the birthday event carrying on. He wouldn't have been dancing and dining with the Prince, but if he could have heard the music and witnessed the laughter, he would have considered that as good as actually being there. While Oakland sat at the window next to his bed on the second floor watching all the commotion going on down below, he saw a door open at the south side of the Manor that was rarely used. In fact, he hadn't remembered ever seeing it open and close. His face had lit up when he spotted who had come out of that door. To Oakland, it appeared that Deklan had been escaping from whatever was taking place inside.

As though trying not to be seen, he saw Deklan sidestepping with his back against the Manor wall. The Prince crept craftily to the corner of the house before taking off with a crouched gallop toward the field where the two of them had recently been running into each other. The thought was crazy, but Oakland wondered if Deklan might have been planning to seek him out again, the mystery man he continued meeting in isolated places.

Deklan's strong physique wasn't easy for Oakland to ignore. He liked the way the man looked and the way his shoulder length hair flipped away from his face as he ran. He thought about following Deklan wherever he was headed, make believe he'd come across him by accident again, but decided to stay put and keep his admiration for the Almond Prince his own secret.

Oakland could hardly sit still, and instead of chasing after the man, only watched Deklan disappear into the thick foliage of the forest. Inquisitively thinking, Oakland wondered why he was running into the woods alone. Was he heading out to meet somebody? A secret affair? Was it he who Deklan might be searching for? Oakland could have only hoped.

Repressing the urge to jump out the window, Oakland sat back at last, pleased with himself for choosing not to dash after his first true heart's desire.

That was the first time Oakland allowed his infatuation for another man to unfold. It was as though a strong force had been pulling the two of them together. He felt it, and the way Deklan acted the other day, he must have felt it too. Oakland's heart was finally opening up to a man he found desirable. He fidgeted nervously before pulling himself away from the window, contemplating one more time if he should stay or go. Even though he hadn't cared for his final decision, principles had won the battle.

He moved to the bed, lying back with his arms angled under the back of his head, gazing into emptiness the ceiling offered, unable to get the images of Deklan out of his thoughts. Even under moon shadowed lighting, he found the man attractive. It was his sturdy features that held his attention. The few times they'd met, Deklan's handsome face and gleaming eyes had permanently lodged in his memory. There was elevated brilliance within his aura that Oakland couldn't quite explain, almost a sheen that hypnotized and pulled him in.

He rolled to his side and stared out the window while listening to the outside noise as if it were inside the room with him. It was the distraction he needed that would bring him back to reality. The stray cat he named Elmer was another helpful diversion, walking the bridge of his body from toe to shoulder and settling on the pillow where he proceeded with the hair licking ritual that had taken place almost every single night. The scratch of the cat's tongue against his scalp had helped curb his thoughts, but only slightly since Deklan was such a prominent image he couldn't shake.

Oakland then heard Wattsworth shouting orders to the staff, telling them everything for Deklan's twenty-sixth birthday celebration had to be in place well before the guests arrived the next day.

As if the party shouldn't have taken place, clouds suddenly covered the sky and defeated the sun that instant. It turned the grounds dark and rain had come down hard.

ᄋᲐ Ᏸᦞ

Into the woods, Deklan had taken off from the manor for good reason, trying to outrun the plan of his future set in place by his parents. He wasn't interested in getting married to somebody he had never met, much less to a female and... "Oh Gawd," coming in contact with her vagina. He wasn't born the man he was expected to become. He was attracted to men, never found that allure with the ladies. His anxiety had gotten the best of him and he needed to get out of that house.

Deklan had eventually come to a narrow brook and clumsily jumped to the other side. His foot slipped on a mossy rock and he grumbled as the water filled his boot.

He left the stream at a slower pace, surrendering to the rain that had suddenly taken hold of him. He'd found refuge under the fullest tree, distraught with his situation, but satisfied he was far away from what reminded him of why he'd run away in the first place.

Deklan reached for a bright red apple dangling from a twig above his head, scrubbed it against his wet shirt and had taken a horse sized bite—the tartness turning his face into a screwy knot. At that moment as if the sharpness of the apple had told him any place he'd run to would be sour, he rationalized and decided it might have been best to return home and face his qualms head on.

Unhappy and miserably wet, feeling nothing less than that of a prisoner, Deklan slogged through the misty woods, feeling wet brush, sticky ground cover, and grabby tree branches. He shivered from the freezing rain trickling down his back, and the cold air skimming his dampened flesh. He sneezed. Strands of wet hair snapped his cheeks.

It wasn't until he was emotionally alone with his gloom when he spotted the illuminated windows in the Manor ahead. He had become hesitant about taking another step toward the lights, and instead, settled under another tree and let the rain take over his surroundings. He was soaked, but hadn't cared. Somehow, saturated seemed better than being flooded by proposals of marriage at home. He wanted to stay where he was— wet, miserable, and senselessly troubled by activities other than those of his own. He stayed put and shivered, slumping to the ground beneath another tree, sitting with his back against rough bark. He closed his eyes and let the scalding anger take claim to him. Rain had mixed with burning tears from a strong man breaking down.

For a long time, he remained motionless before rising to his feet. He looked continuously around the area as if expecting lightning to strike, listening intently while peering out into the downpour. It was cold and hazy, much like a soppy winter's day.

A few moments had passed, and to Deklan's disbelief, the clouds moved out of the sky and the sun quickly vanquished the rain, providing him somehow with the sense of being rescued. When the first rays of light struggled through the low hanging deck of clouds, he looked to the right and then the left, uncertain of which direction he should have gone. Home or further away?

He left the tree and headed for the barn to meet with Chadwick, hopped on and rode bareback into the open fields someplace far, far, away. The late evening sun had warmed its way through the cloud cover, giving him relief from the chilling dampness.

Time had flown by quickly before Deklan realized nightfall had snuck up on him. His eyes had sneakily adjusted to the dusky eve of the sunless sky and before he knew it, he was running Chadwick into the peaceful night.

Chapter 7

It had become noticeably late, and there was nowhere Oakland had to be or anybody he needed to clean up after, leaving the rest of the evening open to himself. A swim up river seemed like a grand idea.

Swimming bare, the chill of the water stimulated him. His feet paddling lightly as he crawled on his hands along the rivers rocky bed, stopping at a place shallow enough to roll over and lay back, letting fresh air caress his exposed body from head to toe and every part in between. He was a free spirit at that moment and it certainly felt good, no doubt. He wasn't sure if it had been the cool breeze racing across his body that made him tremble or because certain areas normally covered had gotten blown by the whispering cool night air.

Even though Oakland was alone in the dark, he was compelled to cover up with the largest water lily he could find. He floundered—his arms and legs outstretched over the surface of the water, helping him float. He listened to creatures of the night communicating with one another. It was a peaceful sound. Relaxation had come to him easily, even with the noises recognized as birds, crickets and creeping bugs.

∞ ∞

While trudging through the undergrowth along the river's edge, ignoring the snapping twigs and spongy mush beneath his and Chadwick's feet, Deklan had come upon a pair of trousers slung over the branch of a tree as well as freshly set barefoot prints on the ground that pivoted into the river.

Deklan's original plan had been to flee the Manor in search of refuge and silence. That specific jaunt was meant to avoid the constant reminder he was soon to marry a powder puffed female and her... "Oh Gawd," wet vagina.

Even though Deklan preferred to have been left alone with his thoughts, his curiosity pricked his desire to find out whose britches had been flung into that tree. Searching for a naked gentleman was a guaranteed and enticing distraction, as well as help keep his mind off home and an assigned maiden waiting for him.

He hopped back onto Chadwick and strolled along the mushy bank while scanning the river the entire trip. The darkness had taken possession of the woods, increasing the difficulty of seeing much of anything, but the slim reflection of the moon across the water's surface had been helpful with locating any possible movement out there.

The soft ground under Chadwick's hooves left his footsteps quiet, and if there had been anybody swimming or lodging nearby, they'd have been surprised by the horse's subtle appearance.

∞ ∞

While Oakland lay in the river, he couldn't get his mind off

Deklan. To him, the man was striking on all aspects of a human being, and the fact he was a gentleman, had made for a more appealing man.

He exhaled, reminiscing over Deklan's aristocratic facial features during the short time he'd been with him before—the square chin and sharp nose, the angular jaw line lightly shadowed with dark facial hair. His fair complexion had absorbed the glistening beams from the moon, and reflected off his flesh like shimmering diamonds—a feature Oakland liked, that of which was much different from his own caramel skin. Deklan's bright blue eyes fringed by long lashes dazzled like polished sapphires behind free dangling strands of long dark brown hair that had fallen loosely from the short ponytail tied at the back of his head.

Going along with his desires, Oakland stiffened below the waist while he thought how strong and solid Deklan's body felt during the brief encounter they had while rolling in an arm-lock down the hillside. Once landing, Oakland recalled getting a glimpse of Deklan's chest through his open shirt, and how it was dusted with hair resembling wisps of fine feathers. His attraction to a man with a hairy chest almost outranked a striking face. He'd also noticed how Deklan carried himself with virile qualities, and the masculine strength had naturally appealed to Oakland.

Snatching Oakland from his fantasy, he'd caught sight of Deklan towering above him on horseback.

Whoa! Surprise! What? When? Where had Deklan come from? Was he dreaming or was reality really happening?

Deklan's stealthy arrival startled Oakland, causing him to shriek while manically trying to stand and cover his male defining body parts. Water splashed and waves rippled inland. He stood knee-knocked, like that of a stork who'd lost its balance. He attempted to cover up with clumsy hands, but his exaggerated male organ wouldn't allow any sort of success at concealing what protruded so grandly between his legs. There was a lot there, he knew himself, and two hands were never enough to hold it all in place.

As if astonished by what he'd seen, Deklan stared. Eyes bulging. His mouth dropped open as if he had just seen the sun come out at nighttime.

Oakland thought he heard, "Holy mother of the blackened forest, that thing is huge."

Deklan quickly blinked and mumbled, "H-hey." He broke contact with Oakland's oversized dick and transferred his gaze to his face. Becoming more composed, he added, "You'll catch a chill if you run around in the night like that."

Oakland wasn't able to identify if Deklan was cracking a joke or if the man was being serious with his comment. To reduce mortification, Oakland kept eye contact away from meeting Deklan's, purposely only letting him see the topside of his scalp. Not only was Oakland embarrassed about standing naked in front of Deklan, he wasn't thrilled about the horseman putting a face to a caramel colored stork with a significantly sized male organ that made him appear deformed down there. He held what he had in place as best he could—struggling to detain eleven inches of thick black dick behind a pair of hands that appeared dwarfed in front of it.

Since wearing nothing and possibly looking different the way he was, Oakland remained hopeful Deklan hadn't recognized him from the night before. He calmly turned and walked along the riverbank to the place he'd left his trousers.

In equal steps, Deklan followed on horseback.

Feeling somewhat awkward, Oakland wasn't sure what to do with himself—walk without saying anything, or strike up a conversation—in the nude. With his bare butt facing Deklan, he sensed the man was watching it flex with every step he'd taken. Mortified from being naked, Oakland wanted nothing more than to put his pants on. It hadn't seemed fair game since Deklan wasn't naked too.

Breaking the silence, Deklan finally mentioned, "Aren't you the one I ran into a couple nights ago in the clover field?"

Oakland wanted to run away. For real. "Unh. I was there."

"Running into you again is a pleasant surprise." Deklan was smiling.

"Yes. It is. For me, too. I suppose. However..." If Oakland had been correct, he could feel Deklan's gaze burning a hole into his rear end and wondered if Deklan liked what he was looking at. Probably true since the horseman followed a few steps behind, taking in a birds eye view of Oakland's better assets.

"I have to admit, this was not the view I had expected this evening, but it bodes better than what I was up against earlier at the Manor," Deklan said as if he'd heard Oakland's thoughts about staring at his dimpled butt cheeks.

Grinning, Oakland wondered, *"My ass? Does that mean he likes my ass?"*

Chapter 8

The big day had arrived and there were only a few hours to finish what needed to be taken care of at the Manor before guests started showing up. It was clear Wattsworth was running on spurts of steam. Nightfall was closing in and soon there would have been wagons pulling up to the house with potential brides for, Prince Deklan.

Oakland hadn't quite figured Deklan out yet, but he was near certain a female bride wasn't part of his future plans.

Noticing the sun had already dissolved below the horizon, Oakland spotted the lighted torches alongside the walkway of the Manor's entry glowing a little bit brighter. Against the darkening sky, the lanterns burned charmingly and had become more vivid as time passed on.

Oakland quietly hummed a ditty of a song he'd made up at that moment while glancing up at the candlelight's flickering in the small windows scattered along the backside of the manor's walls. He could see a few images moving behind the lights while flitting about at getting ready for the fancy evening.

Instead of gazing at what he wasn't part of, he'd taken to the river and floundered face up until his dream seemed real. Oakland found a joyful moment and thought if his fantasy had actually come to life, it would have been best if he met his Prince fresh and clean.

The night was peaceful, with exception of crickets and frogs voicing their opinions as to who could croak the loudest.

Oakland floated on the surface of the water, listening, falling hostage to the tranquility of every tone. It was as if he'd been transported to a magical place. One he might not have wanted to return from.

He dried off with a cotton cloth he'd made from an old dress apron of his mother's before covering himself and creeping back to the carriage house. He aimed head on toward the candlelight he'd left burning in his bedside window that always simplified his return home during nightfall.

Before going inside his cozy cabin, Oakland looked at all the horse drawn carriages lined at the Manor's front entry. The vision was remarkable, and it astounded him to see how many people were actually going to be filling the Manor's ballroom, all of them wanting a piece of the Prince inside.

Oakland let out a sigh, wishing he could have been part of the gathering, however instead, finished out his evening inside his barn-style house with chickens and goats.

The moment he put on a nightshirt, he heard rustling outside his front door, followed by a gentle rap against its frame — the sound resembling that of a wooden stick, perhaps one meant for walking.

"Who'd be at my door this time of evening?" he asked, casually speaking to a chicken standing next to him. He pushed the bird out of his path with his foot and peeked through an open crack in the door where he found a white man his size standing there.

Puzzled by who the person could have been, Oakland paused before opening the door to someone unfamiliar. The gentle rap of that wooden stick he'd heard a moment ago tapped again. Wood against wood echoed inside the carriage house like a woodpecker hammering away at a tree. The chickens ran away and the goats backed into a corner at the rear.

When Oakland opened the door, he found a man he'd never seen before standing on the stoop. Their gazes met eye to eye. He was super thin, or it was the pinstriped pants and jacket he was wearing that made him appear as though he was. By the clothing he had on, Oakland figured he'd come from someplace outside the village. The skinny man looked out of place, suggesting to Oakland an invitation inside would have been a bad idea.

Oakland asked if he'd lost his way, mentioning the birthday celebration for Deklan was across the yard at the Manor.

The skinny man glanced over his shoulder and before turning back around said, "Oh no. I'm not here for any party. I've come to see you."

A little baffled by the man's response, Oakland pursed his lips as if he was about to say, *"What?"*, then pinching his brows together in the middle and questioned, "To see me?" instead.

The man repeated, "I'm here to see you, Oakland. I have a gift from your father." The man's tone was formal when he spoke.

Oakland stood with a puzzled gaze, wondering who the man was and how he knew his name. Knowing his father had passed on years ago, had Oakland second guessing the person at his door was being truthful.

"May I come in before the chickens decide to run free?" the man asked.

Rummaging for words and fumbling with the handle on the door, Oakland waved for him to come inside. "Yeah. Unh, sure. Come in. Guests are always welcome."

Oakland looked at him for several moments, finding quite a resemblance between the two of them. He blinked to clear his head.

A chicken clucked, breaking the sketchy silence.

"I don't have much to offer sir, but you're welcome to a mug of water and a fresh apple I picked today," Oakland nervously said. "Can I get you one or both?"

"No thank you, Oakland. My time here is limited," he

replied, fussing with the large tattered box he had tucked under his arm. He laid it on a rickety table at the right of the door. "This is for you. From your father." He tapped its mushy lid.

"My Father? He's been gone for many years." Oakland wasn't sure what was going on, but it was truly an occurrence out of the ordinary.

First an unknown stranger tapped on his door wearing clothing outside the current times. He looked a lot like Oakland, except the man was clearly completely Caucasian. Apart from their skin tone differences, they could have been twins if the man was more muscular from labor. It was as if Oakland was looking at a mirrored image. The gentleman's face was so close to his own.

The visitor looked at Oakland and said, "It's time to dig deep and believe."

With that being said, Oakland's curiosity of the supernatural spiked. The situation appeared somewhat mystical, leaving him to wonder if he'd drown in the river, and what had been taking place was part of passing on. He pinched himself to be sure. It hurt. Then when the chicken pecked his bare toe? That hurt, too. He was very much alive.

What was happening? It was all so strange.

The man in the pinstriped suit asked Oakland to sit down at the table next to the box he delivered.

Doing what had been asked, Oakland waited for the man to divulge with a reason for his unexpected visit.

The thin man laid a hand on the box top and had taken a deep breath before speaking.

Clutching the seat of his chair, Oakland first glanced at the box and then transfixed his gaze on the peculiar man touching it. His head was hurting, but wasn't sure the pain was physical. None of what had taken place seemed real. With all the unexplained illusions, Oakland found it outlandish to ask the man's name. Instead, he self named him, The Mirror Man. That suited him since he was quite like Oakland's own reflection.

Oakland noticed a faint glow around the Mirror Man's face and wondered if it was coming from the candle light next to his bed upstairs or if the mystery man was actually shining.

The Mirror Man had eloquently spoken, "This old box from your father was to be given to you on a night that was going to be significant—a night you would always remember."

A chill sped up Oakland's back, and just like that, the joy he'd felt in the river earlier had disappeared. For some reason, he had a feeling the man was about to tell him what he was already aware of. The thing Oakland hadn't known was what could be in the tattered box and how it related to what the Mirror Man was planning to say to him.

Should he believe? It seemed farfetched and more like a fairytale.

Oakland wasn't too certain of when it started, but he noticed his neck muscles had tightened, practically strangling his brain and cutting off airflow to his lungs.

The Mirror Man softly rubbed his fingertips in a loose manner over the box top and proceeded to tell Oakland why he was at his home. "This might seem a bit extreme, so I would like you to stay seated, if you please. Think of me as… your godfather, like… a fairy, but without a set of pretty wings."

Oakland swallowed and tried to remain calm. What the Mirror Man had said seemed absurd, making no sense at all. There's no such thing as fairies.

Had death really come to Oakland in the river out back? It certainly felt it had.

"Tonight you are going to meet somebody amazingly special." The Mirror Man moved his hand to the edge of the box top as if he was planning to open it, but hesitated. He carried on, speaking in such a ceremonial manner, Oakland could hardly understand what had been said. "I'm your sentinel for the evening, however, only for tonight. As you might know, I'm a clear resemblance of your father, an extension of his inner spirit, which is meant to ease your acceptance of me. Nobody other than you can see or hear me. I'm here to guide you to the calls of your inner heart. You have grown up to be the man your father expected, and his ultimate wish is for you to be yourself as well as be happy. I come to guide you during a time that won't be easy for you or your heaven selected soul mate. In this box, I pass on to you some confidence that will help charm your harmonized soul. You'll know who that person is the moment you set eyes on one another. Wear the contents of this box to this evening's celebration, Oakland. But know it can only be with you this one time and only until the clock tower strikes midnight."

Oakland swallowed another time, his throat feeling dryer than before. The sensation of ingesting a pinecone had been evident, and it had gone down hard. He stuttered, "B-But wait. I'm… not the kind of person you might think. I'm different from other men. Very different. Exhibiting affection in a public place the way it feels natural to me isn't that simple. I'd be ridiculed, or even stoned, possibly put to death. Whatever's inside that box won't make me what I am not. I can't take anything inside it. This won't work, and I'm not certain I want it to. Not even tonight until midnight." Oakland stammered and his voice lowered, "This won't work for someone like me. I'm…"

The Mirror Man placed a finger in front of his own lips, signaling Oakland to stop talking. "It's all right. Your father and I know everything about you—even the thought in your head this very moment. Sadly, much of this world isn't ready for somebody like you, however, like everything, in time, this world will come around. Until then, you are its stepping stone. Mind you, this journey won't be cakes and cookies, but trust that love will find a way."

The Mirror Man walked around Oakland's backside and positioned both hands on his tensing shoulders. He lowered his voice to almost a whisper, "I come from your father's spirit, as a guide to help you find your soul mate. In this box, you'll have what you need, and outside, there's a horse and carriage standing by. Now… it's time to be the Prince your father knows you to be."

"But…" Oakland started.

"No buts. You must believe," the Mirror Man interrupted. "Open the box. You must hurry. There's no time to waste."

"How will I know I've met my soul mate?" Oakland asked.

"You'll know. Just believe. Now hurry. I can do many magical things, but I can't stop time."

Doubtful of the Mirror Man's comment, Oakland sluggishly released the hold he had on the chair and stood. He gently secured his grip to both sides of the tattered box and lifted. There was a sudden odor of mildew as soon as the cover cleared the box bottom but immediately disappeared, followed by glistening smoke swirling above the opening box. Then, as if the wind had shifted, the scent of roses and cinnamon sticks derived from the mist in front of them.

Oakland had begun to relax as if the magic dust coming from the box was a comfort potion. He was mesmerized, unable to pull his gaze away—becoming even more relaxed. At that moment, Oakland hadn't realized the Mirror Man let go of his shoulders, but as the mystical fog evaporated, he saw his father's image facing him on the other side of the table all over again. It had to have been his angel. His guardian. Or what the Mirror Man referred to as, his fairy godfather.

Oakland stood quietly while peering into the tattered box, where which he'd found the most spectacular bundle of fabrics he'd ever seen in his entire life. He wasn't used to such fine quality dress wear, only the wooly work clothes he'd worn day after day. He held his hand above it as if sensing heat, feeling as though he should only look and refrain from touching.

"Go ahead, take hold of it," the Mirror Man whispered with a smile. "It's yours for the evening. It will bring you good luck, and the one soul who is supposed to notice you, will." His tone had gone much quieter and his whisper sounded that of breathy air when he said, "Believe."

Reaching into its ragged home, Oakland carefully lifted the brilliant gown as though it would disintegrate if handled too roughly. The first piece appeared to be a blouse made of pure white silk, tailored with rich gold thread and the front placket had two double-breasted rows of silver buttons from bottom to top. It had a large wide collar that would stand high and crisp along his jawline with a bow-like scarf to tie around his neck. The double layered cuffs on the long sleeved shirt were fastened together with two silver links. He thought the blouse was too brilliant and he wouldn't feel worthy enough wearing an item so magnificent.

"It's yours, Oakland. Put it on." The Mirror Man's voice sounded different. Like a father's voice. Perhaps his own father's voice.

Afraid he'd tarnish its splendor, Oakland held back a few moments before continuing. Anxiously, but carefully, he removed his nightshirt and put the silk blouse on. The fit couldn't have been more perfect. It was made for him.

The Mirror Man first helped Oakland button it up before neatly tying the bow-tie around his neck.

Oakland reached for the item that had been folded under the shirt, gently removing and putting the shin length trousers on. They were also of the same fine white silk only woven heavier than the blouse. He carefully fastened the front flap by the silver buttons at each hip. Seeing the look on the Mirror Man's face had indicated to Oakland he was doing fine.

"Dashing," said the fairy man. "Keep going. There's more." He pointed.

Oakland reached into the box again and pulled out a lightweight auburn overcoat that looked as though it would reach below his knees. He ran his finger along the gold stitching lining the lapel and then circled the rims of each gold button that had reflected sparks of light around the room.

Oakland's personal fairy godfather assisted him with putting the coat on, fitting it in place just right. He'd left the coat open in the middle to allow the shirt and trousers beneath to remain visible, fastening it all in place with the wide leather belt channeled through the large square buckle crafted of brilliant silver.

There was another item of clothing inside the box as if the bottom of it was never ending. But before Oakland had taken hold of whatever it was, the Mirror Man removed a heavy silver necklace from around his own neck and transferred it to Oakland's. It hung graciously against his chest with an emerald Fleur-De-Lis pendant resting in front of his heart. Unsure if the Mirror Man had known, but the green gemstone was Oakland's favorite.

The Mirror Man steadily stepped backward and motioned for Oakland to retrieve the final article of clothing from the box.

Inside he discovered a vanilla brocade cloak edged in more golden trim work. When Oakland draped it over his shoulders, the coat had broadened his stature by about ten or more inches. He felt masculine, and if he were able to wed a man, that would certainly be his garment of choice.

The Mirror Man handed him knee high stockings of white silk. Oakland hadn't noticed before, but the footwear the godfather had on were made of tanned vanilla leather and fastened with bold silver buckles that coordinated with the belt already fixed around his waist.

The Mirror Man slipped off the shoes and handed them to Oakland, telling him they were his to wear. Once more, the fit was perfect.

"What about you?" Oakland asked while he slipped his feet into the comfortable shoes.

"Don't worry about me, I'm always prepared." The fairy's feet were magically covered in chocolate brown slippers with a gold threaded Fleur-De-Lis emblem embroidered on the topside vamp.

"Where did those come from?" Oakland stared, finding truth in all the mystical events going on around him.

Where was he? Dreamland? Perhaps really Dead? Was he in fairytale land or someplace of the like?

Oakland wanted to see how he looked with all the new clothing on, but there was no looking glass or reflective surface nearby for him to gaze into.

The Mirror Man spun a white gold ring over his knuckle and had taken it off. "One more polished item to refine your ensemble." He held up the jewelry piece he removed from his finger. "Take this ring. Together with the necklace around your neck, you and your soul mate will remain protected."

Oakland held out his left hand and the Mirror Man slipped the ring onto Oakland's marriage finger where it fit best, and seemed as though it belonged there. He gripped the medallion and held his fist tightly against his chest. A deluge of emotion had broken free and Oakland's eyes glazed over. He could feel an endearing soul moving closer to his. It was at that moment he'd begun to believe.

"I know you're not able to see what I see in front of me, but understand when I tell you this. You look striking and your true love will know who you are when you walk into the room." The Mirror Man opened his arms and wrapped them around Oakland's shoulders, hugging him.

"Thank you for seeing what I don't." Oakland hugged back.

"Time to go." Stepping away from Oakland at full arm's length, the Mirror Man swung his left hand toward the door, opening up a pathway for Oakland to follow. "Your carriage waits outside that door."

At first Oakland thought a carriage was a bit much since he could walk to the Manor in a few long strides, but the idea of a horse drawn buggy delivering him to the doorstep of the Prince's palace would have been another magical moment for that evening's fairy tale.

When Oakland stepped up to the open carriage, he caught a glimpse of his reflection in a puddle on the ground. It wasn't clear, but he stopped to gaze anyway, taking a peek at what the Mirror Man had seen. The man had spoken the truth. He found himself unexpectedly striking, and the reflective glimpse had increased the inner confidence he needed to enter the mansions front doors alone. Even though his self-reliance had improved in a short period of time, his nerves were still sputtering from anxiety of the unknown.

The Mirror Man opened the side door to the carriage that had given Oakland passage to step inside. Within moments of closing the door, the carriage rolled away.

Chapter 9

Considering the fuss taking place outside the Manor, commotion had to have been stirring inside. The village people were filing in like an army of ants marching food to the colonies nest at its center. The line of guests started from the carriage parkway outside, continued up the stairway to the entry and flowed down the staircase on the inside. It looked to have been a slow moving line that hadn't seemed to have gone anywhere very fast.

The general society had all been greeted by formal servants on entry, and was acknowledged once again by more servants when they reached the massive lobby at the bottom of the grand mahogany staircase. Beyond that, everybody flowed into the great hall at the main interior point.

As with any extravagant gala, the Royal's remained out of sight until everyone had arrived.

A picture of subtle purity was visible on the main floor. The young intact maidens appeared hopeful at being the Prince's one and only choice. They'd come to the event puffed and overdressed, hardly able to move or breathe in their cheeky ball gowns.

The grand hall had started out with a chill, but the increasing bodies filling the room had let off a heat source that would have kept the place warm if not on the verge of burning up.

The downside to a full room of people was the many different florals mixed with corn starched odors—the smell had swirled everywhere, leaving the halls clean air nearly nonexistent.

All the starchy powders were intended to disguise the odors coming from the ladies as their pasty bodies beneath all the fabulous layers had begun to heat up their lady parts, releasing vapors some men found appealing if not arousing.

Just about every female carried a fan, assisting them at keeping cool or to hide their true gluttonous smile from the Prince.

Finally, the dark of the night had crept in, and the way it appeared, everybody had already arrived. The stairway had become empty, except for a few single men perched against the stair rail waiting to snag any unwanted stray that Deklan found too unsettling to take as his wife.

Sir Wattsworth had left the grand hall and confronted Dante in the master wing, informing him all guests had arrived. The intention was to initiate the family's relaxed position to join the event without further delay.

The mellowing stringed musical instruments were indication the honored guests might have been on their way in. It was formal and verge imperial.

All the milling within the great room had come to a standstill and attention turned to the entry at the back of the room. Everybody waited quietly as if the nations President was about to make an appearance.

Scattered whispers, as well as bashful giggles from excited young ladies in waiting had circulated the room.

Insatiable parents shoved their children in front of the

young groom to be—their way of forcing his future bride into the available lineup. Clouds of odor absorbing powders wafted from the maiden's skirts when haggish mothers pushed their spoiled daughters into any existing spaces.

It was an offensive display to watch parents prostituting their children in exchange for wealth.

As soon as the honored family entered the hall, the quartet had begun playing music at a more pleasing volume.

Guests graciously moved to the outer edges of the room, vacating the center space that allowed Deklan and his parents to easily find their way to the head table at the end of the grand hall. On the way, Deklan greeted almost everyone of interest, his pursed lipped expression indicating no lady had captured his eye. He repeatedly bowed his head and said good evening, keeping his hands clasped tightly behind his back the entire time as though extending an unapproachable charm.

The tinkling music had become more and more droning as time ticked on. It seemed to have been the same racketeering noise that continued on and on and on. The ticky, ticky, ticky of the harpsicord and plucky stringed instruments all sounded as though the same song had been played over and over.

From all the twirling on the dance floor, Deklan's feet had become sore and his stomach felt sickly. He found it senseless to mingle with all the ladies he truly wasn't interested in. Cordial to them, sure, but as a companion that involved pillow talk, not likely.

He was wearing out quickly, and concluded a match for him within that hall wasn't present. As he figured before it begun, the evening had turned out to be a disappointment and he felt it was going to regress downward unless a miracle walked through the front doors and down that magnificent staircase. He was sure of what he wanted and he knew it wasn't any of the selected maidens his parents brought in.

Throughout the evening, Deklan warmly danced with every available lady. Fat ones, skinny ones, even ones with feminine hygiene issues that had him holding his breath nearly half the night. He wanted to pass on all of them. He wanted to run away.

Chapter 10

Oakland had adjusted moderately well to the situation transpiring at the Manor until the door to the carriage swung open, broadcasting invitation for him to exit. Reality punched him in the gut and the event had all become very real. His nerves had gone back to lurching inside him and he started feeling nauseous. He imagined he'd changed to a light shade of green, near to being in ruins.

Outside the carriage door, the Mirror Man had been waiting. He'd given Oakland a few more tidbits of advice while lending his hand to help him out.

Close up, the front stairway was more massive than Oakland thought it'd be. When his foot met the third step, he turned around to pass the Mirror Man a final sendoff only to discover he'd already gone away. As sure as by magic, the carriage, the horse, and the fairy man had disappeared into thin air.

Oakland suddenly felt alone again, stepping back into that dream world he thought he was originally having. He'd returned to believing it was a fantasy all over again.

How could anything come and go so quickly unless it was a figment of his imagination?

To bring himself comfort, Oakland reached for the necklace and held it with the hand that wore the silver ring. It was worth a shot since the Mirror Man convinced him they held some sort of magic. He wouldn't have believed it if he hadn't felt it for himself, but when the two had been brought together, they vibrated and shimmered as he'd been told they would.

"O-oh, this is happening," he warbled, wondering if he'd gone a little crazy in the head. Everything he'd witnessed that evening so far had been out of this world, or hadn't seemed from his time. Anybody in their sane mind would have thought it was all nonsense and they'd somehow been mixed up in a sort of dream-like fantasy.

He proceeded up the grand stairway as the Mirror Man had intended him to do, feeling the pit of his stomach going through bouts of somersaults with every step he'd taken. He had no doubt why that was—hoping to connect with the person he'd been thinking of while pleading that the perpetual magic wouldn't alter the person he was and change him into what others understood companionship between two people should be—all about the boy and the girl. That conflicting attraction wasn't who he was born to be and deep down, he sensed magic couldn't even change who he was meant to love.

Oakland knew the one person he'd like to connect with inside, however, hadn't had any inkling as to whom that would truly be once he'd passed through the mystical abyss of light. As Oakland had been told, there'd be a sign upon their greeting, but what would that sign be and would there be help from the necklace and the ring? Another magic trick he wasn't sure was real.

While climbing the stairway, he looked up into the thin traces of light between the double doors. The closer he'd gotten to the entry, the easier it had become for him to hear what was going on inside. He mostly heard the resonance of a four stringed quartet and the reverberating clatter of a harpsichord—an instrument he hadn't ever cared for. He was able to identify that skull compressing sound anywhere. When those high pitched keys had been struck, his eardrums would vibrate to nearly bleeding. It was not one of his favorite instruments and Oakland could most certainly do without that rackety noisemaker.

What seemed like more than a mile up a rocky hillside, Oakland eventually reached the top of the stairway. In front of him were two massive French style doors that had been left slightly ajar at the center—between them, a soft golden light shone through to the outside.

At that instant, with sound and light, Oakland knew he arrived at the right place at the right time and should enter as if he was initially invited by scribbles on a parchment letter—much like the one he found outside the kitchen door clinging to his cheek. Maybe that note was for him. Put there by magic, not just a fluke, and meant for him to find. Whatever the case might have been, he was where he was supposed to be that day and that piece of paper might have been the initial nudge he needed to set a plan in motion.

Behind those large wooden doors along with that stifling music, he heard several voices muttering no-nonsense babble, all demonstrating tales of fiction in an effort at getting what they wanted and probably hadn't deserved. Even though he couldn't see inside, he knew there were imitation smiles combined with the chatter, all of which displayed acts of misrepresentation in hopes of snagging the man who held the wealth and fortune.

Unsure of the outcome on the other side, Oakland stood a minute before entering. What ticked as only a few short moments felt like stalling eternity.

After inhaling deeply, courage had built inside him. He held his breath, had taken a step forward, and slipped through the opening between the two large doors, the yellow glow instantly feeling like fire.

When he stepped into brighter light at the top of the stairs, he looked down and noticed a few heads had turned toward him with stationary gazes.

Soon after, whispering flowed around the room in a rush,

setting the rest of the heads in motion to look his way. Breathy gasps and pointing fingers had come with whispering, *"Who is that? Where did he come from? And why is he here?"*

He felt his face catch fire. He was burning up. Proving anxious.

Oakland brought no child with him to force upon the Prince, and he clearly wasn't a female, if that was what Deklan wanted. Oakland could tell by expressions circling the room that most of the crowd found him out of place. It was almost as though they were threatened by his staggering existence.

He gripped the pendant with his ringed hand. "Father, give me strength," he whispered to his dad.

Since he'd been spotted inside the Manor, there was no escaping the ballroom. At least not while most eyes had been pinned on him. He was there to stay. Trapped at the moment. He'd been sent to that place for a reason and by what his guidance fairy had told him, he was going to find his lifelong companion under the very roof. Would it be Deklan, or somebody else?

Oakland had become horrified by the selection of companions in front of him. His heart had definitely deflated, not willing to say yes to any of the ladies he'd seen. He continued to stand still while looking beyond the powdery mist that had taken over the large room. He coughed a little bit, feeling as though his lungs were about to burst. Too much talc billowing from undesirable places, and when he thought about that, he coughed again, that time holding out on breathing in.

Down below he could see many female faces that were wrestling behind clouds of what he presumed were starchy powders with added floral fragrances. Those meant to disguise feminine hygiene. The lacey fans they held were without a doubt waving away the puffs in front of them or were used to blow away the many floral odors that were combined into one bad smell.

Oakland spotted Deklan's mother and father leaning into one another at the opposite end of the room. Mister Royal had a finger pointed straight at him, giving understanding to Oakland the father might have been asking who he was and why he had come alone to a party for his son.

In front of the podium where the Royal's were seated, Oakland saw Deklan awkwardly dancing at full arm's length with a pale white fleshy girl who showed off a split-toothed grin. The orange and white cream puff gown she had on was clashing badly with her bright red hair. The busy pattern made him dizzy, bringing on a sense of sickness. Oakland could tell she wasn't of any interest to Deklan. His exaggerated body language and forced distance between the two had made that clear as day. Deklan seemed cordial, but understanding his politeness from their previous engagements, Oakland knew that was why he put himself through the miss fitted partnership. No hesitation on his part at just being nice.

Oakland had seen Deklan close up before, but that time dressed sharply in formal wear, delivered an even more fantastically stunning man beyond belief—like the true Prince Oakland had found in him. Oakland could easily see that while keeping focus on his handsome face and bright eyes.

It had been known that the irises bound through bouts of stress when one spots another person they find attractive, and Oakland knew his had gone spiral crazy when he spotted Deklan across the room.

Oakland's heart pounded rapidly beneath his ribcage, on the verge of busting out of his chest and losing rhythm. For a moment, he thought he'd lose consciousness if he continued staring at the man. Every other time Oakland had seen him, he was wearing heavily woven britches and a loose fitting linen shirt. There at the ball, he was polished in all white, shoulder epaulets with embellishments of silver and gold. Truly Prince worthy, looking much different than he had during their previous encounters, and Oakland was sure Deklan would have found his appearance much different, too.

Was Deklan who Oakland was supposed to meet? Could Deklan be his soul mate? Impossible, but he hoped. They were from two different worlds. How could an exquisite young man like Deklan find affection in a raggedy pauper chap like Oakland? The whole idea hadn't made any sense. That's when Oakland hoped even harder before he lost his nerve and walked away.

While Oakland slowly descended down the stairway, he

kept his eyes pinned on the striking Prince. As he stepped downward, everybody else in the ballroom had become hidden in a murky blur. Only Deklan existed to him.

As best luck had rolled into place as planned, a slanted glance had come from Deklan right at Oakland standing on the straightaway. There had come a stumble to Deklan's dance steps. His eyelids opened wider the same way Oakland's had done when he first arrived and saw the Prince on the main floor across the way.

Deklan's connection with the pale-faced red head had severed. He stopped abruptly and faced Oakland, appearing to have forgotten the chunky girl he'd been paired with or that anybody else had been waiting their turn at the chance with him.

Oakland's feet left the final step while his eye contact remained fixed on Deklan's gaze. Realizing he was staring, Oakland quickly looked away, dropping his focus on the floor in front of him.

An abrupt distraction cut through their line of vision when the next fair maiden waiting in line rudely pushed her way toward Deklan and forced his hand to dance with her. She pulled him close, twisted one of his arms around her waist and vice gripped his other hand with link-locked fingers. The dame seemed determined.

Deklan appeared out of touch with his new female partner since his visual connection had remained on Oakland still standing at the foot of the stairway.

Oakland held back his white toothy grin, expressing a slight one sided smirk instead.

Prince Deklan, as Oakland had named him, let go of the lady and walked his way. Their eyes met again and stayed fixed. As Deklan strolled toward Oakland, the kerosene lamps behind him seemed to intensify to a brighter burn. More magic, perhaps?

Within moments, realization of what was happening had circled the room. The grand hall had gone quiet, nearly silent, along with dropping jaws and hand covered whispers.

What had taken place could not have been expected, and the idea that half the town had witnessed it had put Oakland's anxiety level on an up ticking rise. He wasn't prepared for a public display, however, by no means would he let a Prince like Deklan slip away. If... he... was who Oakland was there to meet.

This was his moment and all the hoping he'd gone through was coming true.

Before Oakland turned and moved to the wine table for a chalice of much needed confidence, he conveyed another nervous half smirk toward Deklan. Looking over the piled fruit in the center of the table, Oakland finally reached for a metal goblet, and at that moment, a white-gloved hand brushed up against his.

It was him.

The Prince of Almond Manor was standing there.

So close.

"Allow me to get that for you," Oakland heard him say, quiet like a whisper. Deklan's deep voice vibrated beyond sensual, sending burning chills through Oakland's entire body, not missing a hair follicle.

What force had his fairy godfather put into play? A strong one, it seemed.

Oakland softened like a thirsty flower when he felt Deklan's warm breath gracing his ear. The heat of his body had sent a terrifying love sick signal through to his bones. He was uneasy, yet at the same time felt secure with him there.

"Sure. Okay. Yes. Please," Oakland stammered, clumsily bowing as if the man was a true Prince. That was his first reaction. He couldn't think of anything else to do. He was new to meeting an heir of such impressive standards. He was terrified standing so close to an attractive man who had hundreds of eyes pinned on him. Deklan was the sort of man Oakland had always been attracted to. It had nothing to do with status or financial security, but a pure heart to heart connection, and by Deklan's actions, it seemed clear to Oakland, he was Deklan's preference as well.

Oakland wasn't sure if Deklan was smiling or laughing at him, knew his greeting wasn't the best, but it was a good attempt considering what had taken place.

Smiling and looking directly into Oakland's eyes the entire time, Deklan reached for the carafe of red wine and with his hand locked over top of Oakland's, poured it into the goblet they were both holding on to.

Deklan's deep voice soothed Oakland's nerves when he said, "I presume you know my name. How about you tell me yours?" That was a decent attempt at starting a conversation.

Oakland found it difficult to believe Deklan hadn't recognized him from their encounter at the river, or from the night he'd taken him home on horseback. Had Oakland's fairy godfather altered his appearance that much as well, or perhaps cast some strange spell on the handsome Prince to prevent identity distinction? The Mirror Man had mentioned that, however, the idea of it actually able to have been pulled off seemed outlandish.

Deklan leisurely released his grasp, leaving Oakland holding the goblet alone. "Thank you," Oakland said. "I mean... Unh... Oakland. My name is Oakland, not thank you. I mean, thank you for the wine, and my name is Oakland," he staggered with his reply.

That time Deklan's true laughter had come out.

Oakland felt a sudden wave of heat cover him and he needed fresh air to cool off. He fanned himself with his free hand while turning toward an open door at the side of the great room. Before taking a step, he asked, "Are you able to follow me outdoors or are you required to stay inside with your invited guests?"

Still holding the carafe of wine, Deklan snatched another goblet from the fruit table for himself. "These people are known by my father and will certainly be fine without me. Besides... I come to believe this birthday party has just served its purpose. Lead the way. I'll be but a step behind you." He looked at Oakland with glazed eyes as if he were trying to see his soul.

Oakland backed up to the facial adhered note he'd read that mentioned Deklan's party was scheduled to find him a suiter. Had Deklan's statement meant he finished searching, and had come in contact with the one he would choose? Glorified with his belief, Oakland smiled, but kept his enthusiastic grin inside.

Their exit was more that of a hurried escape through the side door, taking them to a well-tailored courtyard. Green topiary and floral arrangements were scattered everywhere and the air was much fresher than the dusty odor that had taken over the Manor's ballroom.

They walked side by side along a stone pathway that wove through the garden and circled a pond at the center of the lawn. They marched to the far side and sat at one of the sporadically placed marble benches alongside of the water.

They carried on with the usual chatter that two people do when meeting for the very first time. Likes. Dislikes. Life in general.

Even though Oakland had spoken much about himself, he had however kept the secret about working at the Manor out of the conversation, preferring his status about bathing in a river because he was poor to remain withheld from Deklan's ears. The dazzling clothing he had on was misleading and surely was giving the wrong impression pertaining to his actual character. He wasn't certain if the real Oakland would change Deklan's mind about staying or going. A fine suit surely beat old ragged farmhand wear.

Deklan was charming in the way Oakland thought a Prince would have been and found the handsome man had given the impression he'd like to be more than a social acquaintance. He'd sensed that by the way Deklan smiled at him, and looked at him deep in the eyes. Plus, the way he leaned into his personal space and the way he casually pressed his knee and shoulder against his as he sat with him on the bench. Call it a hunch, but Oakland had a good feeling there was an attraction settling in, felt it the moment they met at the wine table, maybe even before then. The connection was sincere and above all, he could tell it was coming from the heart.

Deklan pressed himself tighter against Oakland's shoulder and surprisingly softly said, "I hope I'm not being to forward, but would you like to dance with me?" He stood and reached for Oakland's hand.

Oakland looked up at Deklan, giving an excuse to avoid leaving his seat. "But there's no quartette playing any music. We left that inside."

Deklan flipped his hand in a hither inviting manner. "Come. Rise up. Music isn't needed to dance. We can imagine our own."

"The truth is... I don't know how to dance," Oakland confessed.

"I'll lead."

"Where you taking me?" Oakland clowned.

"To the stars and back." Deklan's smile was too infections to ignore.

"This isn't going to be good. I haven't any rhythm even with music playing in the background," Oakland admitted, getting more nervous as time moved on. "You'll probably turn me away after this."

"Not possible. Come now. Dance with a Prince." Deklan rolled his hand at Oakland again, signaling for him to rise.

Considering there had been no music playing, Oakland discovered he wasn't doing too badly. He held onto Deklan the same way he had when they were on the horseback ride, with a tight grip and very close.

Something about dancing with Deklan helped Oakland maintain steady footwork. His rhythm remained intact and it appeared as though he knew what he was doing. Deklan was good at leading and Oakland was happy to follow the man.

Deklan pulled Oakland tighter against his body, his heartbeat banging against Oakland's chest. They swayed with their cheeks less than an inch from each other's and Oakland nearly dissolved when Deklan whispered into his ear. "Look see, you have excellent rhythm. Might I be wrong, but this could work out well for the both of us in the days yet to come."

Oakland backed away. If he hadn't, he might have panicked and blown the whole deal. He quirkily smiled at Deklan and sat back down on the bench where he probably should have stayed in the first place. Oakland lifted the goblet of wine for the much needed support he had abandoned earlier.

Deklan sat next to Oakland and commented on his eye color, mentioning the shade of gray was what he first noticed when he saw him on the stairway. They captivated him instantly and were what influenced the uncontrolled reaction that had come out of him.

Deklan had taken the goblet from Oakland's grasp and set it

down on the bench beside them. "I'd like to kiss you," he politely asked, grasping hold of his hand.

Oakland hadn't expected Deklan's request, and at the same time thought he was taking huge strides at getting closer. It must have been the way dominant men operated. He had no idea—had never been in that situation before. His face had gone long as Deklan moved in. Oakland hadn't answered at first, but stuttered, "I... I'm sorry. I'd never kissed anyone romantically before, or actually, a man before." He slightly backed away.

Deklan moved with him, his hot breath had drifted over his skin when he said, "Please."

Oakland stayed where he was, trembling the moment Deklan gently kissed him on the mouth. It felt tender and flawless. The perfect kiss had lasted more than a single red handed spin on a timepiece.

Deklan softly nipped Oakland's bottom lip as he pulled away. "That wasn't so bad now was it?" he had spoken in a soothing voice, on the verge of a whisper, still holding Oakland's hand and caressing the backside with his thumb.

Once again, Oakland's face had gone long, but with certain traces of a slanted smile creeping up one side of his face. He hadn't said anything. Hadn't had to. Deklan might have been able to identify his answer without him speaking a word.

Deklan blinked, leaned forward and pressed his lips to Oakland's again.

Oakland stirred inside and could sense a union of their souls taking place. They'd come together by the blessing of his father and the Mirror Man—some through fate. He'd been directed to where he was, as though the two mysterious father figures had known the way he was and helped him to the man who'd been waiting for him.

"I have much I would like to tell you, but I cannot stay long," Oakland owned up.

"Will I see you again after tonight?" Deklan gripped Oakland's hands tighter.

Oakland hesitated with his answer and attempted to pull his hands away. "I'd like that, but I'm not sure that would be a good idea." He shifted where he sat as if ready to stand up.

"Why would you say that?" Deklan asked, leaning in front of Oakland as if trying to stop him from running away.

Oakland glanced away to hide his eyes. "You must understand as I do. The two of us together won't be easy… at all. People don't understand us. What will your parents think? We'd have to hide in dark places whenever we wanted to be together. Trust me. I'd seen what happens to the meek and unique. I'd dealt with ridicule my entire life because I'm neither black nor white. I one of each, and that alone, people don't like. With your white skin and me a man of mixed flesh, it'll be much worse. For the both of us. How do you think that will look to the majority of the people in the village and those inside the Manor? A cat may love a fish, but how would they live?"

"Hog wash, I say. It's time somebody started making changes in this world. We don't live in medieval times anymore. These days are modern." Deklan stood up, turning away from Oakland while talking to the sky. "They cannot expect me to marry a maiden. It won't work. Men appeal to me, not women. You appeal to me, Oakland. You. You're exactly what I'd been meant to find and everybody needs to understand that. Why should I, or even you, live a lie for anybody. That isn't right." He turned back toward Oakland and had taken both hands in his again, knelt down in front of him and said with a quieter voice, "I cannot go back in that house without you with me. I find it impossible to do that now. It'll never be the same. I won't be able to keep my mind off of you."

Gripping Deklan's hands tighter, Oakland couldn't let go. "This will be a struggle. For you *and* for me. How can we be happy with that?"

"How can we be happy without that?" Deklan argued.

The bell tower had rung in the distance, giving warning that midnight had approached. Oakland looked up toward the reverberating tone and remembered what the Mirror Man had told him. He would lose the magic at midnight and for all he knew, Deklan and his attraction toward him would disappear right along with it. "I'm sorry. I must go."

"NO! You can't." Deklan squeezed Oakland's hands tighter.

"You can't go. I won't let you."

The bell continued ringing and Oakland felt a strange sensation swirling around him. "Tonight was one of the best nights I'd ever had, Deklan. But I must go now." He struggled to pull his hands from Deklan's grasp. The grip was tight, but he managed to pull free.

Oakland had to leave. If he hadn't, he risked being identified as the poor silhouette he was before meeting the Mirror Man.

Deklan appeared sad. He bowed his head to the ground and whispered, "Don't go."

Oakland turned away and ran through the darkness until he reached the stone wall at the edge of the garden. He climbed over and jumped to the ground on the other side. He felt a sharp tug on the cloak he was wearing and noticed that a small piece of it was clinging to the spiky iron framing along the topside of the stocky wall. As quickly as he saw it there, it vanished. Copper embers flickered and lifted to the sky.

Back at the fish pond where Oakland had left him, Deklan had dropped to his knees. In his hand he found the silver ring that Oakland had been wearing. He stood and faced the empty space in front of him, muttering softly, "When will I see you again, Oakland? Will you ever come back?"

Just as the Mirror Man had said, the brilliant clothing on Oakland's back had begun to fizzle and disappear. As he ran away, he lit up like a burning torch, sparks of glowering embers circling him, rising to the sky, taking refuge in a world where they must have come from. In a glimmering flash, it all vanished and he was running barefoot and unclothed. Everything that had happened seemed dreamlike. Oakland collided with anxiety, but he kept running home.

He burst into the carriage house, closed the door and climbed the wooden plank into bed. His heart was aching. Badly. His nose was stopped up, making it hard for him to breathe. His eyes had gone blurry. Tears flowed, unable to hold his emotions from boiling over.

What was happening? He was stronger than that.

Has anybody ever died from loneliness and sorrow?

When Oakland left to visit the party that evening, he was expecting it to be a happier time. Not like it had turned out, painful and uncertain.

Why had his life been selected to be so complicated? God only knows.

He prayed for Deklan's happiness and wished like mad it wouldn't have been the last time he'd seen him. They were soul mates. Had to be. The separation anxiety was too strong for them not to have been. He felt a bond when he was near him, and understood Deklan was who his Fairy Godfather had told him he would meet. The Mirror Man knew that all along.

How had the clothing vanished into thin air but the necklace had not? Everything else, including the Mirror Man was gone. He looked at his hand and found the ring had gone, too. But why?

Oakland continued weeping alone until he drifted into dreamland, holding the only treasure from the night in his grasp—the emerald necklace the Mirror Man had given him. He held that stone and lucidly dreamt his wish.

Chapter 11

Deklan struggled with the hollowness in his chest the day after his birthday. He was supposed to feel better than he had. Birthdays were meant to be happy occasions. His heart ached like he never knew it could and he was clear with the reason why.

Pressing a fisted hand to his chest, he held it there as though it would change his mood for the better. The emptiness was consuming, and the ring in his grasp only enhanced the sadness he'd been feeling. The silver band reminded him of the night before—how content he'd been locked in the arms of the mysterious man he'd met at the ball.

The Prince was missing his mate and his heart was breaking because of it.

"Why'd you run away, Oakland?" Deklan placed the silver ring onto his middle finger where it fit best.

From silence to a roar, a startling bang had caught him off guard.

"What in the name of heaven is going on?" he hollered, spinning his glare toward the crashing door.

Intrusively breaking into his room, two strong ranch hands pulled him from the chair and escorted him by the arms down the corridor to meet with his Father and Mother in the dusty library. By the way he'd been dragged so harshly against his will, and after what had taken place the night before, he was quite certain the meeting with his parents wasn't going to be good, and ridicule pertaining to disappearing with another man instead of a selected maiden was sure to have been heard with heightened vocal tones.

The dark ages were long gone. People weren't dragged to the dungeon beneath the castle anymore. There was no need to be brutal. Should he fight back or just let the goons take him to the underground cell? He hung limply, not making it easy.

As soon as he was pushed through the library doorway, the outburst from his father had come at him like a fired musket, "How could you make a spectacle of us like that?" His father selfishly thought of himself and how the all-male rendezvous would reflect on him and the family. "You have disgraced us and our name. Do you know what you've done?"

Deklan stood motionless in front of his parents, finding difficulty coming up with a response to his father's unsettling rage. He spun the ring around his middle finger and reflected back on his birthday night, then said, "I'm not sure what to say to you, *Pa*. I'd tried to tell the both of you for a very long time that I'm not at all attracted to the female species, but you wouldn't hear me. In fact, I'd suspected you'd always known, but scurried around the subject whenever you recognized I was trying to let you in on who I am. Last night was a once in a lifetime moment, and I wasn't going to let anything stand in my way—again. For you or anybody else. I'm tired of hiding. So… don't blame me for the way my attraction toward men had come out into the open. I'm worn with keeping my true emotions locked up all the time, in fear of what people will think of me—of you and this family. One thing I do know for sure. If you feel the person I was born to be, unsettling, then I guess I don't belong here either. I connected with that gentleman in a way you will probably never understand, and I plan to find him. A man is who I'm meant to

70

spend my life with, not a woman. There, I said it. May I go now?"

"No you may not go, now." Deklan's father stood up with a pointing finger. "This is not up for a one sided discussion and you are not making the decision. You're going to listen and this is what you're going to do." He glanced at Deklan's mother for a brief moment as if he was looking for her to agree.

Gripping one finger with each demand, he spouted out, "For one—you will not see that *black* man from last night ever again. Whoever he is." Dante clearly stated, including a racial slur he probably hadn't meant. "Two—you will marry the lassie of our selecting, and it will be soon to avoid further hostility toward this Family. Number three—you will stay home until the wedding day so we can keep an eye on you, and don't give it a second thought that I won't lock your door. Four—you will apologize to your mother for making her cry and giving her the worst night of her life."

Deklan swiftly interposed, "I don't agree with any of what you said with *your* one sided orders, and you're making a bigger mistake than you might think. You're selfish plan is going to destroy people's lives. Not only mine. Where do you see anything positive about this? To indorse the arrangement only suits your needs. You'll be taking away the chance for some lass at finding true companionship. This false marriage would be wasting her life and mine so this small town can see that your only child isn't in love with another lad. You'll also be making my entire life an unhappy one, until the day you die. How do you see this will be beneficial for anybody? Not even you will be content with that. Hiding a secret will be a lifetime of misery for you. Trust me, I know about that first hand." Deklan lowered his head and sighed. "Can't you see the mistake you are making?"

His mother stayed quiet, but was sobbing while Sir Dante carried out his demands to their son. "You have no vote here. This is MY kingdom and I will run it the way I see that it should. You're getting married as we say, to whom we tell you to, and it will be within the week. This affection for another lad of yours must end today. The sooner the better. For your sake and ours. NOW... you may go."

"Really? This is how it will be? Your big finish." Deklan was sickened by his father's idea of the perfect life for him. It wasn't in Deklan's favor and he knew it, but in the interest and reputation of the Royal Almond monarchy. Deklan tripped backward as Wattsworth and the two hefty ranch hands dragged him away. The heels of his boots left black marks as they skidded across the slate floor. "You've just made me a prisoner in my own home, father," he hollered. His voice echoed loudly through the empty hall.

The servants tossed Deklan into his room like it was a prison cell. He'd fallen to his knees and stayed there as the heavy doors behind him slammed shut. Angered, he twisted Oakland's ring around his finger again. The touch of the ring was the only connection to the other half of his soul he had and it helped him feel less alone when holding it. His heart had become broken more than before, and there was nobody, not even his family, who could help him heal.

Chapter 12

Sitting inside the carriage house, Oakland had been able to see Deklan standing in an upper window at the Manor, the Prince's melancholy expression looking right in his direction. The floor to ceiling drapes wavered on either side of him, the flapping fabric mimicking large wings of an angel. He was holding an object in his hand that Oakland couldn't quite make out. It flashed when the sunlight struck it just right.

As if there might have been somebody rapping on the entry door to that room, Oakland saw Deklan briefly turn away and back again. Deklan's saddened actions could have been instigated by disappointed parents or the fact he was missing the man he'd found an immediate connection with.

It was heartbreaking to witness Deklan like that, as well as upsetting to know his parents might have inflicted that anguish on their child. Thinking that, and not allowing him the chance to be with the person he was meant for, Oakland turned sour toward

Deklan's parents. They had to have known the precious gift being taken away from their son and how much they had broken him down because of it.

Oakland sat in his window down below while Deklan sat in his up above, both connected to each other as if the empty space between them had strung an imaginary tether.

There had come an unexpected tug at the ankle on Oakland's trousers. He'd been so deeply engrossed with Deklan he hadn't realized a goat was chewing his cuff line. "Hey! No, no, Gladys." He pulled his foot away.

When Oakland faced the outdoors again, he was certain Deklan had looked straight into his window, the Prince's squinting glare seemed as though he had been trying to figure out who the man in the carriage house window was. Oakland threw his body backward onto the bed, keeping below the sill. His sudden and rash action tossed a fussy chicken resting there upward into a wobbly flight. The bird clucked and squabbled over the banister, wings flapping all the way to ground level.

"Bollocks!" Oakland almost crushed Betty Lu.

Several moments had passed before Oakland dared to sneak another peak at the man in the window above. As he spied, Deklan's expression and peculiar actions seemed as though he'd been held prisoner in his own home.

Then, Deklan turned with an impulsive jerk. There was noticeable commotion on the inside, but Oakland couldn't make out what was going on. When Deklan turned back around, he'd placed a shiny trinket on the sill and tucked it into the corner at the ledge. He stood with his backside to the treasure as if guarding it from whoever had come into the room.

Oakland looked at his own hand and supposed there could be a chance that trinket was the ring he had on the night before. He thought it had disappeared along with the clothing he'd been wearing, but since the necklace was still with him, there might have been a good gamble the ring stayed behind as well, and Deklan might have it.

CR & BO

Without any call of warning or even an introduction knock, the door to Deklan's room burst open, the inward thrust had forced the angelic drapes to flap to the outside of the open window.

Deklan quickly pushed the ring deeper into hiding, corner tucking it behind the drape. When he turned around, there were two servants standing in the room next to his father and mother, one at either side, as though there to bag and tag him. He back stepped tightly against the window sill.

His father scowled for what seemed like two full minutes before blurting out the reason for his enraged entrance. "It is set, Deklan. Your wedding is being planned and we are sending the carriage to bring back the young lady we have chosen for you."

"WHAT?" Deklan shouted. "Have you all lost your minds? This isn't a dominion, it's a family home," he growled.

"This is the best decision for you and you know it," his father yelled back. "You will not embarrass us any further, you hear me?"

Deklan glared at his father and then at his mother. "An arranged marriage? Where are we and what year is it? The way I see this, you are more worried about yourselves than you are about me. I get it."

"That's preposterous," his father blurted, even though Deklan knew it wasn't a straightforward argument.

"It's the truth." Deklan looked at him and then away, shuffling his feet across the floor to place as much space between him and his parents as possible. At that moment, he hadn't even wanted to be in the same room with them. "You're both on the fence with what everybody in town is thinking about you and your precious family. Or are you more worried about your nutty business?"

"For the most part, we are concerned about you. And of course, considering the business as well," Dante motioned.

"Mostly me?" Deklan's eyebrow lifted. "Of course you are."

"Don't be a spoiled brat, Deklan. You're too old for that. Act your age. Your mother and I made this company into what it is today, so it's in your best interest to hear us out and not destroy what we built." Dante moved closer to Deklan.

Crossing his arms tightly at his chest, Deklan leaned backward as if loud bursts were about to blast from his father's windpipe. He stood motionless. Staring. He'd known himself it wouldn't have been right for three people's lives to become destroyed because of one person's senseless decision? His life. Oakland's life. Plus the poor lassie who wouldn't ever know true love because of the condition Dante had made. It was unspeakable.

"Say something," his father demanded, grabbing Deklan's arm.

"What do you want me to say? That I agree?" Deklan dropped his arms, pulling out of his father's grasp. "Well I don't. It's absurd. Meaningless. Preposterous. Life wrecking. Shall I continue? I won't go through with it."

The temperature in the room felt like it had risen fifty degrees as his father's head begun looming in on a fire fed explosion. His mother covered her mouth as if she was about to vomit, and crossed her other arm over her stomach as if calming down the onset of rumbling pain.

"Don't you dare talk to your mother and me with such contempt. You will get married. To a female. And that's the end of this discussion." Dante turned away, reached for Priscilla and dragged her out of Deklan's room like he had her on a leash.

By the appearance on Priscilla's face, it seemed everything taking place had been orchestrated by Dante. Her expression of concern for Deklan was visible, more than the apprehension she had for how Deklan's attraction toward men was going to affect the family business. It seemed as though she could care less about living if Deklan was in a bad place. It was all about the bond between a mother and her child. It would not be broken and there would always be a tether that connected their hearts.

Deklan stood back and watched both his parents leave, slamming the door shut as soon as the final heel crossed the threshold.

Chapter 13

Another knock had come to Deklan's door not long after his parent's had left, the rap more tamed than the last. *"What now?"* he thought.

Instead of propping the chair under the door handle to block people out like he wanted to do, he whirled it aside and decided to see who was on the other side.

Enormously surprised, he loudly wailed, "Jedidiah? What are you doing here?"

Jedidiah was a friend of Deklan's who had once worked as part of the maintenance crew at the manor. Deklan always had a brotherly regard for him—the two had been platonic friends for several years until Deklan's father unemployed Jedidiah to prevent his only son from carrying out any of his mind locked secrets toward the dark skinned servant boy. At least that's what Deklan understood the day Jedidiah had been dismissed. The tones and words his father used that day had made that scenario known, and since his own mind had been attracted to males, he was certain that was the reason why.

"How'd you get in the house?" Deklan stepped back to open a pathway for Jedidiah.

"I know all the secret doorways of this house. Remember I maintained and oiled half the hinges around here." Jedidiah smiled as he walked through the bedroom doorway, hugging Deklan on his way by. He commented, "Wow, Deklan, you've gotten strong. You're like a wedge of granite."

"Hard labor is what this is." Deklan beat a fist against his chest. "Anyway, you are a pleasant surprise, but what brings you back here?" he asked while backing out of Jedidiah's way.

Jedidiah kept his voice low. "I heard people in the village speaking out of line in reference to what transpired at an event that had taken place here the other night. After what you told me about yourself a while back, I wasn't surprised by their mention of you taking interest in a well-dressed lad instead of an elegant lady, but I was a bit troubled by what was being said outside your presence and thought you might need somebody on your side. I understand this world isn't ready for somebody like you, but there's no reason to swing the cutlass machete at your backside when you're not there to block the strike with another."

Deklan fidgeted. "So you're not bothered by this being out in the open or you being associated with somebody who everybody wants to throw stones at?"

"Why should I be?" Jedidiah answered with a question. His face had gone sharp.

"I just figured"—Deklan hesitated—"well… figured since everybody else was either trying to crucify me or make me change into someone I'm not, I imagined you were here to do the same. Like you said, this world isn't ready."

"I would never do that to you, my friend, and there's no reason to make any kind of a change to the unchangeable. I told you that before. There's nothing wrong with you." Jedidiah had given him a tighter hug than he had before and whispered into Deklan's ear, "You can't change what is supposed to be, my friend, and that is that."

Deklan's eyes welled up as the hug reassured and soothed

his snarled nerves. "Thank you, Jedidiah. I needed this visit. Very much so. My parents are devastated with the news and have decided to do something unbelievably stupid."

Jedidiah hadn't seemed surprised by Deklan's emotional reaction. "I'll take a stab in the dark with this one. It's your father's big idea, isn't it?"

The two of them had taken a seat in front of the fireplace and exchanged stories about what had been going on in their lives over the past few years.

Deklan had a simple life, but lately a trying one. His frustrations mostly pertained to the recent events, whereas Jedidiah had been traveling the river bank on a self-built floatation raft, fetching his own food from the wild while keeping clear of the white folk who still thought slavery was permissible.

For a short time, Jedidiah had been working off and on a plantation north of town. He wasn't much for staying in one place for too long, which made the idea of cleaning other people's water closets on a permanent basis a bit off-putting to him. He had been a free spirit and enjoyed his liberty. He preferred the riverbanks where he could live as his own man, bonding with nature the way he enjoyed.

Deklan had gone on telling Jedidiah about the night of his birthday, starting with how he had to fight off all the ladies who'd come at him in ways he found offensive and how the evening had taken a better turn with the magical entrance of a stunning man.

He finished his story by explaining how the man he met had mysteriously disappeared into darkness, with the only evidence the night had been real was the ring from the man's finger that had fallen into his hand.

Deklan crossed over to the window sill where he left that glinting ring. It let off a faint chime as he scooped it from the stone ledge and placed it in the palm of his hand. "With this ring, I will find him," he said, holding out the unique ring to prove his story was authentic.

"Then you need to find him," Jedidiah bluntly said after hearing the sting in Deklan's voice. "I'll help you."

"That would mean a lot to me," Deklan replied. "I'd like to get started straightaway since my parents had already started organizing my wedding and the plan is to have me married off by the end of the week."

"That soon? Then let's get started tomorrow morning," Jedidiah agreed. "Nice ring. It looks rare." He pointed at it just as Deklan slipped it onto his middle finger.

The plan going round in Deklan's head was to search for the man who belonged to the ring. It had to fit somebody in the village, and he was going to slide it on every finger until he found the man who'd worn it. The ring was unique, and once he found the finger it belonged to, he was sure something magical would occur at that moment of rejoining.

Chapter 14

Morning had come and Oakland slept past the rooster's doodle at the crack of dawn. What all the animals in the carriage house seemed to have wanted, and he hadn't, was to get up and start the day.

An animal's life seemed simple. Their day consisted of eating, sleeping and pooping. That circle of life had played out all day and every day. Animals had a profound way of living. To them, life would have gone on with or without them, and they hadn't seemed to have any phobias about how their neighbor lived, unless however, they were at the low end of the food chain, then that would have been a different scenario all together, but still —

That morning's cozy bed had made it extremely difficult for Oakland to get the day started. Even though it had only been a few minutes past his usual time of rising and shining, it had still seemed comforting to lie quietly in the realm of his feathered bed-wrap.

He'd pushed the cat away with a gentle swish of an arm, opening a spot to swing his legs over the side of the bed to sit. His delayed awakening would have been no match for the kitchen staffs vengeful thundering if he'd been but one minute late.

During the few spare moments Oakland had, his mind traveled back to the night he felt like a Prince of a Prince — a feeling that exceeded fantastic. He imagined a joyful reunion with Deklan, absorbing the warmth of that man's body against his, immersed with security when being held in his arms. The more he thought about Deklan, the more he wanted that man.

Cheerfully skipping down the wooden plank to the cottage's lower level, Oakland sung to the pleasant memories of that enchanted night gone by. He passed through the doorway and stepped outside, the sun shone radiantly, lending to a brighter day. If there were vocals to his song, he'd have sung, "I want him. I need him. I'd do anything to have him."

Then, when he saw Deklan on the Manor's grounds with another gentleman who resembled himself, his whistled tune had been cut short as if a cotton ball had been stuffed in his mouth. His heart missed a few beats and his breathing stopped up. He blinked to clear his vision, taking another look.

Was Deklan thinking that person was him? Where had that man come from?

Oakland stepped backward into the shadows of his home and closed the door, rapidly turning sorrow blue from the gloom he'd suddenly felt. His misguided feelings had run wild and he regretted the way he'd left Deklan's side so abruptly the other night. If it hadn't been for that silly midnight rule bestowed upon him by the Mirror Man, the circumstances might have played out differently for the two of them — he'd have been the one standing with Deklan at that moment, not that mysterious man.

If it had been Oakland's right or not, he placed claim to the man who wasn't his, however, after what had transpired between them at the celebration, it seemed there had been an immediate connection the moment they met that magical night. Oakland had felt it, and he was sure Deklan had sensed it too.

The Mirror Man hadn't been wrong when he said Oakland

82

would know his soul mate when they crossed paths. That certainly had occurred, but, definite anxiety had come when midnight struck.

Facing the inescapable, Oakland headed outside to the chicken coop for that morning's egg run. He glanced briefly at the two men still standing at the front entrance of the Manor, appearing to have been only carrying out a conversation. Oakland stood watching, as though he was secretly spying. A flash of light beamed sharply from Deklan's finger, the spark spiking Oakland's eye. He couldn't look away as if the ray had drawn him to it and locked his gaze in a trance. He blinked, and before the blind spots faded from his retina, a horse carriage arrived and Deklan helped the strange man into the seat before getting in himself.

What was going on and where were they off to?

Oakland trusted Deklan wasn't thinking that man was him—that would surly impose badly on the connection he had with the Prince. Deklan must have known the man he was getting into that carriage with wasn't the man he'd met at the ball. Two connected souls knew those things. Oakland was normally a gentle person, but that moment he experienced an agitated streak and he unconsciously squeezed an egg and squashed it.

That morning, Oakland rushed through his chores in half the time it had normally taken, his intention, eager to dash for the clover field to find out if the two of them had gone there. It was the place he and Deklan continued running into one another, and he figured it might have been where Deklan had taken the man. The obsessive side of Oakland had kicked in and he couldn't bear the thought of his soul mate kissing the wrong man, or worse, joining souls the way only two men could, one putting himself inside the other.

Oakland had become fixated on Deklan. The few times they'd encountered each other in the fields had been splendid, but the enchanting night of the birthday surely tightened the tether between them.

The clothing Oakland had worn that night disguised the real person he was, and deep down wished it hadn't been part of their romantic introduction. But, if he hadn't, the night might have transpired into a direction other than it had.

The entire scenario played over and over in Oakland's mind, beginning with how it all started the night of the ball. The grand entrance down a grand staircase. The gazes between them across a crowded room. The enchanted dance under moonlight. The sensual kiss that had left him weak. The bell tower resulting in a disruptive departure. The vanishing clothing. Then, that morning's carriage ride Deklan had taken with an unknown lad. Oakland's stomach churned, releasing an ugly noise that resembled signs of hunger.

Oakland couldn't wait another moment. He needed to find out what Deklan and that mysterious character were up to. He spun away, running as fast as he could for the clover field, found his favorite tree and climbed it to wait for the two of them to show up. He sat on the same branch he always had, his legs dangling over each side.

Time crept by, feeling as though he'd been waiting for a pear to sprout. It had become obvious to Oakland an outing in the clover field or picking apples and pears weren't on their schedule.

Oakland reclined against the trunk of the tree, plucked the nearest pear and had taken an angry bite out of it. The flavor as usual had helped comfort him and his rumbling stomach had stopped, but the ache in his chest had not.

Was he being silly for thinking the two of them could be anything more than friends?

When a heart knows what it wants, there's no stopping the way it feels.

Chapter 15

Jedidiah and Deklan rode off on a journey to find the man who was the other half of Deklan's soul. During the ride, Deklan told Jedidiah all about the experience he had, how he felt a strong attraction to the man he'd met that night at his party.

Deklan knew the mystery man from the birthday celebration was the one he had found a connection with, it never was Jedidiah, his longtime friend, and certainly none of the ladies who had nearly exposed themselves to him in the open forum of a dance hall. He'd hoped his soul mate was out there somewhere— waiting—and perhaps thinking about looking for him as well.

The first stop had been a quiet place outside of town. It was secluded away from everything, making it seem as though it would have been the place his mate would have been hiding. The home seemed to have appeared out of nowhere, the same way Oakland had that magical night. The house was interestingly odd and Deklan couldn't remember ever seeing it before.

The weather beaten house was pretty much rundown with faded clapboard siding that desperately needed a fresh coat of color as well as a rooftop that required repair. By the look of the dry curling roof tiles, water must have leaked through to the inside during every bout of rain.

Deklan pulled the carriage to a stop in front of the dilapidated old house where both he and Jedidiah had gotten out. They crept to the front door, stepping around overgrown weeds while swatting at flies and bees along the way.

Glancing over at Jedidiah whose face was drowning in apprehension, Deklan hoped the man he'd met wasn't living in the place they were heading toward. He had made it a point not to judge by the exterior appearance, but the place was madly rough on the outside and those thoughts couldn't have been helped.

Just as he thought that, a chubby black man had come to the door wearing a wooly shirt and suspenders that held up his great big pants. He stood the same way Oakland had, thumbs tucked behind the buckles at the waistline. A sign they might have arrived at the right place.

"Hello Sir," Deklan said, fingers crossed with hopes he was at the wrong home and the ring holder was not tucked someplace inside or hidden behind that large man at the door.

Choking out a pipe smoker's hello, followed by "what do you want," the bulky man tightly held the rickety door so it wouldn't blow away in the gentle breeze.

"Gracious greetings, kind sir," Jedidiah had spoken. "Hope we aren't disturbing you on this fine morning, but we are seeking out a friend of ours that might be in the neighborhood. Do you live here alone?"

"No one here 'sept me," the big man answered, sounding as though he missed out on most of his education. "'Tis strange that yer friend didn't tell ya where he was goin'."

Deklan stepped forward and added, "He left in a bit of a hurry, sir. Sorry to bother you and we will be taking up no more of your time."

"Not a probum." The round man smiled. His grapy grin glowed brightly in the dingy doorway. "Good luck to ya feller's in findin' yer friend." He let the door go and the spring loaded hinge snapped it back into place with a wobbly bang.

As swiftly as a fly changes direction, Deklan and Jedidiah stepped away from the swinging door to avoid being chipped inside the house on the inward sweep.

"Thank you, sir." Jedidiah nodded, backing up a few more steps.

Seated back in the carriage, Deklan snapped the reigns, insisting the horse move toward town. "One down. I wonder how many more we'll come upon like that before we find my man," he muttered.

"Prepare yourself. I'm sure there will be a few just like that." Jedidiah nudged Deklan. "Look there. Pull over." He pointed at another house tucked away on a wooded lot. That one looked as though it wasn't in need of as much repair as the last, but still was begging for a little tender love and care.

"This looks quaint." Deklan cast a cautious eye at the gray house over Jedidiah's shoulder.

The place was in decent shape other than a few spots of dust forming on the trim work and its leaf stained rooftop. Since the alley to the front door had been maintained a little better than the previous stop-off, made it easily identified as the pathway to the home.

They stepped up to the front door and Deklan knocked.

Nobody showed up. He knocked another time.

Jedidiah cupped his hands around his eyes and pressed his forehead tightly to the window pane. It was his meek attempt at peeking inside to catch a glimpse of who or what might be coming to greet them at the door.

Nobody, still. Deklan knocked again. Harder that time.

After the third knock, they turned away.

Then, the door knob rattled.

Deklan turned back first, followed by Jedidiah.

Anticipation started Deklan's heart pounding. He had a strong feeling they were at the home of his enchanted mate gone lost.

They waited for the door to open. When it had, a young man stood in front of them. Tall. Dark. A little tattered, but that made him uniquely handsome. His open shirt wavered in the wind, showing off his broad chest likely built strong by hard labor. His gray eyes shone brightly against his dark caramel skin tone and his deep quiet voice sounded pure. "Hello there," he greeted them. "Anything I can help you with today?" The man's expression seemed as nervous as Deklan was.

For a second, Deklan and Jedidiah stood there in front of the man, their blank stares giving up no clue why they were there. Deklan glanced at Jedidiah who had then glimpsed back.

The man stood in the doorway and asked again, "Can I help the two of you?"

Could it be?

Deklan wasn't sure if the guy in front of him was his mystery man just yet. There were a lot of similarities from what he could remember, however, it was dark that night and the costume difference had made it difficult to tell if he was really Oakland.

Jedidiah stepped forward first, eluding the discomfort of the unexpected encounter. Quickly thinking, he made up an introduction that sounded legitimate. "We have come in gracious greetings to thank you for your visit to the Royal's birthday celebration a few nights back. Did you enjoy yourself?"

The man's face displayed certain signs of confusion. "I'm sorry, I hadn't attended any event recently and I don't think my brother had either. Are you sure you have the right house?"

Deklan's heart slowed as he observed the man's hands. They were quite swollen from what appeared to have been overworked, and his knuckles were surly too large for accepting a ring unless it was bigger than the magical one he had circling his middle finger. "We are terribly sorry to trouble you. We must have the wrong address. Our purpose was to pass on our personal gratitude to those who had attended. Please excuse our intrusion."

The man remained cordial. "It made for a nice break in the day. Please know it was not any trouble at all."

"You say you have a brother?" Jedidiah interrupted.

Just as Jedidiah asked, a call echoed from inside the house and footsteps followed. "Who's here?"

Before the man standing in the doorway could answer, the

voice from behind him stepped into view. He stood beside his bigger brother looking just as handsome to Deklan, causing his heart to race all over again. Wind furrowed over his brow as if some sort of magical sign had just presented itself.

Could this chap be who he was looking for?

Deklan noticed the man's hands while watching him button up his linen shirt. They appeared the right size, but trying the ring on would have only gotten him closer to the truth.

"Is there something we can do for you?" the younger man asked, pressing his brown hands down the front of his shirt, presumably trying to iron any visible wrinkles flat.

In a nonthreatening manner, Jedidiah moved his hands behind his back and linked them together. "We are looking to find the person who lost a ring at a recent event and we'd like to return it. It appears to hold some value and it wouldn't be right if we didn't get it back to the rightful owner. Did either of you lose a ring recently?"

Deklan shakily held out his hand as Jedidiah reached for it blindly.

The two men admired the glistening jewelry piece. As they had, Deklan twisted the ring from his finger and held out a hand for the younger man to take it. If the ring was going to fit either of the two chaps, it would have been him.

"Go ahead," the older brother insisted, pushing his younger brother's hand toward Deklan's. "It looks like yours," he might have been lying.

The younger brother hesitated while the older brother grabbed the ring and tried forcing it onto his own smallest finger. Even pushing with extreme force, it wouldn't fit past the man's second knuckle. Besides, he had already admitted he wasn't at the Royal's party a few minutes before his brother showed up with smaller hands.

The younger man held his hand out, fingernails up, motioning Deklan to place the ring on his finger as if it was a proposal.

It seemed to have been a longshot, but Deklan had gone through the fitting anyway, noticing the man's hands were gentle to the touch, bringing back memories of the night he held Oakland's at the garden. He hesitated a moment, rotating the ring between his fingers as if a feeling signaled him with having the wrong guy. But he'd gone ahead and placed it onto the young man's ring finger where he remembered it had come from. It fit loosely and had nearly fallen off.

The handsome young man lifted his hand upward into view and switched the ring from the finger it was on to his thumb. "Perfect," he said. "You have found the owner."

Disappointed those two good looking men could have been so dishonest had Deklan more than disturbed. He held out his hand to retrieve the ring. "I am sorry, but that is a promise ring and belongs on somebody else's ring finger. May I have it back, please?"

The young man pulled the ring off his finger and placed it gently into Deklan's open palm. "Not mine," was all he said as he quietly turned away.

Before the older brother had a chance to close the door, Jedidiah and Deklan moved away quickly as if they were two mice being stared at by a cat.

They continued going from one home to another throughout the afternoon, hopeful, as well as desperate, to find the person who owned that ring. The day was physically and mentally exhausting. Nobody seemed to have matched or connected with Deklan's soul the way it had at the birthday celebration, nor had the ring fit any of the men they visited. Or at least the ring hadn't brought about the magic he was expecting when it was slipped onto any of those fingers.

"After the next visit, let's call it a day. Please?" Jedidiah begged. "There's always tomorrow."

Glowering, Deklan agreed. He was getting worn out as well. "One more stop?"

The final visit of the day was high on a hilltop with a long drive lined with juniper trees. The pine scent was evident and made the air smell of Christmas.

It appeared there was no need to knock on any doors with all the young children playing kick-the-ball along the front lane. Every one of them were fleshy white, raising belief there was a slim chance the owner of the house was the skin tone they were looking for. But, no telling by what they'd seen, really. There could have been servants or ranch hands hanging around who might have been black.

The children had taken off running to the front porch and stood there staring at the carriage coming up the drive. The smallest child, who appeared to be less than thirty-six inches tall had run into the house.

Shortly after the door banged shut behind the kid, a tall man reopened it and stepped out onto the porch. Quite a change from what had run through the doorway. Call it a magic trick. It surely seemed like one. Standing with his hands on his hips and the tiny kid wrapped around his leg, he waited.

"Should we just turn around and go?" Jedidiah had a pleading tone to his voice. "This doesn't look promising."

"We can't turn back now. If we do, the man will find it strange and likely chase us down. Keep going. We'll talk our way out of it when we get there," Deklan replied, scanning the place for any odd activity other than the rambunctious kids racing around like jungle animals.

"That man doesn't come close to matching your description of the fellow you met the other night. Look at him. He's huge, and white." Jedidiah pointed out the fact in front of them. "This visit seems futile, and the seventy two children he has running around should tell you he prefers not to share his bed with another gent. Let's get out of here before this guy murders and buries us down tiny holes in the back yard."

"We mustn't be rude." Deklan had become distraught with Jedidiah's nonsense. "If we turn around now, he'll only think we're up to no good."

Jedidiah pulled back and sat tight. "I'll stay here. You go." He flicked a pointy finger.

As soon as they arrived at the front porch, the man that appeared to be towering seven feet tall marched up and leaned over the two of them like a full grown redwood tree. "What brings you here?" he growled with a big voice that sounded like timber cracking.

Covering his eyes to block the sunny halo behind the great

big guy, Deklan had given him the reason they were there.

The tall father of eight, nine, or maybe ten plus, confirmed there wasn't anybody on the premises matching the description. Politely, but firmly, he asked them to leave.

They had taken his advice and turned the carriage around. The double snap of the reign's pushed the horse to move faster.

Heading home, the night closed out the day quickly, evident by the sun melting into the horizon like a blob of gold, allowing the moon to take over the place it had left.

Chapter 16

With interlocking arms across his chest, Deklan's father had been standing on the stairway landing evoking a temper anybody would have hoped to avoid. Mouth pursed to one side and eyebrows on the downward slant at nose bridge center.

"I don't think this man will ever be happy with me," Deklan revealed to Jedidiah.

"He's only looking out for you. Give him time." Jedidiah looked past Deklan with one eye trained on Dante as the man tramped from the top of the stairway to the last step at the bottom.

Deklan stopped the carriage with a tug on the reigns, sitting a moment before climbing out, whispering to Jedidiah to follow slowly.

Dante glared at the carriage with one eye squinting. "Jedidiah, Is that you?"

"It is, sir," Jedidiah addressed him as if he were the true King of a castle. "How have you been?"

"Very well, thank you," Dante replied. "What brings you to town?" Even though he might have his suspicions about the two men, he still showed a cordial welcome to Jedidiah.

"I heard there was a celebratory event for Deklan, which I had missed, but decided to keep my plan in motion and still visit," Jedidiah answered. "I'm glad I did. Deklan and I had a pleasant day."

"It's good to see you." Dante seemed genuine toward Jedidiah, ignoring Deklan the entire time. That seemed discourteous, but considering the situation between Deklan and him, and since he hadn't seen Jedidiah in quite a while, made the interlude acceptable. "So, what have the two of you been up to?"

Deklan interjected with honesty, "We had a few hours to spare so we took the carriage around town. Caught up on lost time. Met a few people. It was nice having Jedidiah here again."

"Did you tell Jedidiah about the wedding while you were out?" Speaking to Deklan, Dante made it a point to mention that.

"Father!" Deklan raised his voice. "Please. Can we put that aside for now?"

"It's inevitable, Deklan," his father lectured.

"Not now," Deklan reprimanded, followed by an apology to Jedidiah for the unnecessary outburst. At the same time he bantered back and forth with his father, he turned the horse and carriage toward the barn.

"There is no need to argue with me, Deklan. You know this won't end well for you." Dante made certain Deklan heard him with a stern hand grip on his shoulder.

Deklan tugged back, trying to break free, but his father's grasp was too firm. "Whatever you say, Pop." He looked him in the eye and repeated what he'd mentioned before. "Remember how many lives you will ruin if you go through with this nonsense."

At that moment, Deklan felt a downward spiral with his father's usually robust temper, bringing about a brief interlude of weakness that was evident in the hold he had on his shoulder. Deklan pulled free at the instant he felt his father's grasp loosen.

Was the king crumbling by his son's rightful statement? Had he realized the push for that wedding was wrong for so many people?

The entire time Deklan and his father disputed, Jedidiah stayed quiet, the expression on his face and the way he was looking upward at the sky indicated he must have been feeling uncomfortable while the two contended their differences.

Deklan's father suddenly stopped arguing. The look on his face was one that could have been realization of what he was putting his son through, or he'd become discouraged he couldn't get through to him.

Why wouldn't Dante understand like Jedidiah could?

"I wish you good fortune, Jedidiah." Dante turned to walk up the stairs, but before he left, he walked back to his son, hugged him tightly and kissed him on the forehead. "You too, my son," he whispered, and then ascended up the stairs.

The sentimental gesture concerned Deklan. His father never showed affection like he just had, and for him to wish good fortune made Deklan think his father had sent him out to pasture for good. What had he meant by that? On the bright side, he hadn't heard the door lock as his father entered the Manor. Was there real reason to worry?

"I am tired of fighting," Deklan confided to Jedidiah. "I need a day off. Maybe I should just get married to a mademoiselle like my parents want me to. It would certainly make things easier."

"Don't you dare." Jedidiah spun Deklan around, their eyes met squarely. "That will not make it easier or make it right for anybody, and you know that. It would only be a short term fix. You'd be miserable for evermore."

"Is it better to have them hate me?"

"No, but it isn't good to live a lie all your life just to make them happy. What about your happiness and the honest way of living your life?"

Deklan dropped his head and led the horse to the barn. "I don't know. I'm tired. I just want this over with so I can move on."

"Getting married to a female you don't even know isn't going to bring this to a close. It'll only make matters worse. For you, as well as everybody involved. You said it yourself." Jedidiah was right. His mention of the whole scenario was more rational than Deklan's was. "Let's get the horse put away and you can sleep on it. You'll be fresher in the morning. It's been a long day."

"I suppose you're right," Deklan lazily agreed.

"I know I am." Jedidiah helped Deklan disconnect the harness from the carriage and then helped remove the bridle from the horses head. He hung the gear over the large hooks on the wall while Deklan walked the horse into his stall. A quick brush across his neck and back and the job was done.

"Are you able to go out with me again tomorrow?" Deklan asked, hoping he'd receive a positive answer and wouldn't have to continue alone.

Jedidiah bowed his head. "Unfortunately not. I have to get back to the plantation as early as possible. I could only stay for the day."

Disappointed, Deklan slouched. "Well, thanks for going with me today. I'm not sure I could have accomplished what we had alone. Having you with me was a big help. Prepared me up for tomorrow."

Jedidiah reached over and wrapped his arm across Deklan's shoulders. "Hey, you would have managed. I'm glad I helped you get started. I know you'll find him. You're on the right track."

"However, I'm yet so far off that track," Deklan added. He looked up at the great big house he lived in and wondered if he should have stayed outside in the barn with Chadwick. The tension on the inside seemed too great. In his imagination, the house was pulsating as though angry and alive.

Jedidiah squeezed his shoulder, transferring confidence to his friend. "Come on, let's go inside."

Deklan tried the door, pleasantly grateful his father hadn't locked him out like he thought he would. It seemed Dante was in a better place with him than he understood.

Deklan and Jedidiah had gone straight to Deklan's bedroom without addressing his mother or speaking to his father again. His goal at the moment was to leave well enough alone to prevent any more arguments.

Closing the door behind them, Deklan fell backward on the

bed with a huff, arms stretched high above his head while Jedidiah dropped in a chair in front of the fireplace—his feet lifting from the floor and back down again. A billowing puff had come from him as well.

Even though it was a long drawn out and tiresome day, the two of them reminisced for hours before retiring for the night. Long stories, a few laughs, even a hug or two.

Chapter 17

Bright and early the next day, Deklan saw Jedidiah off in the minicab carriage back to town before he himself had gone out on his own to search for his true mate. It amounted to a repeat performance of the day before, with exception of different people and without the support of his good friend, Jedidiah.

It was difficult to believe how deceitful people were. Beyond Crafty. Some presented fictitious stories as to who they were in hopes to ease possession of a ring that hadn't belonged to them. Sure it was only a ring with a white gold band, but that particular jewelry piece Deklan had was more than special. It belonged to no thief, liar or swindling hooligan. It belonged to the man he was connected strongly to, who he'd met in the garden — unexpectedly and couldn't dismiss from his thoughts. He wasn't about to let go of the ring until he found the man who'd lost it. The one his heart had linked itself to. The one he desired back in his life.

Deklan continued the search in and out of the city, each rejection prolonging the feeling of loneliness. With the unsettling understanding he'd remain forever alone, enforced his persistence to locate the owner of the jewelry piece. He pressed on, however, his exhausted body and mind overpowered his determination to extend his search into the evening. Before the sun had fully set, he turned the carriage and headed home.

The day hadn't ended the way he'd hoped, but grateful the ring was still circling his middle finger instead of some stranger's who'd made up a tale to take it from him. He had a deep sense he'd know the man who owned it the moment they reconnected, certain the strong feeling he had that other night would return and prove he'd found his mate.

ଔ ଓ

Oakland returned home from his evening swim in the river, bare-chested with a small cotton towel draped over his shoulder. From the time he first set toe into river until the moment he left it, the day had changed from sunset to nightfall.

He wouldn't normally take to the open field undressed, but he was in a rare mood to let it all hang out, and the darker than usual evening enabled his caramel completion to seamlessly blend with the night. His existence of wandering the woods unseen would have been more conspicuous if he'd added the ivory smile.

The way he always had found his way during his nighttime strolls, Oakland identified illuminated lanterns placed in each of the Manors windows, but that night, he noticed additional lanterns flickering in the barn out back.

"Bollocks," he griped while swiftly ducking behind the biggest tree he'd been able to find. Of all evenings he decided to walk home without clothing, somebody had to be lagging out in the horse barn. He figured it was Deklan putting the horse and carriage away, repeating what he'd done so many nights in the past, but wouldn't bet his smile on it being him that time. It seemed too late for that. Oakland remained quiet, hiding his nudity from whoever was in the barn.

One by one, each lantern in the barn had gone out, shocking Oakland into believing whoever was closing the place down would have exited at any moment.

He reached for the towel he'd placed over his shoulder to find it wasn't there. "Bollocks," Oakland said again, hand gripping the bulge between his legs while running toward the carriage house, aiming for the back corner to stay clear of shining lights.

Piloting a crouched run, Oakland had finally made it to the carriage house, however, by the time he reached it, all the lanterns in the barn had been shut down. He stood against the house with his backside pressed tightly against the clapboard wall, sidestepping with slow proficiency toward the front door. The only way in.

Oakland lowered his breathing and quietly crept along the wall, keeping his footsteps as silent as he was able. Dry leaves under his feet crunched, making unwanted noise. His favorite word of the night had come out again, "Bollocks" — then — "Sshhh!" He crept toward the door, keeping his movements slow and steady, feeling his exposed butt scraping against the rough woody surface of the carriage house. He winced while trying to cage his long black dick behind both hands.

He finally reached the door, naked and mostly uncovered. All the animals inside the house met him the moment he stepped over the threshold, wanting food or at least a friendly pat on the head. He pushed them out of the way with his bare hip and one swish of a foot.

"Move, move, move," he nagged, adding a word of pleasantry to get the animals to do what had been asked.

Before Oakland made it in and successfully dropped the lock bar into place, he heard a deep voice behind him speak, "Hello there, kind sir."

Was it Deklan? It sounded like him and there was only one way to find out.

"Could this predicament get any more charming?" Oakland sarcastically mumbled beneath his breath, his face heating up from being mortified.

Oakland turned around smiling as if nothing odd or

awkward had taken place. His tone was sharp when he said, "Good evening." He stood anchoring the door in place with his foot and a shoulder while struggling with one hand to prevent putting the enormity between his legs on display for the man at the door.

When Oakland realized it was Deklan standing there, his heart felt as if it almost stopped. With a bang, a hand hit his chest as if by doing so would have kept it beating. It seemed to have worked—the loud thump in his ears booming similar to a wake up slap to the back of the head.

"Oh. It's you. Hello there." Deklan backed up, clearly appearing staggered to find it was Oakland standing in front of him, and without any clothes on. His forehead wrinkled. "What are you doing here?" A second night in a row he'd asked that same question to a black man in an open doorway. First it was Jedidiah and then Oakland. He looked up, down and around the place to confirm he was standing in his own back fortress.

Oakland stood awkwardly, like a one legged stork, wobbling and on the verge of tipping over. "I... Yes. Um... I live here. I do. In this coop. With the animals." Remaining truthful with Deklan, several broken phrases that hardly made any sense rolled off his tongue. He sounded uneducated while fidgeting to hide what he had packed in his crotch, trying to deter humiliation and a rising erection from looking at Deklan standing with his shirt dangling open. Oakland followed the hairy trail down the center of Deklan's abdomen. He liked that. A lot.

With his forehead wrinkled, Deklan chuckled. "Really? How long?" He looked down at Oakland's large hand while it scrabbled at keeping his impressive manhood from being exposed. His gaze shifted higher, slowly observing Oakland's body as though he was ready to move in and have his way with the entire package. Every ripple and bulge shone physically fit. Deklan lifted an eyebrow that might have been an approval for what he was seeing for the second time.

This could be good.

Oakland had gone on, still sounding rash, "Um... been here a while. I work in the garden and part time in the kitchen when needed. Here." He pointed to the ground, but meant that he worked at the manor, not actually there in the coop.

"Wow," was all Deklan said while he rubbed his hair shadowed chin.

Oakland wondered if Deklan was upset with him for holding back the truth from the start or if his expressive word was because he'd been thrilled to have seen his near naked body standing in front of him. He asked, "Would you like to come in?"

Deklan crossed his arms over his chest, not saying anything, but eventually had given in to the invitation. "Sure, why not. It might make the circumstance a little bit less absurd."

Following his comment, Oakland had a laugh. He opened the door wider to make it easier for Deklan to cross the threshold, keeping his body hidden behind the shadows of the door. A slight gust drifted in, opening the front of Deklan's shirt more than it had been, giving Oakland a glimpse of what he already knew he liked. What Oakland had seen perked his temptation and his male bonding instincts were to reach forward and touch him, but the time hadn't seemed right for exploring with eager hands. Instead, he properly stood at ease and only transferred a reserved glance from Deklan's blue eyes to his well-groomed hairy chest.

Deklan looked around Oakland's small living space. "Nice. Cozy." He nodded, dropping his arms at his sides. A sparkle ricocheted from his hand and poked Oakland in the eye. He was wearing the ring.

Another, *"Oh bollocks"*, voiced in Oakland's head. He reached for a towel draped over a chair and wrapped it around his waist. "Sorry about this." He looked back over his shoulder and caught Deklan staring at his cocoa rear-end. He spun back around, grinning. "I just returned from swimming in the river, so as you can see, I wasn't ready for guests. Sorry for my unsightly appearance."

"Don't be silly. I'm a man with similar equipment. There isn't anything I hadn't seen before. Plus, you look... fine." It sounded as though Deklan stumbled for the perfect word, and had exercised fascination when he said it. There had been noticeable anxiety that had taken over his ability to conduct himself as ordinary. He wrangled the ears of a nearby goat and the ring sparkled again. He pulled away, looking at his hand for a moment, slowly spinning the ring around his finger.

Time stalled for a few seconds and all sound had gone with it. Soon into the silence, Oakland secured the short towel at his waist, positioning it low at his hips to effectively keep his oversized dick from swinging freely below the trim line.

Was it a burden or a gift?

Oakland's dark broad chest remained unprotected and he was convinced Deklan hadn't minded it being left bare. He caught him looking on occasion, but seemed as though he was shifting his gaze from one part of the room to the other. Oakland was enjoying Deklan's sneaky method of observing his body. It lifted his spirits—had given him the proof he needed as being a desirable man to someone like Deklan.

Oakland glanced at the ring on Deklan's finger and couldn't believe it'd come back. The Mirror Man told him the pendant and the ring would remain connected and the two people wearing them would too.

"Don't just stand there, come in. Please." Oakland rolled a hand into the empty space between them. "Have a seat at the table and don't pay any mind to the animals. They'll relax as soon as they feel comfort having you here."

Deklan had taken two steps to his right and snagged a chair from the dining table, spinning it with some talent on one leg so it faced him. He dragged the chair with one hand across the floor, sat down and scooted himself forward with his knees tucked neatly beneath the table. The ringed hand dropped to his lap.

Oakland watched him intently, finding it interesting how he kept the ring hidden from view.

"How come I haven't seen you around here before?" Deklan asked. "I thought I knew everybody at the Manor. You are definitely an employee I would have noticed." He sputtered, "I mean, not because you look different than most of the other servants around here. Or I mean... I'm sorry, I didn't mean that." His hand lifted to his forehead. "It's just that... I meant to say, you're a good looking gent who doesn't seem like he'd be shoveling pig poop to survive." Another hand slapped his forehead. The ring flashed. "Oh, Dagrats! No, wait. I don't mean people shy of good looks should be doing the dirty work. Dagrats!

What I wanted to say was… Oh forget it." He huffed and made it a point to stop speaking.

Oakland held back laughter, and acted as though he hadn't heard a word Deklan said. He had however answered, "I keep mostly to myself and the animals I live with. I don't socialize with anybody, servants or employer. I just do what needs to be done and then return home where I belong."

Oakland increased the flame in the lantern sitting on the table.

"I was wondering—" Deklan shifted in his chair and brought his hands to the tabletop, unconsciously exposing the ring "—when I brought you home the other night, why didn't you want me to know you lived here?"

Oakland glanced at the white-gold band shimmering on Deklan's middle finger. Instead of answering, he stood up and mentioned he should go put more clothes on since he was feeling out of place in the nude.

"Stay!" Deklan anxiously blurted. "I mean… you're fine the way you are. I don't mind. It's warm in here anyway so less clothing makes more sense. I should loosen some of mine, actually." Following through, he rolled up his sleeves and pushed the shirt tails behind his back, exposing himself even more.

Oakland found Deklan's restless response a validation of his attraction toward him. "I'll be right back." Oakland sprinted up the wooden chicken plank and exchanged the towel for a light linen pant. Even though they hung lower than the towel and showed off every bit of what he had beneath them, he felt more comfortable out of that cotton towel.

He'd gone back to his tiny kitchen and found Deklan sitting with the front shirt panels dangling toward the floor at his sides, finding the man extremely attractive.

Deklan leaned back in his chair with a smile directed at Oakland. "It's gotten hotter in here, don't you think? We should open a window, or at least the door."

"Oh, bollocks" What was he up to?

Oakland stared at Deklan, becoming choked up at how sensually good-looking he was with his shirt nearly off. The contrast of the white linen shirt against the dark hair neatly feathered across his chest played with his mind, causing his own dick to twitch beneath the linen pants he had on. If Oakland had said anything at that moment, the words would have come out as senseless jumble. He stayed quiet and stared at the man's stunning body, imagining the treasure he'd find once all the fabric had been discarded. He quickly looked away before his fascination for Deklan had become evident, putting the front of his flimsy pants on the rise.

From the corner of his eyes, Oakland had noticed Deklan staring at the smooth dark muscles across his chest, tracing his torso with his gaze, following the deep gutter of his abdomen until his eyes met the black hair sprouting above the linen waistband. Oakland stood still a moment and let him gawp. It seemed to have been what Deklan wanted.

Deklan cleared his throat and turned away, then repeated, "So, why the secret?"

"Secret?" Oakland mimicked his word. "What secret?" he said it again, sitting down in the chair across from Deklan, exhibiting his limited understanding as to what Deklan meant by secret. What had Deklan really been talking about? The attraction he had for him and his stunning body, or that he kept hidden in the shed behind the big house?

Deklan smirked, most likely trying to find out if Oakland had a secret liking for him by keeping his phrased question so limited. He clarified, "How come you didn't want me to know you lived here?"

"Oh, that secret." Oakland was relieved, leaned back in the chair and answered, "I suppose I wanted to keep to myself. I don't know. I liked you the moment I met you and was thinking if you knew I was a servant around here, you'd treat me differently, or perhaps define that the employer and the help should not socially mix."

"What?" Deklan looked him in the eyes. "Knowing you lived in this stable wouldn't have changed what I thought of you."

Relief stricken, Oakland stood up and reached for a pear. "Would you like one?" He held up the biggest and shiniest fruit from the bowl and offered it to Deklan.

"I'd like that," Deklan replied, smiling and looking at Oakland's torso again. He seemed to be hooked on what he'd seen.

Oakland inhaled, expanding his strong black chest for Deklan's sake, feeling the burn of his blue eyed gaze becoming fixed on it. He grinned as he turned to retrieve the sharpest knife he owned.

Deklan shifted in his chair and Oakland noticed him watching his hands cutting the pear into wedges. Oakland flirtatiously asked, "What's going on behind those blue eyes?"

Deklan seemed tense as he pulled himself out of the locked gaze he had on Oakland's hands. His own hand was trembling as though nervous, continually twisting the ring around his finger. His hooded eyes turned soft while staring at Oakland for a stretched out period of time, holding the same dreamy trance Oakland had on him.

Oakland's head slowly lowered, recognizing the ring Deklan had been spinning around his knuckle. He kept the knowledge he knew about the jewelry piece to himself, knowing it was the ring the Mirror Man had given him on the night of the celebration—the one he thought had vanished along with midnight. Oakland gently placed his open hand over Deklan's, instilling comfort in him to speak whatever was on his mind. He found the contrast of his dark hand over Deklan's incredibly sensual, and he silently prayed he wouldn't pull away.

Deklan lifted his gaze to meet Oakland's, and had given in to his oncoming smile. Slipping his hands from beneath Oakland's, he removed the ring from his finger and softy whispered, "Let me have your hand."

As in marriage? Oakland fantasized.

Without reluctance, Oakland placed his palm into Deklan's. The warmth he'd felt from him was beyond anything he could have imagined or explained. At that moment, he connected with Deklan even more, as though a ghostly influence had passed between them.

Deklan looked straight into Oakland's gray eyes and slowly slipped the ring onto his finger. Rays of light beamed around the room as if a force of magic had derived from the matrimony.

Coming from the makeshift bedroom at a higher level, there were additional light beams shining. The flashes of light were known to Oakland, coming from the pendant on the bedside table. It had the same reaction when the two jeweled trinkets were together before. The pieces fit.

At that moment, he understood there was a definitive connection between two people. The right two people. It had become clear to him their souls had finally met and a bond secured with the return of the ring.

Oakland dropped his gaze, hiding the signs of his weakening emotions from Deklan's view. He was a grown man, supposed to be strong, but sentiments deeper than he could have ever imagined had taken over. It was a reaction of happiness — one that only factual love could have produced. His eyes welled up. He blinked to disguise what had come on so abruptly. At the moment a tear had fallen to the wooden surface, he felt his hands had been squeezed by Deklan.

"It's you," Deklan had softly spoken. "My striking Prince I thought I'd lost. I missed you tremendously. How had I not known?"

Oakland spun the ring and glanced at the upper deck where he knew the necklace lay. He looked back at Deklan with a boyish smile.

Without losing Oakland's gaze or grasp, Deklan stood majestically in front of him and asked, "Can I kiss you?" like he'd done once before.

Oakland was in the exact place he wanted. The very place he was supposed to have been. With the man he was meant to have been with. He stood, moved in and had taken Deklan's lips against his. The kiss was warm and the man's touch felt gentle, yet exuded masculine strength.

"I'd missed you very much, Oakland. Like an important part of me had been taken away that night," Deklan's voice had reached that of a whisper — the warmth of his tone embracing Oakland's ear.

There were no objections from Oakland when he felt Deklan drawing him closer, the hair on the man's chest lightly brushing against his, rising anxiety with a necessity to feel more. Deklan's tongue turned aggressive, seemed enthused to take what had just become his.

Giving in to Deklan, Oakland let the man take charge. Because of sexually prolonged weakness, Oakland's erection had grown a whole lot bigger within seconds, firmly climbing the deep gutters of his and Deklan's abdomen.

Excelled anticipation to lay with his Prince had developed when the returned pressure of Deklan's dick had immediately grown stiffly alongside his. Their responsive erections had proven an attraction for one another had gone way beyond a cordial glance between two men.

The affectionate feelings for men Oakland locked away for so long had all come out at that very moment he was kissing Deklan. He'd dreamt of that incredible day so many times before, but had never been free enough, or had met somebody he could have trusted to travel that penetrating path of discovery with. He'd undeniably had the emotional frame of mind to open himself up for another man, however, practicing caution during those times were vital. There had been nothing open about two men falling in love, much less sharing themselves intimately in the privacy of a single bed. He'd wondered for a very long time what the pleasures of somebody like Deklan moving deep inside him would feel like, and during that passionate kiss, he was sure he'd found the one man who'd take that first step with him.

Chapter 18

The morning had arrived too soon for that first night Deklan and Oakland spent with each other, neither of them had any desire to go their separate ways. Fact be known, Oakland hadn't wanted Deklan to ever remove himself from his body—the internal sensation was too great.

By far, it had been the best night of Oakland's life, and he wouldn't have traded it for ownership of the great big world. He'd known for a long time he was physically attracted to the male gender, and when he connected with Deklan, found they fit as perfectly as a locket and key, and his distinction for that stunning man had intensified.

In days past, Oakland had only imagined what it would have been like to obtain another man's touch, self-confessed the idea wholly, however, had never acted on his desires for reasons he'd been informed that two men in love was an abnormal act against nature. He never understood how desires of one's heart could have been identified as such bad behavior. It hadn't computed. To him and probably many others, that conception was indeed absurd, as well as pain inflicting whenever mentioned that two devoted souls must remain apart.

In his day and age, Oakland had been forced to keep his secret locked away, only commencing his hidden urges behind closed doors where nobody knew what he would have been up to. Even though most of the human race had considered him a rapscallion, he fulfilled his sexual desires with the use of his own black hand, imagining he was being dominated by a real man laid out over top of him, penetrating him, pushing his passions to the limits of no possible return.

His imaginative fantasies had finally turned real when he connected with Deklan that night, and the way the man had introduced himself to his body seemed all too natural to have been considered anything other than the way it was meant for the both of them. After feeling the incredible sensations Deklan had put him through, Oakland's own hand and buttered zucchinis would have never been able to fulfill his sexual pleasures again.

Deklan and Oakland slipped in and out of slumber the entire night, at each waking moment making body joining intercourse from dusk to dawn. Their newly learned connection couldn't have gone unexploited once they'd found how magnificent it was sticking their erections inside one another, Oakland gladly at the receiving end more than Deklan had been.

From that initial butt filling insertion, Oakland had a difficult time letting Deklan remove himself, and as luck had flourished, Deklan seemed to have preferred giving his stiff dick to Oakland. There'd been no denying the two of them interlocked perfectly that way, Oakland instantly feeling most natural having Deklan bearing down on him, and Deklan seemed more than thrilled it was his cock pile driving the black man beneath him. However, those claimed positions had satisfied each of them without a doubt, Oakland had given away his favored place to Deklan's paralleled desires by burying his thick black cock inside the man's tight white hole once or twice that night. The entire time Oakland maneuvered all eleven inches in and out of him, Deklan's eyes had glazed over and his teeth ground harshly together.

Deklan's verbal moans, growls, and gleaming face had given all the clues he wanted Oakland moving inside him, and the moment Oakland proposed to vacate, Deklan gripped sturdy and held him in place, verbally begging, "Don't pull out. Stay. I've waited too long for you, Oakland. Way too long."

Lying together in sexual lockdown was well past due and the thrill of their novel discovery of one man's dick is another man's pleasure, figured their energetic bodies had fused with semen transferals at ten times minimum throughout the night.

As they'd pleasantly found out, Oakland's body had effortlessly drawn in Deklan's nine inch erection. The bond he'd experienced when Deklan introduced himself for the first time border lined on a dream, however, what he'd felt inside had confirmed it was all very real. From that exploratory moment Oakland laid back and spread his legs, he was hooked and couldn't get enough of the Prince sliding his erect cock in and out of his butter slickened asshole. Repeating what Deklan had cried out earlier, Oakland begged, "Please, don't pull out" — he released a pant — "Ejaculate inside me this time."

At that moment, Deklan paused. "You sure it's okay I do that?"

Oakland gripped Deklan's ass cheeks and pulled, drawing in a sharp breath from the striking pleasure of his dick sinking deeper. "It... should be fine, I'm sure." — he exhaled — "I'd swallowed my own semen many times and I'm still good."

"Positive point. I'm guilty of that myself, but this time, it'll be my sperm in you." Deklan picked up his rhythm a little bit. "Oh, jeez." His face scowled. "I feel it coming. I want to shoot in you real bad, like I'm claiming you as mine."

Feeling the exquisite pressure returning deep inside his rectum, Oakland moaned, "Oh, Gawd. Do it. I beg you. Put your claim on me."

"Done." Increasing his pace, Deklan pumped his hips into Oakland, groaning his answer, "You're gonna get every spurt up that black ass, then. Omigawd, I'm almost there." He grunted and hammered Oakland's exposed taint, making his entire body boogie with each forceful thrust. The course hair above his dick scrubbed with stimulating effects to Oakland's cock sucking butthole and big black nuts.

"That's it. Shoot it in me. Keep hammering. I'm there. I'm there. Here it comes. Oh, BOLLOCKS," Oakland hollered at the moment his orgasm buzzed through his entire body, spiraling up his spine and back down again where it squeezed his pelvis like a strong grip had been kneading dough. He moaned as though it was the best feeling ever experienced. He couldn't maintain his mind blowing outburst. The overcharged sparks racing through his pelvis had been too incredible.

His upper body jolted forward at the moment the bulbous head of his thick black dick expanded and spit semen everywhere, shooting white froth across his dark chest and face, the contrast appearing that of large corded pearls. The scent of his own sperm clobbered his septum, setting his mind into orgasmic overload. Deklan's prodding dick positively pumping the semen out of him. Oakland continued ejaculating, several spurts arcing clear above his head, slamming into the wood planks covering the wall and dripping downward like thick maple syrup.

"Your gorgeous, Oakland," Deklan gruffly said, and then winced. His face immediately contorted. "Here it comes. Gah! Suck the sperm from my thick white dick. Jeez." He fell against Oakland's chest, body jerking. His pelvis struck Oakland's chocolate taint with a hard inward bang, gluing him stiffly in place, then, instantly changing to short rhythmic thumps that matched each palpitation of his power pulsing prostate, each spurt of white hot spud sent deep into his new boyfriends butt chute.

Deklan grunted. He growled. He roared. His entire body had gone completely firm, back bowing that forced his dick deeper. He couldn't pull out if he wanted to. He stiffly held on while he flooded Oakland's rectum with semen.

Oakland was nearly crying—the sensation so great. He begged, "I need that, Deklan. Shoot everything you have inside me. Please." He locked his legs around Deklan's back, holding the man in place. He'd taken Deklan's kisses. Each jolt from his Prince's hips had matched the rhythm of his penetrating tongue.

Deklan's body tremors had taken control, his orgasm

obviously reaching its peak. He growled, "I'm still unloading. Omigawd, your tight ass is sucking me so good."

Their dick connected experience had drained them both, taking some time before able to regain a coherent state of mind. They'd played every role in bed as though they only had that single night together. One lay back with his legs in the air, while the other had driven his dick in and out of ass and mouth. They flip-flopped positions. Side saddle spooned during hip thrusting penetration. Ramming tight holes on hands and knees. Taking horse-style rides on each other's erection. It was all new and exciting. Every position they could think of, tried—ejaculating each time before moving on to the next. Oakland had even sucked on Deklan's stiff dick, swallowing his spurting semen and telling him how good it was.

Before Deklan pulled out of Oakland, he asked, "Had I poked all the right spots inside that beautiful body of yours? I can keep going if you want me to? I have more to give. Did you like how hard I was inside you? Hope you can walk okay?"

Those were some overloaded questions all at once, but Oakland had approved them all by saying, "Hadn't my plentiful discharge and crazed bodily reaction been enough of a positive answer for all those questions? That's how great you felt sliding in and out of me. Even though you had my legs bowed most of the night because you were thrusting those hips between them, I could have kept going. I really believe my asshole was made for your dick. I think it likes having your erection probing around as much as I do."

Deklan laughed. "That asshole of yours had done a grand job, felt like it was sucking on my dick the entire time I was in there. It was an amazing feeling and when I stopped to watch out of curiosity, I saw it literally opening and closing around my erection. There was a squeeze and tug sensation I couldn't get enough of, the same way my hand milks a cow. Like that. The visual and the feeling together was so erotic, I'm surprised I hadn't ejaculated sooner. How'd you make it suck my dick like that?"

Then Oakland laughed. "I had nothing to do with the way my asshole had reacted, no control over my cock greedy sphincter. The sucking rampage I felt happening was all down there. All I knew, I could feel it pushing and pulling all over your cock. Did you feel it really milking you once I started ejaculating? There is something up inside my asshole that rocks me wild and I believe you can feel it too. Crazy good, right? I was darn tootin' my rectum had a plan to suck you right on in. I'd have gone hog wild bonkers if you'd come up missing."

Deklan nearly busted a rib in two with laughter. "Omigawd, that was hysterical. And yes, the first spurt out of your piss slit was when your hole had gone suck crazy, like it was starving for my semen and if it hadn't gotten any, it would have croaked. I'll definitely come back for more of that cock-sucking action. I liked it a lot. I'm glad I helped you out with perfectly lacing your beautiful chest with strings of pearls—you're amazingly attractive under all the glistening whiteness."

Oakland winked. "Are you referring to my manly discharge or your extraordinary pale body over top of me?"

Chuckling, Deklan dropped down on top of Oakland and said, "Both. But… mostly your discharge. I liked watching you ejaculate all over yourself. It was just as sexy as watching my dick gliding in and out of you." He kissed Oakland again—gently as though in love with him.

"You think I'm sexy, huh?"

"Damn tootin' I do. Very sexy."

"Compared to you? I don't think so."

"Please. You are stunning."

"All right. If you say so."

Behind a grin, Deklan kissed Oakland again. It was short and sweet. "I have another question I'm curious to know."—he paused—"What was it like when I ejaculated in you? What had it felt like?

"Loved it. I felt a permanent tie to you after you ejaculated inside me—a feeling I'd been wanting for a very long while. I was brimming with extreme pleasure when your erection expanded and contracted with every spurt, each shot going in was like the first powerful blast of a water pump being cranked. I'm sure the pressure was because you ejaculated with a lot of force, like it's the actual water getting pumped up my ass. I can't explain it, but when your dick moved in and out of me, there was a spot you continued nudging that intensified my release more than when I hand stroke my dick to ejaculation. You had me feeling so incredible, wanting more, as though there'd never be anybody on earth who could make me feel like that ever again. When the time comes for me to stick my erection in you, you'll know what I'm talking about."

"Oh. Well. Great. As much as I like the positions we just held, I can't wait to know what you feel like. I'll be ready when you are."

"I'm not a small guy between the legs as you can see, so get ready to be split wide open,"—Oakland grinned—"Since you asked a slew of questions, I have one for you," Oakland mentioned before he rolled over to finish the night's sleep.

Deklan replied, "Shoot. What is it? I'll answer anything you ask."

"You had me in a bunch of positions last night, all those of which I loved, but which was the style you liked best?" Oakland felt a little bit shy for asking such an intimate question, but he wanted to know.

Deklan seemed enthused about giving his honest answer. "To be frank, every way I put you was incredible, and I enjoyed getting you on your hands and knees while I drove my cock in and out hard and furious from behind, but my preferred position was lying on top, feeling us chest to chest, your eyes looking into mine, like we were completely in love. I liked seeing your face and getting to know how good I made you feel. I felt an extreme closeness to you, as though we were one person. Does that make sense? Plus, we were able to kiss while my erection slid in and out of you nice and slow."

"Makes a lot of sense, and I agree. All for the same reasons, however, with me on the bottom and you on top. I think we work best that way."

Deklan quickly interrupted, "Bottom and top. Hmm. I like how that sounds. Maybe we should start something, here. I'll be the top, you be the bottom. It can be our secret labels."

"Done deal. I'm a bottom, you're a top. I wonder if that

would ever catch on for all same gender couples like us? The world will eventually need to know who's doing whom." Oakland laughed at himself. "Well, since that's mentioned, this bottom really liked your slow rhythmic motion because I could feel every inch of you moving in and out of me. When you did it like that, there was something amazing that had happened I'd never felt while hand stroking myself to ejaculation. You kept rubbing up against a specific spot inside my asshole that nearly shot me through the roof of this place. I can't quite explain it, but that internal rectal massage was mind blowing, like I was ejaculating the entire time you were reaming me with your dick. I liked it a whole lot, and I loved watching you work the sperm out of me like that. Your masculine body is incredible, you know? The entire stunning bundle over top of me, doing me, makes me stay stiff and ejaculate."

Deklan grinned. "So… other than my thick white dick, you like my hairy chest and abdomen too, do you?"

"Heck, yes. I love it, and it feels so good stroking my dick and torso as you rhythmically rock over top of me. It's an added bonus." Oakland laid a hand to Deklan's chest, raking the silken hair with his fingers.

"Glad to hear that. Why don't you roll over so I can hold you from behind while we get some sleep?" Deklan lifted the quilted cover and Oakland backed into him.

"Holy corncobs, you feel good," Oakland slurred.

"Was that spoken subliminally because my dick is hard again?" Deklan ground his hips into Oakland's butt, his hard cock dividing the man's ass crack and snaking up his spine.

"I was speaking about everything in general, mostly referring to the hair on your chest against my back, but the corncob stiff dick feels great, too." Oakland shimmied tightly into Deklan and mumbled again how good the man felt against him.

"All right, then. Corncob. Now, go to sleep, my stunning black angel." Deklan's arm had come around to Oakland's front side—his hand smoothing the semen deposits into his dark skin like it was body ointment.

After attaining the sleep he needed, Oakland had woken first that morning, finding he was lying tightly on top of Deklan's left side. His head lay on Deklan's chest, comforted by the hair against the side of his face, hearing his heart thump, adding to his tranquil wakening. His cocoa leg crisscrossed over Deklan's and his hand tightly gripped the thick base of his Prince's erection, the silken hair above his dick was warm against his fingers.

Oakland left the idea of making love again up to Deklan. He'd found out during the night that Deklan was certainly more aggressive than he was when it pertained to sexual encounters, and if Deklan so much as pressed the head of his cock against Oakland's black anxious sphincter, he'd have his legs over Deklan's shoulders without a second thought.

Deklan let out a groan, stretched hard and thrust his strong rugged hips upward, his slate hard erection sliding in Oakland's straining grasp that could barely reach finger to thumb. The man was thick.

"Hello, Love." Deklan kissed the top of Oakland's head and scrubbed his tangled hair with his scruffy cheek. "Your warm suggestive body has me stiff and ready to put it in you all over again. I can't seem to get enough of that beautiful ass now that I've had it."

Oakland hadn't objected. He immediately rolled over onto his back, taking Deklan with him, positioning the man's magnificent body over top of his. Oakland ankle locked his legs around Deklan's waist and placed his hands against his strong chest, the soft hair soothing his fingertips as he gently stroked each muscled mound.

They kissed with mingling tongues.

Deklan rocked with moderate grace above Oakland until his erection freely slid inside him again. It happened that easily. No effort whatsoever.

Oakland's breathing had turned to short huffs when he felt Deklan slipping in, burrowing deep, the man's thick invasion feeling extraordinary.

Passionately and slowly, they moved together—Deklan rhythmically rocking on top while Oakland shifted to his beat beneath him. There was groaning and moaning, wet tongue tied kissing, but most of all, talented internal stroking that led to all male body flooding discharges within a short few minutes.

Oakland gushed heavily across his chest at the same time Deklan power squirted deep within his sex-hole. Oakland could feel his Prince's cock expanding with every injection, as well as sensed each spurt aligned with a grunting growl that sounded angry. He heard Deklan holler a few, "Oh yeah's and Oh gawd's," indicating the raspy growls were more pleasing than not.

They concluded with a long bottomless kiss, and discovered their chests had been bonded together by Oakland's sticky semen.

"I said it before and I'll say it again. You are so sexy, Oakland." Deklan commented as he pushed himself up and balanced on the heels of his hands, centering his body above his favorite man. Oakland's clearing discharge somersaulted through the hair on his chest and dripped down his torso, sparkling like diamonds from the reflective light of the full morning moon outdoors. He confessed to Oakland, "This is probably a foolish thing to say since you seem to thoroughly enjoy my stiff dick stuffed inside of you, but pardon my eagerness with climbing on top of you again. I couldn't help it. I needed to feel myself inside you one more time before I departed."

Oakland shifted beneath Deklan and asked, "Why are you apologizing? You must have known I wouldn't have said no. I'll always be ready for you. No questions asked. Couldn't you feel how starved my body was to get the semen out of you? For the love of Peter, we ejaculated within minutes. Might be a record."

"It was a quickie. I seriously had no idea an asshole could suck a dick like that. Yours... well... my love, can suck an erection dry in the best possible way." Deklan grinned. "After that, I'm never leaving you."

Oakland smirked, then turned serious. "We fit seamlessly, Deklan. I really believe we *are* meant to be together. No query about that."

Deklan rolled his hips into Oakland one more time and held still, burrowing his dick as far as he could make it go. "Where did you come from, Oakland? Where from heaven had you come from?"

Throughout that night, they had exchanged real love and kept it going well into the morning, giving each other a part of themselves that neither had transferred with anybody before.

Their hearts and their souls collided exactly at the time they were supposed to — sharing and giving life to one another. They offered their bodies with intimate love and by doing that, a part from within them traded places. It was their body's distinctive way of joining their souls as they were meant to.

"You feel incredible, Oakland. I could stay inside you forevermore. It's like a closeness I'd never felt before and never want to go away."

"It won't go away, and the strength of that connection will bring you back to me."

"You can bet your chickens on that," Deklan added. "I suppose… as much as I regret leaving *your* hind end right now, I better get home before the rooster announces the rising sun and my parents find out I made love to the servant boy in the barn all night long." Deklan chuckled while slipping free from Oakland's exultant body.

The void Oakland felt at the very moment Deklan withdrew had him literally feeling empty inside. He'd been left with a lonely sensation as he watched the Prince get dressed.

Deklan kissed Oakland softly on the lips and whispered into his open mouth, "I'll be thinking about you all day long, and 'til the next moon rises in the sky, my love, hold my essence within thee and keep me in your images."

Oakland weakened.

Deklan departed.

Chapter 19

"What are you doing in my bedroom?" Deklan crept through the door at five in the morning and found his father standing there.

"You don't question me? This is my house," his father crossly reacted. "Where have you been all night? I know you weren't here where you belong." His fists tightened into hard balls. His breath leaked out like it was stuck there for a week or more.

"I was out," was all Deklan said.

"That isn't answering my question." Dante moved closer to Deklan, his eyes pinched closer together, a tight knot at the center of his forehead.

"What more do you want to hear from me?" Deklan quarreled, keeping the real facts to himself, above all, the part where he had his erection shooting sperm inside the ass of the servant man living out back in the cottage house.

"I want you to be honest with me."

"I am being honest with you."

"You are not."

"I am too."

"You were short."

"What?" Deklan angrily wondered.

"Yes. Short."

"I don't even know what that means?" Deklan huffed. Exhausted and wearing out from all the bantering back and forth with his father. "I don't want to keep doing this."

"Doing what?"

"Arguing with you." Deklan tossed his thick belt into the chair next to the fireplace and then dropped into the one next to it, his skull pressing against the seatback, gazing at the ceiling as if trying to find a way to fly through it.

Moving in front of Deklan, blocking his view of the fireplace, Dante worked at reasoning with him. "You need to listen to me," he pleaded. "This world isn't friendly and everybody here will try to hurt you by what you are doing."

"They need to mind their own business." Deklan squeezed the arms of the chair, anger escalating. "I'm not doing anything wrong."

"But they won't mind their own business, Deklan. Don't you understand that?" Dante stepped closer to Deklan, appearing more concerned about him than Deklan thought.

"It's time they minded their own business." Deklan leaned forward and dropped his head into his hands. "We of all people are in a position that can change the way people think. We are influential in this forsaken town of ignorant fools."

"Is that what all this is about?" — his father asked — "you and Jedidiah trying to make a change?"

"No, Pop's." Deklan looked up. "I can't help the way I am or how I feel. I've known I was like this all my life — as far back as I can remember, or back when I actually realized what it was."

"This is preposterous." Dante's fists returned to knots of steel. "You can't? It's not right."

"What do you mean it's not right?"

"The whole vulgar boy liking boy's stint." Dante waved a finger up and down at Deklan. "It isn't natural."

"It is to me. I may not be like you, or anybody else, and mostly what I'm not, is vulgar." Deklan turned away. "I'm disturbed you even chose that word as a label for your own child—makes me wonder what else you think about me. For your information, I can't just magically snap my fingers to change the way I am. You may not believe this, but I was born this way. I'd always known that. When I was eight or nine, I wanted to hold a boy's hand instead of some bratty little girls. At the time, I hadn't realized what that meant, but when I was about twelve or thirteen and looked back on all the thoughts I had at a younger age was when I'd realized the nine year old desire to hold Johnny's hand instead of Nelly's was actually deep hearted admiration for that boy."

Dante appealed, "There is no such need for finger snapping, because you are not supposed to like men the way you do."

"There's more to love than boy meets girl, father. I'm proof of that. Ladies and their vaginas just aren't for me." Deklan faced him, angrier than before.

"Deklan. Enough. There's no getting through to you right now. The marriage will go on as planned." As if he were a child, Dante stomped across the floor, carrying out his tantrum for not getting his way at that opportune moment.

Deklan stood up and blocked his father from walking out the door. "Let me ask you. Do you love mother?"

His father turned. "Of course I do. What kind of a senseless question is that?"

"Hear me out and answer me this. Stop right now. Don't love or care for mom anymore as if she never existed and replace her with a man." Deklan pierced his father's eyes with his own. "Could you do that?"

Dante stammered, "It's not the same thing and you know it."

"Sure it is," Deklan pointed out. "It's exactly the same thing. You cannot change the way you feel about love toward another person any more than I can, because it is in your nature to love her, a female, and it's the way it's meant to be. For you."

"You're right. That is the way it's meant to be. A man with a woman. You are coming to your senses. Good to know."

"You're missing the point, father," Deklan tried to reason, disturbance evident in his tone. "I'm talking about internal souls, not the exterior vessel. Two souls meant to be together. No matter how hard you try to separate them, you cannot. They will always be drawn together even if the tallest wall is built. One more thing—God doesn't differentiate man from woman. You'd told me that yourself. So why should we distinguish that in the human form? We're all equal souls to him with slight modifications to our bodies in order to progress with his plan to populate the planes. If I wasn't meant to be here as I am, he would have made me differently. I'm exactly the way he wanted me to be, and neither you, I, nor anybody else should be questioning his reasons for what he's created. I am perfect in his image, as are you."

Dante hadn't said a word. Only stared. That of which had given Deklan the impression he might have gotten through to his father regarding romances between the same genders. The message Deklan had illustrated for his father was clear and made a lot of sense. He'd understood his own mind and body more than anyone, and known it would only function the way it had been intended—pairing off with a female wasn't in the cards dealt to him. Deklan had become infatuated with another gentleman and he'd have done anything to have prevented separation from that man, or crucified for the soul connecting love he had for him.

Deklan watched his father quietly walk out of the room. No further vocal debate had been spoken, not even a good bye.

Should he be thankful or worried? Had it really mattered?

Earlier that morning, Deklan had identified Oakland's smile as extreme fondness for him, and after sharing his body intimately, that of which included erectile penetration, Oakland was most likely feeling connected to him more than ever, too. He wondered what Oakland might have been thinking at that moment while out of his sight. Was the man imagining him in his arms again? Kissing him, and loving him the same way he had the night before? Since Deklan was, Oakland must have been envisioning the same.

Chapter 20

The morning breakfast routine was in motion when Oakland had unexpectedly come across Deklan in the kitchen—it was the first time he'd seen him there since he'd been working at the Manor. He knew that visit was no coincidence, had understood Deklan purposely planted himself there for good reason—to see his new boyfriend he made love to the night before. It had only been a short while since he'd seen Deklan, but as he remembered, the man was as good-looking as all get out—that face was downright too handsome for Oakland to ever forget.

The first thing Oakland had done when he encountered Deklan standing in the way of where he needed to pick up the buckets of scrap, he politely asked him to step aside, looking him square in the eyes for a brief moment. The previous evening's exotic memory returned like a lightning flash to the face. He glanced at the man's well-built chest peeking through the tie backs of his partially open shirt, remembering how pleasant the soft hair felt pressed against his own chest, fighting the massive urge to reach out and run his hands through the feathery silk all over again.

It was grating for Oakland to act as though he hadn't been acquainted with Deklan on a personal level, keeping their extreme relationship a secret. Frankly, the few times Oakland sneaked a glance at Deklan, every ounce of him wanted to kiss those lips the way he'd done the evening past. Oakland's chest burned just thinking about how truly far away from Deklan he was, even though the man was but a few inches from his side.

Taking a risk, Oakland brushed a shoulder against Deklan's chest as if by accident, and with that covert move, the man's rugged scent had hit him like a hand across the cheek. If he hadn't moved away as quickly as he had, he'd lose his senses and there'd have come black erection overload aimed in Deklan's direction.

For the first time with added reluctance, Oakland removed himself from the kitchen, and without surprise for reasons obvious, nobody misbehaved with a plunging foot to his rear end that would have sent him cartwheeling out the door. Oakland was grateful for the bootless bottom that day, however, repulsed by those slippery mice only mischievously playing when the pussy cat was away.

Since Oakland wasn't sure what would have transpired next, he figured the best idea should have been to head back to his chicken coop and pretend everything was as it had been before he kissed Deklan. Out of all the people the Prince could have selected, Oakland found it outlandish he ended up being the one man in the crowd of many Deklan had chosen.

Could the day get any better?

While Oakland hung out in dreamland, he'd been pulled back to reality when he realized the space around him wafted rotten. "Pee-yew" he bawled. "What on earth?" There was an offensive odor in the air that had been elevated by his own overheated body. Working in the morning sun had ripened him beyond rancid, putrefying the air around him. It wasn't the animals that smelled bad that time, but he who desperately needed the bath.

Grabbing a detergent bar and towel, Oakland had taken off

for the river. His joyful whistling kept him company until he reached a place more secluded than usual. Instead of tossing his clothing over a tree branch, he'd gone for the river fully clothed. Unconventional he knew, but found it easiest to achieve a speedy wash and rinse of both body and cloth.

After the initial scrub and dip, he removed his clothing and swam to a shallow part of the river where he floated face up to absorb a few moments of isolation. He chuckled when he felt the stony river bed tickle his bum. The day was brighter than usual, providing undeniable exposure to every bit of his man sized features. A little part of him hadn't cared if he'd been seen by anybody, but his more modest conscience kept him on slight alert.

It hadn't taken long before he started thinking about Deklan again, hoping the man would have appeared out of nowhere and ravished what he'd mentioned was a black body of grandeur. Just thinking about what Deklan would have done to him pumped his black erection up his abdomens center. After glancing around and figuring nobody had been watching, he curled his body forward and had snuck an extended suckle to the head of his dick, stopping before ejaculating into his mouth.

That brief self indulged mouthful had shifted Oakland's thoughts to the man he preferred wrapping his lips around the head of his cock, sucking, and swallowing his sperm. Undeniably, he found satisfaction by the way Deklan showed interest in every part of his body, especially the well-endowed bonus that hung thickly between his legs. That craving for his big black dick was a no brainer the first moment Deklan had seen its glory and again when he'd taken it down his throat with minimal complications. Eleven inches had been a jaw breaking mouthful for sure, and that first encounter, Deklan had mentioned he was up for the great challenge of swallowing as much of him as he could, even if choking on it was the outcome. The guy had been determined, and hadn't done too badly at his initial attempt, managing the massive task like a champion, easing the bulbous head past his tonsils, consuming a little more than half of Oakland's length, but had wished he'd been able to have taken more. A semen coated throat had established a job well done. Eating down half a huge cock was better than none at all, and Oakland had resumed full penetration when he switched to Deklan's never ending asshole instead. That sex-hole was perfectly deep and had come without a frustrating gag reflex that would have prevented total cock insertion.

Oakland's dick was larger than the average chap to the point of looking horse hung freakish. His extreme size had always left him feeling self-conscious, and because of that, he'd done whatever he could to conceal his long black appendage from being a spectacle at somebody's small town circus. He'd remained private about that his entire life, until Deklan had come along and expressed how much he liked the new challenges that had come with an erection of his size. More than relieved, Oakland let Deklan explore every thick inch without reservation.

Glancing around while floundering on his back in the river, Oakland checked the surroundings again before skimming his soapy hands across his bulky chest, slipping them down his rock splitting abdomen, and tending a back and forth grip over his eleven inch dick, wishing the entire time Deklan was there doing it all for him. He stirred just thinking about the man's slick hands rubbing him from top to bottom, not missing his thick black dick, maybe taking the bulbous head into his warm wet mouth. Those thoughts had triggered another rise in Oakland's male extension, turning it stone stiff like before—the massive beast climbing up the gutter of his chiseled abdomen.

Once more, Oakland lathered his entire body with the lavender bar, stopping short when he felt the prickling sensation of semen about to burst forth. He eradicated the stroking, held his breath a moment as an effort to seize the urge to ejaculate. He rinsed the soap away as he crawled to the edge of the river on his hands and knees. Small rippling waves carried the foaming soap away. He laid his head back against the grassy bank while letting his naked body absorb the heat from the sun above. He'd become content, feeling compelled to close his eyes and appreciate relaxation.

"Well hello, good looking." Deklan had shown up as if he'd come right out of Oakland's split second fantasy nap.

Oakland blinked, clearing his vision. He scrambled for words, "Wuh... Oh. H-hullo." Turning onto his knees, he fumbled to cover his swinging organ with both hands—his never ending challenge.

"No need to change your position just for me. As you were. Please." Deklan chuckled behind a glistening smile while staring at Oakland kneeling naked in the river. He blurted, "Damn, you're memorable. So, so, memorable." What was he referring to?

"Thank the heavens it's you," Oakland said as he stood up, shifting his hands to bunch as much of what he could behind both hands. Even though Deklan had seen him without clothing before, Oakland still felt that impulse to cover himself. There was something about the daylight that made everything look differently than how it appeared at night time. The eminence of light accentuated every bulge, gutter, and plane. "Why are you still laughing?" his self-conscious character had returned full speed.

"You're cute. That's all." Deklan dropped his hand away from his mouth.

"Cute?" Oakland tipped his head. "I look silly is what I think."

"No, you look cute. Plus, I like what I see. You should already know that."

"How about handing me that towel unless you are planning on coming in here with me?" Oakland reached a hand out toward Deklan, anticipating a bath event instead of having that towel given to him.

"Actually, I could use a wash," Deklan said, followed by unlacing his boots that led to unfastening his belt.

While watching Deklan unbutton his shirt and taking it off, Oakland's dick started swelling to the point he couldn't keep it hidden behind his hands any longer. The man's splendor was more than Oakland could handle and there was no stopping the reaction that had become more and more evident as the moments passed. There was no chance at concealing anything between his legs—he had too much hanging there. A major erection was on the rise, determined to bust through the gated fingers that had been trying to hold it all in place.

Oakland's eyes had become pinned on Deklan's strong chest, fascinated all over again by the soft hair that lay across it like tiny feathers. An added benefit to all that gorgeous chest hair was the trail traveling the center of his abdomen that joined the darker curls sprouting above his opened pants.

It seemed like forever and a day by the time Deklan's entire body had become exposed, the exquisite site had turned Oakland's dick to solid stone.

When Deklan stepped into the water, his reaction appeared as though there was a chill that reached his bones. His stunning chest expanded as he inhaled, muscles swelling and bunching all over, revealing everything he had to the entire outdoors.

Oakland reached for him with an open hand. They stood together in broad daylight, naked and kissing. Black against white. Oakland felt every inch of Deklan, impressed by the size of the Prince's erection and how well it battled with his own.

"Mm-mm. You smell real good." Deklan had broken away, taking in the warm air whirling around Oakland.

"Lavender." Oakland picked up the floating detergent bar and led Deklan to a deeper part of the river.

At a snap, Deklan had taken a dip below water, resurfacing moments later dripping wet. The water had run down his face, dark strands of glossy hair had come down with it, dangling in front of his eyes, the blue glimmered more brilliantly than Oakland remembered. The water drizzled from his broad shoulders and down his chest, weaving in and out of the feathery wisps, his entire body sparkling beneath the afternoon sun.

As if it was the first time Oakland had seen him, he anxiously grabbed hold of Deklan's hand and towed him to the opposite side of the river. "Come with me."

Standing in the soft sand in front of Oakland, Deklan couldn't seem to hold back his emphatic grin. The look on his face appeared ready for intercourse as if they hadn't breached one another in several weeks. He had a rising erection that indicated his determination to use Oakland's sexy black hole that would move him to ejaculation.

Skillfully, Oakland buckled down onto his back, pulling Deklan on top where he wanted him. He spread his legs wide open and moaned extreme pleasure when his Prince had driven his thick erection straight into him all at once, hardly flinching at the resistant water-slickened entry. As had occurred before, the erotic high of Deklan's erection sliding rhythmically in and out had pushed Oakland to that orgasmic edge in a great big hurry. The stimulation inside him was too great to handle. There was no holding back. He whimpered like a pet, falling apart so quickly from the punishing sensation of being speared by Deklan's dick. He grunted, spraying his chest with his own semen at the same moment Deklan's tensing body and quick thumping thrusts had indicated he was pumping sperm into his impatient sex-hole, too. The raspy growling confirmed the man was ejaculating. Spurting inside him. Shooting deep.

River water sloshed.

Semen spit, while body's thrashed.

Grunting and groaning had come with each spluttering jet.

The scent of semen overpowered the freshness of lavender.

Oakland had eventually gone limp, his black dick slumping heavily over his hip, the bulbous head submerged below water.

Deklan collapsed. His body convulsing as he ejaculated the final spurts into Oakland's sucking butthole. He growled, "Ohmigawd, that sweet tight ass. I'd never felt anything so spectacular before. Can I keep you?"

Chapter 21

Back at the Manor, Deklan sat directly across from his mother at the dinner table, putting him to the right of his father who sat at the head. Servants had come and gone, bringing meal courses as well as keeping the drinking glasses maintained.

There hadn't been a single mumble of socializing at the beginning of dinner. The loudest noises heard were silver utensils clinking against dishware. It was almost ear piercing to Deklan, the high pitched chimes tormenting his already spiked nerves.

The first to break silence was Deklan's father when he said, "It's a pleasure having you at the dinner table with us, Lady Gretchen. Knowing you'll be dressed in pure white, the wedding will be more beautiful." He raised a brow while glancing at the girl's father.

Deklan glared at him, catching onto the subliminal suggestion that questioned if the chosen lassie was an intact virgin, for which if marrying him, she'd undoubtedly remain that way since his cock would only get stiff for Oakland.

"Thank you, Mister Royal." She giggled shyly, most likely not understanding the meaning of the compliment the same way Deklan had.

Sitting next to Lady Gretchen, Deklan felt complete discomfort, couldn't relate to her at all, and had only been able to think about the black chap he'd made love to in the river earlier that day. It had become difficult to even concentrate on his meal or anybody at the dinner table since his mind wondered if the sperm he injected into Oakland was still cozily tucked up inside him. Deklan's true life fantasy was to continue penetrating that man every chance he could.

How would Deklan get through the unsettling arrangement his parents had planned for him? He couldn't like that girl. He hadn't even had a chance to get to know who she was. His parents organized everything without his consent. Picked her out of a laundry lineup for all he knew.

Deklan tried being cordial to the girl and her family, but the situation he'd been put in had cut at his insides like an old wood chopping hatchet. He stayed quiet most of the evening, speaking minimally when necessary and pretty much only when spoken to. Much of what had come out was only, "Hello, yes, no, Thank you," and eventually, "Good bye."

The thought of what had taken place at the dinner table had upset Deklan. A female for him to marry was absurd. Everybody there had to have known that. He'd already taken claim to the person he wanted to be with. He and Oakland were meant to be together as he had recently proven, not him and some handpicked lassie. He'd known she'd be deprived of his erection, never able to get it to rise if aimed at a vagina.

Deklan had resented the girl sitting at the table next to him, even though he hadn't had any chance to get to know her. It hadn't seemed right to dislike *that girl* as much as he had, but his parents had put her in that bad situation, not him. His loathing was well engaged, for the entire bunch sitting at the table, and if Lady Gretchen had the willingness to have gone along with such nonsense, perhaps she too deserved being disliked by Deklan.

He had a crazy imagination after that antagonistic thought.

The picture painted in his mind was that of his masculine boyfriend busting up the dinner party like a hero and claiming him—taking his man to a faraway place. But of course, that would have been imprudent. Oakland would only look borderline wild standing in the middle of the dinner table reaching a marriage proposing hand to the one he loved. Deklan had a smirk on his face at that heroic idea, wishing like mad it would have actually come true.

It had taken about ten minutes after dinner had finished for Dante to escort everybody to the parlor adjacent the dining room. The seating was more comfortable there and a better place to deliberate about the wedding plans for Deklan and the new Missus Royal.

The two fathers had gone off together in front of the fireplace, and behind them, the mothers were sitting in facing chairs with cups of tea, chit-chatting about their pretty jewelry as if they had no say in the wedding matters.

Deklan and his new girl roamed the room in a purposeless manner, hardly speaking while looking at items placed here and there as if they were in a small town marketplace. It was a scratchy interlude for the both of them, clearly not going well for Deklan, but the parents and the giddy girl seemed to think it had.

They all smiled while he was drowning in anxiety, nearly turning blue at the whole idea of marriage to a girl. He had a sudden panic attack when he thought about how true royal's inaugurated a marriage and wondered if that would have taken place for him and Gretchen, where an audience stood around a bed chamber and watched the newlyweds lose their virginity to one another. At that moment, his pretty shade of blue had turned green and he thought he was going to cough up his liver. He held his stomach and mumbled, "Ohmigawd, I'm going to be sick."

"You were saying?" Miz Gretchen asked.

Deklan waved a hand at her and said, "Oh, it was nothing. Just pre marriage frights."

As though there was limited time on everybody's clock, wedding plans had been made quickly and agreed before the group had broken up—the ceremony would carry out over the coming weekend—taking place that soon.

It had been decided.

No further questioning asked.

Deklan was getting married.

To a lass.

In four days.

After everybody left, Deklan caught up to his parents in the second level hallway. It seemed as though they were trying to get away, but he wasn't letting that happen until they heard him out. He yelled, "Why are you doing this? Don't you know this isn't going to work?"

His father retorted, "You don't seem to understand, Deklan."

Deklan followed. "Understand what? That you are doing this for your own benefit and not giving any thought to mine? I can't marry Gertrude, Greta, Grace or whatever her name is."

"It's Gretchen, dear," his mother clarified.

"My point. I don't even know the bird," Deklan's voice increased an octave.

"I can clearly see you don't understand," Dante jumped back in. "This *is* for your benefit and you will need to go along with the plan."

"And then what?" Deklan fought back.

"And then you will live happily ever after. That's what," Dante assured.

"You are confusing the message, Father. This isn't a fairy tale. Neither Happy nor Ever After will exist in this situation. They don't go together and shouldn't be used in the same sentence."

"It does for your mother and me." Father knew best.

"Are you sure about that?" Deklan turned his gaze to his mother's saddened face. There had been no expression of happiness, but more a frown of concern. Mother had been the one who knew best, and by her appearance, she hadn't agreed with any of it. A Mother knows, and if Deklan had been correct by what he'd seen in her, she'd known the marriage to a girl wouldn't have been right, that he needed a boy as his companion, not a girl. Deklan had known she'd been aware of his male attractions long ago. He had identified that by her polite comments and the way she had never pushed girls on him, and how she'd always tried shifting the subject when his father tried to bring it up.

"Your mother is fine with this, Deklan. I know her better than anyone." He put his arm over her shoulder like he would have done if she was a chum, jostling her closer to his side. Her tense body was a certain sign she wasn't content, but Dante was oblivious to it or hadn't wanted to see what he should have seen.

Deklan mumbled, looking to the floor, "You're wrong."

"What did you say?" His father tilted his head. "Be sure you are ready for the weekend. You're getting married to Lady Gretchen and that's final."

"Why are you treating me like I don't have a mind of my own," Deklan yelled.

Dante raised his voice above Deklan's. "What I am witnessing right now, I can clearly see you don't have a mind of your own. Since you're not thinking, somebody around here needs to do that for you."

"Forget it." Deklan turned away and left. It was as if he was falling uphill, stumbling all over the place but not getting anywhere. "I need to go. I can't stay here right now." He kissed his mother on the cheek and walked away.

"Don't you go out and muddle this up, young man," his father hollered.

Chapter 22

A knock at the door hauled Oakland out of his evening slumber. He jerked and for a moment felt as though he'd been hovering out of sync with the real world. He pulled his trousers on with a clumsy effort and answered the door without a shirt on.

It was Deklan standing there. The evening had instantly gotten so much better.

"Run away with me," Deklan blurted out, squeezing through the doorways open crack, and kissing Oakland as he passed.

"What? Now?" Oakland squabbled, his tone had reached a higher pitch than normal.

He pulled both of Oakland's hands into his. "Yes. Now. Run away with me. Tonight."

"I'm happy to see you and would love nothing more than to take to the hills with you, but I have already made up a bed for the night. Other than that, you're supposed to be getting married in a few days. Shouldn't you be storing energy for the big night?"

"Then let me stay here. With you. I can't go back into that house. They've all gone mad." Deklan gripped harder. "I can't marry that girl. I don't know her, nor will I be able to share a bed with her the same way I share one with you."

Conflicted with emotions as to how he should have felt, Oakland pulled away. He'd become angry. Confused. Sad. Infatuated with a man the world wouldn't allow him to have. He wanted to run off with Deklan so nobody else could have him, but it would have only made matters worse, for him and for Deklan.

The moment his face had turned gloomy, Deklan spun toward the door as if he had a plan to leave.

Oakland's heart rate sped up, beating hard and loud. "Wait," he mumbled. "Don't go." He reached out and placed both hands on Deklan's shoulders, squeezed comfort into his tensed muscles at the moment his head tilted forward. Oakland moved closer, pulling Deklan into a hug from behind, feeling a tremble when his arms wrapped around him. There had been noticeable sobbing coming from Deklan. The man was breaking apart.

Deklan reached up and gripped Oakland's wrist, his touch felt shattered to Oakland, a weakness he hadn't sensed in him before. Oakland's source of strength had normally come from Deklan, however at that moment, the Prince was leaning on Oakland. The home Deklan lived in had trampled his spirit, and by what his family had planned to put him through, revealed they hated him the way he was.

Deklan spun around in Oakland's arms and looked at him, tears streaming down his face. "I'm so lost right now I don't really know where I belong."

Oakland stroked Deklan's face with the pads of his thumbs and brought him tighter to his chest. Their hearts raced against each other's as if attempting to swap places. Backing away, Oakland held Deklan's face in his hands, looked him in the eyes and kissed him. "You belong here with me. We both know that. You can stay as long as you need to." He offered as if the home was his.

Deklan nodded. His watery blues had begun to dry. He chuckled, shyly telling Oakland how much he loved him.

What did he just say?

Oakland stood frozen, waiting for his blood to flow after it'd stopped up from lack of a beating heart. Since he was feeling the same about Deklan, it hadn't come as any surprise to hear him speak those three words, but shocked that Deklan had said them so soon. Oakland gushed from hearing what he'd said, however, glad he was the one Deklan had confessed that to.

Deklan kissed Oakland one more time before letting him go. A smile crept over his face.

While holding Deklan close, Oakland sensed a change in him—he sensed the man was troubled when he arrived, but after finding comfort in his arms, sensed his mood switching almost instantly. There was no refuting they were two halves of the same soul, predestined to walk together. There had been too much of a connection between them to be anything other than loving mates.

As though shy and afraid of hearing a denial, Deklan softly asked, "Do you mind if I sleep here with you tonight?"

At Oakland's admission, Deklan wouldn't have had to ask twice, or even finish the question. "Of course you can. You honestly don't even have to ask."

Deklan's gaze had been deeply concentrated on Oakland while running his knuckles down his dark bare chest and around to his back where he locked his fingers in place to hold him close. "Thank you. I promise I won't be a bother."

Oakland's head tilted to one side when he said, "The real bother is that I don't have any nightgowns for you to wear. You'll be forced to either sleep in what you have on or take to the sheets in the nude like I will."

"I'll be most comfortable sleeping with nothing on. Less confining. Plus, I wouldn't mind a repeat of how we slept before. Hope you won't mind a naked man in bed beside you again?" Deklan perked up a little bit and dragged a sleeve under his nose to wipe it clean. He sniffed and then goofishly chuckled. The Deklan charm was slowly coming back.

"A repeat suits me perfectly. I'll agree with that decision," Oakland replied.

"It's settled then. Since we were all over the place the last time I slept over, which side of the bed will be mine?" Deklan asked, dabbing his eyes with his cuff. He smiled, his white teeth shining.

"I'm a lefty, so that means you get the right side by the window. The bed is small, so we will have to sleep pretty close."

"That won't be a problem. Cuddling is good and I'll probably be holding on to you most of the night anyway." Deklan started undressing.

Oakland doused the lanterns around his tiny home except for the one on the table next to the bed. It let off an easy yellow flicker that mixed with the silver-blue shimmer coming in the window from the moon outside. Oakland liked the way it made Deklan's skin radiate blue-violet on one side and white-gold on the other. The trail of hair marking the center of his abdomen acted as a division line between the two subtle tones. Oakland's caramel skin, however, appeared royal-blue next to Deklan's, and the sharp contrast between the two of them painted one erotic image.

It had taken no time for Deklan to claim his place on top of Oakland. They kissed the way a new couple would, which led to a pleasured connection with Deklan sliding right inside Oakland and moving his erection back and forth at the pace of a snail.

The same as before, their time together had been the finest and wouldn't have been easy to separate once that awful moment had arrived. They made love in Oakland's bed a few times throughout the night, transferring semen the way two men could only have done. If Deklan had been a wolf, he'd have certainly marked Oakland off limits to the rest of the pack by the amount of sperm he spurted inside and on him.

Oakland had become preferential to receiving Deklan, watching the man's rhythmic movements over top of him, observing the way his chest expanded and his abdominal muscles flexed with each thrust. There hadn't been anything better on earth than to have his Prince moving his stiff dick in and out of him. It was that same closeness Deklan had mentioned that he couldn't quite describe.

When the man ejaculated with such unbounded intensity, Oakland valued every bit of that life Deklan had injected into him.

It seemed as though Deklan's intention had been to make Oakland a part of him, giving his body the energy it needed to stay alive.

The satisfaction of feeling Deklan's molten semen flowing toward his heart and settling in was exactly what Oakland valued necessary.

Was it possible for two people to bond so quickly?

Their draw had become uniquely tied during those moments spent together, and Oakland wondered if that was because the two of them were held so far apart by the human race, or if it had been because they *were* true soul mates, unable to live apart. The pull so strong, they'd inevitably remain linked somehow throughout their lives. Be it next to one another or far apart.

After the shared affection and amusing conversations, sleep had finally come to them—Deklan's fleecy torso tightly pressed against Oakland's backside, his wrapped arms holding him with warmth and unbreakable affection.

Chapter 23

"Oh, wounded hell!" Oakland groaned, frantically pulling himself out of his sleepy slumber. He nudged Deklan a few times, trying to wake him, but the weight of his body kept him pinned in place.

Moaning, Deklan shifted but hardly moved.

"Deklan, get up," Oakland grumbled, keeping his voice close to a whisper.

"What the…?" Deklan slid off of Oakland and sluggishly sat up, rubbing his eyes like a young boy. The morning sun persistently mined for his soul like a dagger shucking a walnut. Digging and prying.

"Stay still. Shhh! Somebody's at the door." Oakland kicked the bedcovers off his feet, gripping his perpetual erection against the center of his abdomen until the swelling had gone down. He pulled his trousers on at the same moment the second hard knock reverberated around the carriage house. At least he understood it to have been the second rap. He'd been sleeping so soundly, it could have been the third, the fourth, or even knock number five. Who'd have known except the person trying to bang the door down?

"Who could be here this early in the morning?" Deklan sleepily asked while holding one eye shut to block out the intrusive sunlight coming in from the window next to him.

"I'm late," Oakland answered, tripping over his big feet as he made a zigzagged route for the door. "It's probably somebody from the kitchen staff coming here to fry me for not having their breakfast ingredients at the counter on time. They get antsy if it's a minute late."

Deklan dropped back, and griped, "Really?" He laid his arm across his forehead. "They disturbed us for that? Off with their heads. I'll order it done."

"Well… it is my job, and your family would starve to death if I wasn't gathering your morning eggs popped out of those chickens' asses. Now, shush." Oakland's hand flapped behind him, politely hushing Deklan. "Don't let them know you're here. I'm dead if these people found out I was sleeping with the boss's son."

"Forget them and come back to bed. I'm stone hard and you're the only one who can relieve me of the misery that's purely your fault. Get over here and take a seat on my center. Your spurt ready post awaits you." Deklan boldly voiced his orders, pulling the covers back. His full blown erection sprung forward with a heavy thud against his abdomen, it too, begging for Oakland to hop on.

"Jeez, that's a beauty and I'd love to sit down on it again. But… I can't. I have a job to do." Oakland imagined another great ride where he'd bounce like a jackrabbit until they both ejaculated another time. "You have my semen stuck in your chest hair, by the way. You should clean that up before somebody see's it."

"No. I like it there. They'll think it's mine, not yours." Deklan glanced at his chest.

As intrusive as a blow horn and interrupting the sexual fantasy ride on his boyfriend's big cock, an unfamiliar voice had rung from the other side of the door. "Deklan. You in there?"

"Holy cow patties piled higher today than yesterday." Deklan sprung out of bed, his erection immediately arcing forward as it deflated fast. His eyes bulged wide open as though he'd never been sleeping. Sober as ever. Erection by then, totally collapsed.

"What the... who the?" Startled, Oakland mimicked one of Deklan's famous phrases he'd heard before, and backed away from the door as if it was on fire.

"My father," Deklan whispered. "It's him. He's out there. Looking for me. Oh, Fiery hell!"

"Buggers to your hell. Oh, my hairy bollocks, instead." Oakland panicked. He spun in circles, making no headway.

"Quiet." Deklan held two fingers over Oakland's mouth. Any other time Oakland would have taken them between his lips. That time, not a chance. Somebody was getting nailed and it wasn't him that time.

"I'm dead," Oakland squeaked. "Period."

"You're not dead." Deklan softly paced the floor, holding his linen shirt in front of his swinging dick. "I need to think. Sssshhh!" He pointed a finger to the ceiling. "If he knew I was emptying my hairy nuts into the guy who was serving his meals, I'd be the dead one."

Like a child, Oakland clamped both hands over his own mouth and tiptoed backward away from the door.

"Just stay quiet." Deklan had a look on his face that seemed he hadn't a clue what should have been done. Should he act as if he wasn't inside the carriage house, or should he answer the door and come up with something stupid?

He'd chosen stupid.

Oakland walked the plank and hid in the bed corner with Bettie Lu, holding her beak to keep her silent.

"Pop?" Deklan opened the door. "What are you doing here?"

"I should be asking you that. Get dressed," his father ordered. "You're coming with me." He tipped his head around Deklan, looking inside. Maybe looking for Deklan's boy toy, who was keeping quiet while Dante's eyes scanned the place. "Pee-yew." Dante sniffed. "Remind me to have this dump cleaned up."

Deklan might have made up a story about how much he wanted to be left alone, but since his father continued barking orders, he kept his mouth shut. He turned a full circle, glancing in Oakland's direction as he spun. "I'll be right back," he told his father.

Deklan skipped up the chicken plank, grabbed his trousers and boots from beside the bed, and leaned in with a gentle kiss on Oakland's lips. He whispered as he pulled away, "I gotta go. Love you, Oakland. Keep my babies safe." He rubbed Oakland's tummy before turning to leave.

Oakland smiled and hid the onset of an emotional weep, not too sure if the reason for the tears were because he was so in love with Deklan or because he might never have him in his bed again. Whispering alone, "Love you too, Dek." It was the first time Oakland said those words and the first time he referred to his boyfriend as Dek. It was a strong name, suited Deklan, and seemed to have been only his to call him.

Oakland heard the door close, which by that, had given him the approval to make a move.

It was sad to think Deklan and Oakland had to hide who they were because other people in the world couldn't or wouldn't understand them.

With Deklan gone, Oakland wondered if he'd ever see him again the way he had that night. As a loved one. As a companion. If ever possible, as his husband. His heart tightened the moment he heard Deklan exit that door. Sadness erupted within Oakland. He couldn't seem to stop the overflowing sensation of losing the man he'd fallen in love with. He sat on the edge of the bed holding Betty Lu, fighting those weepy emotions that would not ebb no matter how hard he tried to detain them.

There was no joy when it had come to being love sick.

Chapter 24

As if he was an untamed animal on a chain, Deklan had been led from Oakland's small cabin to the great room where the wedding was to take place. His father was a few paces ahead of him, yanking on the imaginary links.

Wattsworth on the other hand was already there directing traffic and pointing out where he wanted tables and chairs set up, giving out orders like a commander of a regiment.

Laid out on a table closest to the door was a large parchment page illustrating the great room's layout, marked how Wattsworth wanted everything organized.

He sketched out the typical layout for a large wedding ceremony, starting with long tables lining the front entrance that would collect the gifts. That was tradition, even though the filthy rich had no need for much of anything more than what they already had.

In the middle of the room was a sea of chairs that formed

three elongated V-shaped sections, wide in the back, narrow at the front. Wattsworth created two outside pathways that angled from the rear corners to a finer point at the front platform—an unexpected twist to the traditional wedding waltz down a center aisle.

The great room had been set up based on a typical wedding chapel, except with far less religious artifacts that had been replaced with a repertoire more glamorous.

Deklan's stomach churned at the thought of that day being his last happy one on earth. The marriage to a girl was so wrong for him, and as far as he'd known, the only person at the Manor who could understand that, was Oakland. Separate bedrooms could always be an option—one for her and one for him. How could he carry out wedding somebody he didn't know instead of the man he really loved and could easily hold an erection against? It was unsettling to him. He had half a mind to run away with Oakland and never return. Screw the business. To hell with the wealth. None of that was worth a life of misery and erectile dysfunction when in the presence of a vagina.

Next to his father, Deklan stood at the table with his arms crossed, expecting his own hands to tremble and his jaw to grind, but neither had. Since his nerves had been barraging in on high vitality, he found the lack of the jitters, odd. His eyelids reduced his vision to small slits and he said nothing. There wasn't any point in voicing his opinion since there hadn't seemed to have been a single person with any plans to listen. The event was *everyone else's* wedding, not his. He'd understood that very much to have been true.

Deklan looked around the great room, completely uninterested in anything that had been staged in it. He started breathing heavily and then left his father and Wattsworth standing at the table. He unconsciously headed down the right side aisle toward the fabricated platform at the front of the room and stood there for a while staring at what was in front of him. *"Why can't all this be for Oakland and me?"* boomed in his head. *"He's the one who has my heart."*

"Deklan!" his father hollered, voice echoing. "How does everything look to you?"

One tear tried to break free, but Deklan wiped it quickly with his floppy sleeve. He sniffed and turned. "Uh... good," he honestly muttered, sniffing again to hide the fact he was unhappier than he'd ever been in his life. "Everything looks good."

To keep from breaking his parents' hearts, especially his mothers, he'd gone along with their plan to get married to the unknown lady bird named Gertrude, or Greta, or... Gladys was it? He still couldn't remember the name of his bride. A bad sign and should have been everybody's clue that the marriage was a bad idea. His true wish however, was that his parents would realize what they were doing, to take notice of his own breaking heart, and not let the marriage go on as planned.

"It all looks good, Pop." Deklan walked toward him and Wattsworth who were standing over the floor plan, still. "I wouldn't change a thing."

"How many times have I told you not to call me Pop?" his father pointed out. "You know you're to address me as father when the help is present. It shows respect."

"Sorry, Mister Royal." Deklan turned cold, purposely going against his father's ridiculous demand. "You're doing a great job organizing your wedding. Call me when it's my time to walk the aisle with whomever it is you have chosen for me to marry." He turned and left the great room, heading outdoors.

Chapter 25

Watching from the carriage house window, Oakland noticed Deklan leaving the Manor in a hurry. If he hadn't been caught up with morning chores, he'd have gone after Deklan like he wanted to.

Deklan's actions had given Oakland the impression he needed somebody on his side, like he just lost the biggest battle of his life and every friend he had just died under gunfire. It was killing Oakland that he couldn't follow Deklan right then and take away the brunt of anguish he was certain his family had inflicted on him.

Oakland sped through his chores, delivering eggs, vegetables and grains into the kitchen before grabbing the trash and running back out. During his blurred race around the room, he noticed a few eyes glaring at him, especially the daggered beams coming from the one who missed the opportunity of kicking him in the rear before he'd left the place.

"Maybe next time, Chap?" he mumbled.

Oakland found it difficult to imagine Deklan walking hand in hand down matrimony aisle with someone other than himself. It wasn't right, nor was it making any sense. The picture perfect marriage was all wrong. Oakland was the one who'd been kissed by Deklan, not *that* strange girl. It was his hand he held, not hers. They'd even slept so close their bodies merged, one deeply penetrating the other — transferring semen from one body to the other, the way it was meant to have been done between two men who had a deep passion for sharing more than just their bodies alone. Oakland at that moment was carrying Deklan's ejaculate seed, protecting and keeping it safe. The two of them related to the other so well, the seamless connection was effortless and purely natural. That was holy matrimony.

Oakland had taken off running around the back of the barn with a bucket of water for the vegetables in the garden and one with food for the animals. He was in such a rampant rush, he'd tossed the food at them without watching where it had landed. If he had even a single minute to spare, he would have sat with them, but understanding Deklan was troubled by what occurred inside the manor, he hadn't the time for socializing with a pig, a chicken or a goat. They had to survive without him that one time. The distraction of food should have helped clear their little brains from hopping right into playtime.

Oakland had overheated like deserts dirt, sweating like the downpour of a rainy day, smelling like day old pig poop. He quickly grabbed a change of clothing and had taken off for the river to rinse off that morning's workout.

"Holy, bollocks!" The water was colder than an old witch's tit in a leaded breast wrap. He'd done what he could to ignore the chill, rushing the rinse to finish quicker.

As he hurried, Oakland pictured Deklan finding refuge under the pear tree they'd mutually had come to like, pretty much deciding it had become their favorite place on earth. It seemed fitting at the time for Deklan to have gone there, and Oakland would have been surprised if he hadn't.

While running through the clover field, Oakland's straw hat caught wind as if signaling him to slow down. The cord spun the hat around his neck where it then flopped and rested at his back. He stopped at the hilltop and as if by magic, spotted Chadwick grazing a few feet away from that pear tree. His mental power had told him Deklan was there, too. He had to have been. Those two were like fuel and fire—always together when not at home.

Shifting his hat back on top of his head, Oakland strolled down the hillside to meet Deklan, letting the wind behind him carry out most of the work at moving him forward.

There was one thing he needed to do—console Deklan's breaking heart and bring him back to life. It had become his desire to take care of Deklan. He *was* his soul mate even if others understood it differently.

Fate can't be interrupted no matter how hard others try to stop it.

Keeping his footsteps light against the ground, Oakland walked quietly up next to Deklan. With his hands in the usual place he'd always carried them, tucked behind his suspender straps and closely above his waistline, he stood in front of Deklan and waited for him to react.

It hadn't taken long for Deklan to respond. His eyes had given off definite signs of being unhappy, but quickly changed for the better as soon as his gaze shifted to Oakland. "I'm glad you came," he said, his hand reaching up and pulling Oakland down to the ground next to him. In the other hand he held a half-eaten pear.

Oakland leaned over and had taken a small bite of the crunchy pear while still held in Deklan's hand. He side hugged Deklan, feeling the Prince's anxiety level relaxing as the moments passed.

They'd reluctantly broken apart, but still held hands, fingers locked together over Oakland's knee.

Leaning back against the tree trunk, Deklan started speaking, softly at first and then strengthening his voice, "I'm not sure I can go through with the wedding, Oakland. They are making me marry that maiden. It just isn't right on many aspects. Why can't they see people's lives will be destroyed just to satisfy their own self-regarding reasons?"

Oakland kept his hand on top of Deklan's, gripping it tighter, nudging his shoulder, too. "I honestly believe the light will come on some day. It may not be straightaway, but it will illuminate."

"Huh?" Deklan seemed to have been thinking so literally at the moment that Oakland's outlandish analogy appeared to have made no sense to him.

Oakland said it in a simpler way. "What might seem like an event that doesn't align the way you think it should right now, will soon fall into place the way it's supposed to later on. Two souls meant to share a life together cannot be kept separated. Love will find a way."

Deklan's forehead formed a knot between his eyes. "You lost me. What?"

"I meant to say that life is funny sometimes. We all climb different mountains, but will end up on the other side where we are supposed to be. This whole messed up situation will all work out as it should. We've gotta believe that." Oakland said differently to Deklan, hoping he'd understand.

What Oakland recently found out and Deklan hadn't seemed to have known, was that he had a mystical fairy guiding him through life. Everyone does, however, Oakland was fortunate enough to have met his guidance fairy face to face. At least that's what he'd thought.

Worry lines ornamented Deklan's forehead. "What's going to happen to us when I'm forced to be with and share my bed with that lass?"—his face turned white—"When I think about the parts a girl is made of versus the equipment on a man that I enjoy, prefer, and don't want to live without, I go cold. The thought of lady bits makes me queasy, Oakland. There isn't anything wrong with them, by no means, I just have no interest. My brain and body aren't made to function that way. Not a single part of the female anatomy does anything for me. You know, right?"

Oakland watched Deklan worry, noticing him wincing and turning a couple shades of gray. It wasn't pleasant. "Of all people, Deklan, you should already know the answer to that. I can definitely relate."

"Will I ever see you again?" Deklan asked.

Oakland wasn't prepared for that question. He sputtered, "Je... Jeez, Deklan. Of... of course you will. I'll be right outside your window, slaving away."

Deklan's face had gone sour. "I don't like that word. It never should have existed."

What Oakland said had come out wrong. For one thing, he hadn't meant he was headed back into slavery as it sounded, or had he meant to make Deklan think he'd only see him from his bedroom window. "Wait. No. I didn't mean that," he shuddered.

Deklan had sunk backward against the tree, pressing his shoulder into Oakland's while laying a hand on his knee. "There's too much segregation in this world. I don't get it. I think I was born way before my time. You and I think differently than most people do. Our era isn't ready for men like us. Hopefully this all changes in the future."

Oakland thought optimistically. "Somehow we will figure this out." He laid his hand over top of Deklan's, giving it a squeeze. "We're stronger together. It won't be that easy for anybody to tear us apart." He rotated Deklan's chin toward his and delicately pressed their lips together.

Deklan breathed Oakland's kiss in. "Never let me go, Oakland."

"Not possible," Oakland whispered back. Lips remained connected, but enough of a gap to have been able to speak.

Deklan stood, lifting Oakland with him. "Let's take Chadwick for a trot along the river. Maybe take a swim. Yeah?"

Oakland walked tightly at Deklan's side as though they had been tied together by rope, holding his hand the entire time, nearly squeezing away its blood flow.

Chadwick was still grazing as though he hadn't eaten for weeks, having no worry in the world except for making sure his stomach was full.

"I want you in the front this time as we ride. I need to hold you." Deklan leaned into Chadwick and gripped the reigns.

No argument had come from Oakland about taking the front seat. He liked the idea of Deklan's strong arms wrapped around him from behind, keeping him securely in his place.

Deklan turned Chadwick around and Oakland climbed on first, the saddles handle jacking up the bulge between his legs when he scooted forward to leave space for Deklan comfortably in the back.

Deklan wormed a toe into the fendered stirrup, grabbed the handle and lifted himself into the saddle behind Oakland. "You okay up there?" he muttered into Oakland's ear.

"Doing well," Oakland replied with a twisting undertone. He found it comforting having Deklan positioned behind him, even though the strain on his genitals had taken a beating and any more pressure would have caused a pitch change in his voice.

Reaching around front of Oakland, Deklan cupped that bulge in his pants with a single hand, even though normally two would have been needed. Rubbing gently, he asked, "You sure about that? I don't want that magnificent black dick sustaining any damage."

Chuckling, Oakland replied, "I'm perfect like this."

"That it is." With one hand full of chocolate nuts, Deklan wrapped his other arm around Oakland's waist and tucked three fingers inside the front of his shirt. "Now it's even more perfect," he said, giving Chadwick a gentle squeeze to the ribcage with his heels — the directive to start walking.

While they rode on horseback, feeling every footfall Chadwick made, Deklan rested his chin on Oakland's shoulder — his scruffy cheek firmly against his ear. "I like holding you, Oakland. It feels so... well... so natural."

"It does feel natural, and very soothing, I'll admit." Oakland could feel Deklan breathing as his chest pumped against his back. He tunneled his fingers into his shirt over Deklan's and held his hand.

Within a split second, Oakland felt defeated. A nauseous sensation had come over him the moment he thought about the ignorant people who planned on taking the love of his life away from him. He'd just finished lifting Deklan's spirits, only to feel his own spiraling downward as if he'd just been pushed over a mountainside cliff. Oakland turned his head and kissed Deklan, hopeful to have hidden what he had felt and put both their worries to rest.

As though Deklan had sensed fear, he pulled Oakland tighter against his chest and whispered, "As long as we have each other, we'll be okay."

Oakland stayed quiet and let his handsome Prince keep hold of him from behind.

Chapter 26

Instead of heading to the river as earlier mentioned, Deklan led Chadwick to a secluded lake somewhere in the middle of the woods that Oakland hadn't known was there.

The lake ended up being a place so far away from everywhere they'd ever run away from, it seemed as though it had been their very own private kingdom. A secret place. One only a moment from the sun that nobody but them could touch.

Oakland's adoring actions needed no words.

His fairy godfather would have been proud.

Deklan tugged the reigns and Chadwick stopped.

Oakland looked everywhere, as though he'd been taking in the pine and cedar scented air around him. "This place is stunning. I'd lived here my entire life and had no idea this oasis was even here. The grounds look untouched. Like Genesis."

With his cheek pressed to Oakland's, Deklan hugged him with both arms. "I found this a while ago and knew someday I'd share it with someone extraordinary, and that person is you, Oakland. This could be the place we call our own. A secret hideaway we can come to and be together whenever we want. Nobody else but us. What do you think?"

Oakland had lost any ability of speech. He only stared directly through the space in front of him.

Deklan gripped Oakland tighter and gently rocked with him. "What do you think, my love?" he asked again.

"Yes. Our secret place. Of course." Oakland stammered, but Deklan had detected a troubling behavior in Oakland's reply, likely that a private hideaway was needed for the two of them to be together. It wasn't right, or fair, but sadly, the world wasn't ready to accept two men holding hands. Deklan was definitely in love with Oakland, and if a hidden valley was the only way to be with him, he would go with that.

Oakland's Mirror Man had told him the relationship would be a struggle, and so far, that magical man had been correct. Oakland had broken out of his trance and mumbled, "Sorry. I just find this place so spectacular. It's incredibly tranquil. A place right out of heaven."

Deklan tossed the reigns over Chadwick's head and they dangled to the ground in front of him. His muzzle followed the straps and he started eating grass.

Deklan rounded his leg over the horse's rear end and jumped down. "Your next, my handsome Prince." He held both arms out to lure Oakland into them.

"You're going to catch me, right?" Oakland cartwheeled his leg up and over the horse's mane, putting himself sideways in the saddle.

Deklan started by placing his hands on Oakland's thighs, then securing them at his waist as he slid down the side of Chadwick until his feet touched ground. With the weight of his body, he leaned in and pinned Oakland's back to the horse and kissed him.

Slowly, Deklan backed away and pulled in a deep breath. "Omigrace, I love you, Oakland. I can't even explain how much I do." He'd gone in for another kiss, more ardently than before. His eyes closed, his hands connected with Oakland's chest, feeling the beat of his heart thumping at the rate of a running rabbits.

Backing away, Deklan had taken Oakland's hand and navigated him toward the water. "Let's go for a swim and forget about everything."

Oakland had gone along with Deklan's plan, tripping over his own feet like a love punched schoolboy. They had come to a large pine tree where its root system had given way and the surviving trunk extended gracefully out over the Crystal Lake.

They had taken turns removing each other's clothing, Oakland unbuttoning Deklan's shirt first, exposing the hair blocking the man's perfect chest. His palms caressed slowly as he worked the shirt up and over his broad shoulders. He tossed it into the wind and it drifted like a fabric kite, coming down over the leaning tree trunk.

Deklan had then taken his turn, slipping the suspenders over Oakland's shoulders, letting them drop freely at his thighs. It cleared the way for removing his shirt, strangely unbuttoning it from bottom to top. It was Deklan's quirky way and might have been what made Oakland smirk. He clutched Oakland's shoulders and dove in for another kiss. He couldn't help himself. There was a charge between Oakland's legs that had pushed with force against Deklan's own erecting dick.

Deklan unfastened the clasps that kept Oakland's pants in place, eager to get at his semi-hard cock. It sprung free, banging against his thigh before slowly rising even further. "There's my boy, or wow, I mean my man." Deklan grinned as he'd taken Oakland into both hands and squeezed. He indicated ultimate liking for Oakland's black cock when he commented, "This beautiful thing is so damned thick. I can't get over how big it is."

Oakland had returned the favor and untied Deklan's fly, and like that of a caged bull, his heavy dick busted free too, flopping out of his pants, protruding thickly to the right.

Oakland dropped to his knees, taking Deklan's pants with him. "How about I swallow you whole?"

"Jeez, yes. Go on. Give it a try." Deklan laid the oversized head of his white dick onto Oakland's extended tongue, and it had taken less than a few seconds for Oakland to close his lips around the shaft and start sucking, his cheeks expanding and yielding each time Deklan's plumb sized head moved back and forth across his pink tongue. Deklan's butt cheeks dimpled as he pushed forward, forcing his erection to the back of Oakland's throat.

Oakland moaned with each wet stroke, taking Deklan's erection deeper with each forward glide. He continued until the entire shaft of white meat had gone all the way down his throat, proving he was professional at sucking his boyfriend's dick, not choking once.

Looking down, Deklan cried out, "Jeez."

The whites of Oakland's eyes had expanded as he looked up at Deklan grinning back at him. He pulled off his cock and gasped for air. "No good? Should I stop?"

"Gawd, no. That mouth of yours is doing a fantastic job. I'm amazed you're able to swallow the entire thing. Keep it up. I want to sperm coat your throat, if okay with you."

"I'll take what you can give me. I'm truly surprising myself, too. I must want it bad. Why you showing off a toothy grin right now?"

A smirk. "When you had taken me all the way in, the hair above my dick had given you the most attractive mustache I'd ever seen on a black man. You looked mighty fine with a brown hairy lip. It had softened your appearance somehow."

Oakland chuckled and mentioned he was relieved it wasn't about his newly discovered talent. "If you enjoyed it that much, I best be gettin' back to it so you can appreciate it again." He'd commented in so many words once before that Deklan was hairy in all the right places, from his impeccably groomed chest to the velvety hair surrounding the base of his erection that had given him an attractive mustache Deklan liked seeing.

The more Oakland swallowed him down, Deklan's facial expressions changed, contorting with extreme pleasure. A few growls had been released as the man on his cock sucked on him harder than he had before. The suction of a wet mouth around his dick was a brand new incredible sensation.

"Gah, Jeez," Deklan growled. "You sure do want my semen flooding that throat, don't you?"

Oakland couldn't answer at that particular moment, only nodded, and the way he'd been sucking on every inch of Deklan's dick, he might have been more thrilled about swallowing his sperm than the Prince had known. The strength in Oakland's oral suction nearly turned Deklan inside out. He'd been doing well, going at that white dick in a frantic manner, acting out his determination to swallow every bit of Deklan's ejaculate.

The sexual drive Deklan had for Oakland helped him forget about the upcoming event. His breathing had become erratic, caused by his oncoming orgasm, and before it all ended too soon, pulled back to catch wind. The head of his cock slipped from Oakland's mouth with a wet pop, the swish of his heavy dick smacked Oakland across his cheek.

Oakland looked up and gulped, "I'm not done."

"Neither am I. But there's something I want to do with you," Deklan said as Oakland stood. The guy had been gasping.

It was noticeable that Oakland was observing every part of Deklan's body, ending with a long hard stare at his square bulky chest. Deklan stared back, moving his hands to Oakland's jaw, down his neck and skating over every inch of his blocky chest. "Omigrace, you are extremely beautiful, Oakland." He kissed him quickly on the lips and at a snap, had taken off toward the lake. As he ran, hollered back, "Let's swim. No clothes allowed."

Just like that, Oakland followed, running straight into the water at the same speed, holding his junk—that damned freakish two handed burden had gotten in the way again.

As Oakland ran, Deklan grinned with his gaze pinned on the stunning black man running toward him, watching every muscle bunch, imagining the man could have been his if the world wasn't so sheltered with how a person's life was supposed to have been lived.

Deep down, Deklan adored every part of Oakland, from his sidewinders smile to his enormous feet.

They swam to a deeper part of the water where the surface rippled level with their chests. The tiny waves pricking at them sounded like musical bells being tapped by a metal pick. The moment had been glorious, one Deklan knew himself he wanted to last forever.

Oakland and Deklan had both taken a few quick dives, mostly adjusting to the water temperature, which had first felt cold on the initial entry.

"Come closer," Deklan commanded, finger combing his wet hair away from his face.

There had come a moment that Oakland seemed to have hesitated, as though he was teasing or wondering if he should have taken the relationship further than what they had. Deklan immediately reached out and pulled him to his chest, looking intently as he laid a hand to Oakland's cheek. "We need to figure a way to be together, Oakland. Not just here in hiding, but always." He kissed him.

Oakland whispered, "We will, Dek. I promise." His body leaned into Deklan as if the water from behind had given him a push. Their chests pressed tighter against the other and the kiss had gone deeper that time. Passion had taken over and they begun to spin, the force of the turn lifted Oakland higher above water as if riding a wave.

Soon after, Deklan slowed the spin, and when Oakland ascended, he was centered perfectly for penetration—Deklan's skyward erection tapping at his sex-hole as the shifting water wrestled with it.

The moment Deklan felt Oakland dropping down, he lifted his hips into him. "That's it. Open up. Let me in, Oakland. I need you to take me one more time."

Oakland's reaction had elevated with tremors. It must have been his unrestrained pleasure from Deklan's erection forcing its way inside him. The large head had broken through the sphincter ring with slight resistance as Deklan angled his dick upward, determined to get every inch as far as he could inside his stunning black man.

Oakland inhaled sharply and his body quaked. He cried, "Yes. Right there. Hold it right there." His head dropped to Deklan's shoulder. "Omistars. So good."

Deklan held still, his cock penetrated with pressure where Oakland wanted it. He could feel a pulsing sensation around his dick, as if Oakland's rectum was sucking for sperm. Deklan whispered, "I want to ejaculate inside you so bad, Oakland. I'm almost there. I can feel your rectum flexing, trying to take it from me."

Oakland whispered back behind kissing lips, "I want it. Shoot it in me."

Jacking their balance while stuck together, a sudden noise that hadn't come from either of them echoed from the woods.

Oakland stiffened and pulled his mouth off Deklan's. He breathed, "Bollock's. What was that? Footfalls?"

Deklan held his breath, his hardened cock weakened, partially snaking out of Oakland's sex-hole. He whispered, "Not sure. I thought this place was secluded. Thought we'd forever be left alone out here."

"Omigawd, somebody saw us." Oakland panicked. He lowered himself until the water met his chin.

"Maybe not. Stay down." Deklan spun, holding out a hand.

"Omigawd," Oakland repeated. Then he screamed.

Deklan shouted, "Jeez."

They laughed.

"Damn Deer," Oakland griped.

"At least we'll have pets when we come here." Oakland faced Deklan after watching the deer take off into the trees. "My heart," Oakland whined. "I think it stopped."

"Follow me. I'll start it up again." Deklan relocated to shallower waters, bringing Oakland with him by the hand. He laid him back on the sand and climbed on top, water washing over their extended legs.

The full body contact had turned Deklan's cock extremely hard all over again. Feeling so close to ejaculating, he needed to put his erection back inside Oakland before his dick started spurting sperm all over the man's bare chest. He bore down on top of Oakland, opening his legs with his own knees. Angling slightly, he slipped a hand between their abdomens, grabbed hold of his own erection and aimed it at Oakland's tight black hole without looking, punching the tip of his cock head in and out to soften the knot for entry.

Sexually ready beyond anything he'd ever imagined, Deklan pushed his nine inch dick harder into Oakland until the ring of his black sphincter clamped hold good and tight. As he nudged the head in and out, there was a sloppy sound of suction that was as erotic as a tongue wet kiss. He moaned, "Oh my gawd, Oakland. I need to ejaculate. I've gotta stick my dick all the way into you. Like... right now." He ran his hand over the deep gutter of Oakland's abdomen and wrapped a hand around the man's stiff black cock. "Jeez! You want it, too, don't you? You're dick is a rock." He stroked Oakland's erection, his palm becoming wetter with pre-drizzle leaking from his dick. He transferred it to the head of his own dick and rubbed it in.

Deklan licked his fingers, the scent and taste of Oakland's semen nearly pushed him over the edge. His voice had gone jagged, "I really need to ejaculate right now. Inside you. Hurry. Open that hole for me." By the time Deklan finished begging, Oakland's fingers had gone to circling and poking at his asshole, stretching the seal for the massive intrusion of Deklan's big white dick.

Oakland's legs opened wider—his fingers pumping in and out of his dark chute in a speedy manner. His hand a blur. The slurping sound Oakland's fingers had made while they punched in and out of his asshole fractured Deklan sexually, pushing him closer to that unwanted early sperm release, fearing he wouldn't get his dick inside Oakland's butt in time. "Jeez, I'm so aroused by what you're doing, Oakland." He grabbed hold of Oakland's ankles, spreading one leg out to the side and lifting the other over his shoulder. His butt crack opening right up, exposing his inviting black hole.

Deklan pushed his hips into Oakland, bumping his hand aside and feeling the silkiness of his softened sphincter smooching the head of his dick. "Oh my Gawd, your hole feels good. Let me in." He was hyperventilating. Losing his mind. He needed to spurt. Every second counted.

Yanking his hand out of his hole, Oakland ordered, "Shove it in. Hurry. Fertilize my-yaaAAH..." he couldn't finish speaking. At that moment Deklan sunk his cock into his man's water slickened chute with one ass splitting plunge, burrowing deep. All at once. He couldn't wait another second either. He needed to ejaculate or his balls would explode. Even though he had gone nuts deep, he heard Oakland cry out for more, pleading for his thick white cock to hammer the mercy out of him, begging to blow semen into his pulsing sex-hole. Oakland had turned noticeably enthused once Deklan was inside him.

Oakland's squealing and ass sucking sensation motivated Deklan even more. He moaned, groaned, and growled like a fanatic, pulling out once and shoving his cock back in, slamming his hairy pelvis into Oakland's butt cheeks so hard he nearly bumped his cock gripping rider clear into the forest.

Deklan shouted like a grizzly madman, "Jeez, that butthole! My, Gawd!" His hips ground forward in short thrusts, becoming glued to Oakland's rear end. His body tightened, turning solid. He couldn't breathe at first. His entire body buzzed from his whirling orgasm racing through his entire body, extreme pressure in his groin. His head felt like it was going to explode. He grittily groaned, "H-here it comes. Gah. I'm shooting."

Deklan's erection had gotten the best of him. It happened that fast—sperm filling Oakland's manhole after the first few strokes of being inside him, ejecting semen with force. He roared louder. Voice echoing. Nearly causing fish to fly from the lake like birds.

Oakland was whimpering, his voice cracking, "Aaah-yaaah! Oh, Gawd!"—his body squirmed and jerked under Deklan— "hammer my hole. Make me lose it." He sounded wild, practically weeping.

Deklan's hips forcefully pushed into Oakland, his entire body holding stiff as he ejaculated. "Oh, my Gawd. Take... my sperm... HUH!" His pelvis continued jamming into Oakland's butt, uncontrollably thumping as if a magnetic force had pulled him in. His body wouldn't let him pull out if he tried. He kept spurting as if he'd never empty. Fertilization had definitely taken place. "Uhng. Jeez. So much semen going in. Take it all. Suck my dick dry."

Oakland cried and coughed as if Deklan's sperm had shot clear into his throat. He gurgled, "Gawd. So good. Keep that dick in me."

Within moments after Deklan started ejaculating and the pulsing of his expanding cock thumped at the internal spot that made Oakland lose his mind, Oakland ejected semen clear over his head as if shot from a sling. He was whining, thrusting his ass into Deklan's hairy pelvis, pulling the man's dick in as if begging to take his nuts, too.

Deklan felt his cock being squeezed and sucked. Oakland's chute had greedily taken the man's sperm as if his life depended on it to survive.

While hand jerking his own cock, Oakland ordered between gasps, "Give... it to me. Aaaa-gaaah!" — he lost his breath for a moment — "Gaaah.... Pump the sperm out of me, Dek." He shot a few more loads, saturating his guttered abdomen. "Ruin my hole with that horse hung cock. Sperm breed me."

The verbal slander out of Oakland's mouth kept Deklan stone stiff, and if he hadn't released his semen already, he would have spurted then.

In less than ten minutes after they'd gotten started, both were whipped and cock empty.

As soon as he'd caught his breath, Deklan snaked his dick from Oakland's butthole — backing out slowly, trying to keep his deposited sperm from spitting out along with his cock. It was important it stayed — keeping his man marked for the rest of the day and maybe into the next. "I'm sorry. Sorry for ejaculating so quickly, but your hole felt so damned incredible."

"That was the best sexual few minutes I'd ever had. I'd wanted your sperm blown up my ass as much as you wanted to pump it into me. So, there will be no apologizing or critical blaming for how quickly you ejaculated."

"You are just too sexy, Oakland. That black body. That black ass. Your beautiful black dick. The scent you had given off when you ejaculated. All of you. I'm still rock hard as though I'm not done using your hole." Deklan glanced between him and Oakland, finding his own dick still stiff and leaking semen into the course black hair above Oakland's dick.

"Well. If you're not done, stud, my ass is still yours if you need to use it." Oakland laughed. "Go on. Use it." He laughed again. "Use it."

"A five minute rest is all I need, and trust me, I'll be ready to go back at it, squeezing another few shots inside that sweet used butt of yours."

"As I said… A Stud."

"Stud? Studs don't ejaculate within seconds of penetrating their boyfriend's butt. I promise to last longer the next time." Deklan's erection snaked upside Oakland's, pressing firmly against his abdomen, still slick with semen.

"If you weren't such an awesome stud, I wouldn't have spurted within seconds either. I'm pretty sure I had never shot so quickly in my life—not even as a teen when I first learned how amazing ejaculating felt. Speaking of those teen days of discovery, I used to give myself hand jobs a dozen times a day. But, it's definitely better enjoyed with a real man's cock shoved up my ass instead of a few of my own fingers or homegrown vegetables covered in butter. The moment you put the big guy in me, I'd lost all strength to hold back. You know, there's a spot a few inches passed my sphincter that makes me go absolutely crazy when the head of your dick glides over it. I have the feeling I'm ejaculating the entire time you're inside me. The sensation isn't as intense as it is when I actually shoot, but it is one of the best feelings and makes ejaculating that much more intense. I'm not sure what it is up there, or how you're doing it, but you must keep that zone in mind every time you put that dick inside me. I wonder if that happens to anybody else, or just to me?"

Deklan articulated, "I had noticed how you reacted when I hit that spot, so I stayed focused on it while inside you. There was a wilder side that had come out of you, and you spilled a little bit of semen every time I nudged it. Seeing you go crazy like that made me want to drive into you even harder. I liked making you feel that good."

"Well, you succeeded. Look how much had come out of me."

Dragging two fingers through the semen on Oakland's chest, Deklan said, "You did shoot quite a lot. You should see it all. It's amazing. I don't think I'd seen so much semen come out of a dick—speaking of myself since I'd never seen another man ejaculate. Well, except for you. Plus, I don't think I ever ejaculated so quickly and with such volume before either. It was as if my body was on a mission of its own, with a need to breed the man

I'd fallen in love with, making sure your body was receiving what it'd been missing all your life."

"I'm sure you're right," Oakland replied. "I suppose when two people connect so deeply with each other as much as us, the bodies crave what's needed and takes it without waiting or asking."

Deklan groaned into Oakland's ear, lazily drawing out his words, "Ohwww, ye-eaah." He reached between his legs, gripped his thick white cock and shoved it back inside Oakland's black butthole. He let out a growl combined with grizzly lip biting grunts in time with each thrust. "Mm. Mm. Mm. So good. Yeah, you tightened right back up. Mm. Huh. Huh. Hnguh. You like that? Mm. Mm. Hnguh. Mm. Hnguh." He banged.

"Gah, Jeez. Yeah!" Oakland squealed. "Yes I do. You trying to make me shoot again? The hammering is working."

"If that's what you want, but truly, I just needed to be inside you again, make sure I plugged that hole to keep my semen up there where it needs to stay. I need other men to know you're mine if they come sniffing around that rear end. It's mine now. All mine."

"Nobody's but yours."

"Good answer. Are you okay with me pulling out?" Deklan asked.

"Not really, but go ahead."

"I'll pull out slowly. You'll never realize I left that beautiful tight ass."

"The hell I won't. Nine thick inches of dick isn't easy to ignore."

"A tight ass that sucks dick isn't easy to ignore." Deklan admittedly interrupted, slowly pulling out as he'd done once already a few minutes earlier. He looked down at his glistening dick slipping free. "Ease up, sweetheart. Let it go. Loosen that manhole. That's it. Looking good. Ah, here comes the head. Set the python free."

Oakland had chuckled and pouted at the same time. "Sadly, I'm dickless."

"Oh, you're not dickless. Trust me on that. Eleven black

inches isn't rightfully labeled that, but being without my dick in you will be all right. You have my sperm to keep you company for a while." Deklan made a popping sound with his mouth when the head of his cock squeezed out of Oakland's hole. "There's my entire dick." He chuckled, too.

A fast sexual encounter made for physical exertion and neither one of them noticed the strain on their body until it was over. Oakland groaned when he budged and so had Deklan. A bit of laughter too.

Realization of sexual exhaustion had come when it was too late. They collapsed in the sand, gasping for air. Eventually, their breathing evened out and a sleepy desire had come over them both.

It was Deklan's idea to lie at the lakeside completely naked — completely exposed to the elements and any viewers if there had been any watching. He held Oakland's hand the entire time they enjoyed the few clouds floating in the sky and listening to the few birds chirping overhead. It was tranquil, almost unworldly.

Deklan rolled onto his side and faced Oakland, gently combing his fingers through the course hair above Oakland's softening dick. His voice lowered, "I'm so glad I met you, Oakland. I can't imagine what my life might be like if I hadn't." His finger traced the hairy abdominal trail that diminished a few inches above Oakland's navel, stopping with his palm flat against his farm firmed chest.

"Me too," Oakland answered, looking his way. His arm bent behind his head, lifting it off the ground.

"If you hadn't come along when you had, I don't know how I'd have survived. I'm in such a mess, Oakland." Deklan rubbed the large mounds of Oakland's cocoa chest, the smooth dark skin felt soothing. "You mean a lot to me." He caught Oakland smiling.

Even though it had been less than ten minutes since Oakland ejaculated, his dick had turned thick and rigid all over again the moment Deklan repositioned his body back on top of him. It wasn't difficult to understand why. Deklan was beautifully fit, masculine, and extremely sexy.

Pensively, Deklan looked at Oakland and told him, "I don't want to leave this place, but since my keepers are going to start wondering where I'm at, I should probably move out."

"I suppose... you're right," Oakland pumped the words out between gasps. The weight of Deklan's body had put a strain on the flow of air in and out of his lungs.

"Leave your door open tonight. I'm sneaking back to you." Deklan lifted himself off of Oakland, kissing him on separation. He whistled, and Chadwick had come running.

Expressing regret, Oakland let him go.

Chapter 27

"Where've you been, Deklan?" his father's voice had come across as testy. "You'd been gone all day without word as to where, and the second time this week you've done this. No more running off into the wilderness without letting somebody know where you'd gone off to."

"I needed some space," Deklan shortly answered. The good time he had with Oakland quickly beaten down by his father's storming voice.

"We all need space, but we don't always get what we think we need," Dante replied. "Your mother's been worried. Don't do that to her again."

"I'm trying to make sense of, as well as come to terms with, what you're forcing me to do. I wish there was a vile word I could use to stress how I feel, but I don't know any."

"You need to listen and know this is right for you."

"Really? Right for Me?" Deklan hissed. Glowering.

Before Deklan's father had a chance to reply, Wattsworth walked into the room with a handful of parchment pages outlining his busy list of what was yet to be done. Mother was following him, but she hadn't fully entered the room. She stood in the doorway with her tiny hands clasped together in front of her thin waist. She seemed okay, however, there was a certain amount of concern in her eyes. She hadn't wanted the marriage to proceed any more than Deklan had, but father seemed to have thought he'd known best as he had clearly put into words more than once in the past days.

Wattsworth seemed frazzled — parchment crinkling in his hands. There was only one full day left to get the place ready for the wedding, and looking around at an unfinished chapel might have been what had triggered the man's anxiety.

As it was, the grand hall looked splendid. It was smothered in white and shimmering silver, the typical wedding hues in the day. Any light coming in from the windows would catch the silver, reflecting luminescent diamond patterns throughout the hall. Tiny rainbow sparks pinged every surface, appearing enchanted. All seemed perfect for a new beginning between two people that hadn't had a moment to really get to know one another.

The layout was clever. The seats had been arranged to welcome one hundred guests. There were two outside aisles running in a V-formation that would take the couple from the far back corners of the room to the same spotlighted point up front where the parson would be waiting.

Draping every chair were silken white fabric covers held in place by a large wide gleaming ribbon of silver, bow tied across the back.

To create a wall of burning light along the back section of the marriage platform, there stood twenty wax candles on tall silver sticks, resembling a mountain peak crowning high at its center. Shorter wax pillars had been plated and hung sporadically from the ceiling by fishing cord, presenting the illusion they were floating in mid space — Wattsworth's idea at bringing the outside stars to the inside.

Deklan and his father were blatant opposites — like night

and day. His mother on the other hand was similar to him, the reason why the feelings they both had about the wedding had been quite the same.

Hearing his father carrying on about how perfect everything was, Deklan forced himself to ignore what had been said. He moved away, putting distance between the two of them, setting foot on the first step of the alter. His mother followed and stood beside him. He looked her in the eyes, finding her expression as devastating as his own.

She reached down and had taken his hand in hers. "Deklan, I can practically hear your thoughts, and I hear nothing cheerful."

"Then why are you letting this go on?" He looked to the floor and had taken the next step onto the platform.

Priscilla had gone with him, stopping in front of the wall of candles. "This is beautiful." She looked up at the highest one. "I just wish it was for you and somebody you really wanted to be up here with."

"It isn't too late, mother." Deklan turned to her. "You can help me stop the procession of such a huge mistake. I can't do it alone. Father is too pig headed."

"I wish it were that simple, Deklan." Priscilla dropped her head to one side as if giving up. A sigh was expelled. "Your father has a will that is firm, and when he has an idea, he always finds a way to make it happen. Look at the business he built. Just one example of his great achievements that started with a single seed he decided to plant instead of consumed."

"Talk to him," Deklan begged.

"I tried talking to him, but he won't listen. You know that. We'll figure a way to make it work."

"But this is major. It's not as if he's bidding on a horse at auction. This is my life we are talking about. Other's too." Deklan's eyes were beginning to burn. Tears had surfaced at the same time his body started shaking. It was a tangled emotion. One of fear that had knotted itself around anger.

Still at the same table in the back, Wattsworth and Dante were standing. Deklan and his mother rejoined them, listening to their suggested changes.

Dante placed a strong grip to the back of Deklan's neck. "It's perfect isn't it, son?" He had spoken as though there was no quarrel between them a few moments earlier, nor had the man probably cared for any answer other than, Yes.

Deklan almost lost his balance when his father shook him. "No Pop, it isn't. It's ugly, because the whole idea of what you are doing is ugly." He was finding it difficult to believe his father had purposely put up blinders to the enormously screwed up situation in front of them.

Dante's big hand spun Deklan around. He'd spoken to him face to face. "Now you listen to me. You will not disgrace this family any further than you already have by acting out your foolish fantasies. It just ain't right. You can't show a sweet liking for other men the way you've been?"

Like a strong soldier, Deklan gripped his father's arm and yanked it from his neck. He backed away and put his hands to his temples and pressed. "Stop it. Just stop it," he yelled. Squeezing his eyes closed to block out everything around him. The place had literally gone black to him.

His father stood taller. His expression tightened with anger. His face turned beet red.

Next to Deklan stood his mother with both hands over her mouth, crying.

"Stop. Stop. Stop!" Deklan swayed as if honing in on a mental breakdown. "Stop everything." He fumed, extending his arms at his sides like a pair of wings. "You may not like this father, but your son, that is me, is a homosexual. Yes Pop, I like lads. There, I've said it." His arms had extended at his sides and he backed up a few steps. "You've known this for a while now and you need to stop denying it. I am what I am and no marriage to a female is going to magically change how I feel toward other chaps."

"This cannot be. It's not possible." Dante lowered his voice and corralled Deklan to a more secluded corner of the room. His mother followed closely behind, still crying.

"It is possible, because here I am. Right in front of you is your homosexual son. The new word for who I am is, gay. So I'd heard."

"Don't say that. You are destroying a perfectly good word."

"The word is gay, Pop. You need to say it. I am GAY!"

"I won't say it. It doesn't make any sense. The word means happy and you cannot be happy like this."

"You're right Pop, I'm not happy." Deklan bit his lower lip and turned away.

"Then marry this pretty damsel and you will be happy."

"No, Pop. That is why I'm not happy. I don't like the maidens the way you think I should. I'd rather be with the boy next door."

"No you wouldn't."

"Yes I would."

"No... You wouldn't"

"Yes... I Would. Why are you arguing about something that cannot be changed?" Deklan fought back.

"There is nothing to change."

"I'm glad you agree." Deklan's fists loosened a little.

"That is not what I meant and you know it."

"Pop, I don't have the answer or the solution you are looking for, but I do know I was created this way for a good reason. Call it Gods way of preventing over population of life on the lands. I don't know." Deklan had gone serious. "All I know for sure is that I cannot change no matter how hard you or anybody else tries to make me. I also know that you cannot force what isn't supposed to be."

Deklan's father pursed his lips. He had nothing to say after that statement from his son. His eyes turned dark. He looked from Deklan to Priscilla and back at Deklan again. "Be here tomorrow for this wedding or don't come home at all." That was the first sensible ultimatum Deklan had heard from his father in days. At least he'd been given a choice to be excused from marrying a female.

As his father turned and left like a retracting lightning bolt, Deklan bowed his head and huffed. He'd shaken his head with total disappointment at the same time his mother grabbed his arm and squeezed it.

Deklan's hands had gone back to his temples and his

fingertips tried circling the tension away. There hadn't been much more that could have been said and it had become apparent he would marry some damsel his father handpicked off the street the same way they selected fruit at the market, however if it spoiled, tossing it out wouldn't have come that simple.

Without saying anything more, Deklan kissed his mother on the forehead and walked away. As the doors closed behind him, he caught a glimpse of his mother still standing there with the crumpled handkerchief in her fragile grasp. It was tarnished with tears brought on by a vile display between Dante and her only son. She'd taken a deep breath, glanced around the beautiful silver room and quietly crept out the door after Deklan, practically tracing his exact foot print.

Chapter 28

Oakland felt a void when Deklan wasn't with him. A crack had been cut down the middle of his heart when he heard Deklan was still going through with the wedding. It hadn't come as a shock since Deklan's father had such a strong grip on him and was able to nearly dictate every move he made.

It had taken time for some people to realize paired souls cannot be kept apart. In their case, Deklan's father was one of those people, and the degree of acceptance was higher since the issue had hit home instead of at somebody else's front door.

Oakland had been sitting quietly on the wooden bench outside his front door when he spotted Deklan walking the drive and kicking stones. Small dust storms twisted off the ground like tiny tornadoes each time a pebble hit the dirt. Even though he'd grown into a man who'd undoubtedly become sad and terrified, he projected charm that was boyish and cute when toe met stone. The sting it generated would still hurt if contact was just right.

Oakland's heart had sunk at the sight he'd seen, but selfishly perked up at the first sign of him angling his way. Oakland sat taller and forced a courageous smile. He had to, for his own sake and for Deklan's.

Deklan stood in front of Oakland, casting a shadow that blocked the sun. His hair was a mess. He sat down without a word and sneakily slipped his hand beneath Oakland's thigh. His touch as usual eased Oakland's nerves like nobody else could.

Oakland leaned back against the house, listening to the birds chirping springtime songs. It was pleasant considering the circumstances were far from the best of times. He dropped his hand to his side on top of Deklan's, his grip tightened as he looked around, finding it absurd he couldn't simply show affection to his boyfriend during the light of day.

They sat together in tranquil silence, watching two roosters walking side by side as if they were more than friends. At the same moment, Deklan and Oakland glanced at each other with grins, delighted that a sign such as that had been presented to them in such a mysterious way. Oakland and Deklan were meant to be together as much as those silly birds were. It was clear that the two roosters weren't interested in tagging a hen any more than Deklan and Oakland were up to pinning damsels. It wasn't a natural feeling for either of them and by the looks of it, for the two roosters either. Strangely enough, roosters are territorial birds and typically break out into a cock fight if more than one is in a hen house trying to manage the lady birds. Seeing them together in harmony indicated there must be an appetite for the other.

Deklan and Oakland sat on the wooden bench observing the two roosters ignoring the hens that were trying desperately to get their attention with flapping wings and fluttering tail feathers. It was comical to watch the roosters caringly interacting with each other while completely snubbing the females. The actions of those roosters suggested they were homobirduals. A made up word, Oakland had come up with.

It wasn't long after the roosters had run away together that Deklan asked Oakland to follow him to the barn for a visit with Chadwick.

Ludicrous it would have been to say no. Oakland stood,

letting Deklan identify he'd accepted the invitation. They'd taken off running for the barn like lovesick schoolboys, Oakland chasing his heart's desire, bringing him joy when he heard Deklan laughing.

Chadwick had been standing majestically in the stall when they arrived, but his stillness immediately changed the moment Deklan and Oakland had come through the door. His nose bobbed along with what seemed like excited whinnies. His hooves beat the ground as he pranced in a circle.

Once the horse had settled down, Oakland pulled a brush through Chadwick's mane while Deklan scraped mud and soot from the underside of his hooves with a wooden gouging tool.

Deklan had come up missing for a few moments, but returned with a scrub brush and a bucket filled with sudsy wash water. He started scrubbing Chadwick's rump, moved down around his knees and legs before telling Oakland he might want to look away for what was about to take place next.

What could be so bad that it was necessary for him to put blinders on?

Then it happened.

Oh sweet surrender. Shock horror.

Oakland's jaw immediately dropped when he witnessed what Deklan had done. "Holy bollocks," was all he could muster. *"That poor horse,"* he thought. It looked more than painful. It was a horrific deep cleaning from what Oakland could see and knew for sure he wouldn't want that done to himself, specifically not with a bristle brush that appeared as though it could scrape dry paint off the side of a house.

"I warned you," Deklan bashed. "First timers are usually shocked by this process."

"Shocked? Jeez, Dek. More like horrified. Take it easy on him," Oakland winced.

"It needs to be done to prevent buildup of dirt. This thing can get infected if not kept clean and then there'd be a bigger issue in hand." Deklan extended the horse's genitals to its fullest length and continued scrubbing it with the soapy brush. The horses' ears pricked as if getting ready to break down the stall and kick down the walls.

Oakland couldn't stop staring at the size of the horse's genitalia. It was huge. No, it was enormous. The thing couldn't have been a fraction less than eighteen or twenty inches long. It looked massive in Deklan's soapy hand. It was offensive really, but Oakland couldn't seem to look away. His own genitals started to hurt from watching that bristly brush being scrubbed up and down the poor horse's private parts. Oakland crossed his legs, attempting to sooth his imaginary pain. "Holy, bollocks!" he squealed again. "How much longer will this go on?"

Deklan laughed at him and finally let go of Chadwick's great big generative organ. It hung like a rope for a second and then quickly retracted into hiding as if something frightened it away.

After that horrific wash job, Deklan moved behind Chadwick and flushed his tail with the remaining water in the bucket. A clean hind end helped keep the flies tamed. As dreadful as the bath had been, the added laughter helped lift the dark cloud hovering so sinisterly above.

After the brush bath, Chadwick seemed energized. He perked up and started dancing again. Then dropped down into a bed of hay and rolled around, his hooves galloping at empty space out front of him. He quickly stood and shook, flicking straw bits everywhere. He whinnied and stared with a huge toothed grin at Deklan.

"Are we done?" Oakland asked.

"Yep, that's it. We're finished." Deklan tossed the dripping scrub brush into a wall bin about twenty feet away while he heaved the large bucket upside down over one of the stalls posts.

To Oakland's impressed surprise, everything had landed where it was supposed to.

Deklan dried his hands on his pant legs, stepped up to Oakland and kissed him on the lips. "There now. Chadwick is squeaky clean and infection free."

Oakland's entire body had gone as stiff as a barn plank floorboard. "Sorry, I'm still in shock over what I just witnessed. I had no idea Chadwick was such a big boy. Omigawd, that was awful. You really need to wash your hands."

Deklan kissed Oakland again and laughed. "You'll get used

to it." He tapped Oakland on the nose with his horse cocked finger.

Shifting backward, Oakland screamed. "Ho, hey. Whoa!"

Deklan laughed louder.

"That isn't funny. GO... wash your hands." Oakland pushed him away and pointed to the water pump outside.

"Yes Mumsie." Deklan smartly obeyed.

As Deklan turned away, Oakland spanked his rear-end. "Good boy."

Deklan held his hands out beneath the spout while Oakland started pumping the handle. It had taken a few thrusts to get the water out of the ground, but when it finally flowed, it had come out like the Grand Rapids falls.

As ordered, Deklan scrubbed. Once done, he said, "How'z 'bout we sneak into the house, grab us some grub, and a change of clothes?"

The look on Oakland's face should have told Deklan it wasn't a good idea for him to be making an appearance inside the manor. "What if somebody sees me with you?"

"Everybody's too busy to notice if someone doesn't belong." Deklan shook his hands, flicking water droplets to their feet.

"Are you sure about that?" Oakland asked, glancing at the huge house.

"No, but who cares. They are bound to meet my true love someday anyway. And with a family like mine, it's bound to be a spectacular introduction." He wiped his hands on his pants.

"Aren't they prepared to set fire to any man you bring home who'll get in the way of your marriage to that girl person?" Oakland mentioned the bride-to-be as if she was an undesirable object. Truth told—the female gender was unfavorable entities to him. He doesn't do bouncing boobs or dark scary vaginas.

"Don't be silly. They may have their issues, but nobody is going to get injured or killed over this. Now come on," Deklan asked again.

"I'm kind of on edge with the whole thing, not quite sure what to expect. Ya better stay close or I'm bound to lose my way."

"You're going to fit in fine. I know this. Now, let's go."

Deklan took hold of Oakland's hand and led the way.

"I feel sick." Oakland held his stomach.

"My place is yours. Since I found my way into your delightful entrance, comfortably through the rear, it's now your turn to make your way into mine, sneakily through the back." Deklan snickered.

"Did you hear what you just said?" Oakland's mind wandered. He liked it.

"I know exactly what I said. Glad you were paying attention and understood what I was referring to. Follow close behind me and keep your eyes on the prize."

Looking at Deklan's fit rear end, Oakland said, "Not to worry. You can count on that. My eyes are definitely on the prize."

Chapter 29

At the high front entrance, the Manor's door opened and Deklan's father stepped out on the stoop yelling at somebody inside.

It wasn't clear what he was hollering about, nor had it mattered, but the way Deklan reacted, it seemed best to dodge the oncoming arrow and stay out of his way. He pushed Oakland aside into the bushes at the base of the stairs.

"Aaagh, bollocks. Roses." Pricked by thorns, Oakland leaked itty spots of blood.

Deklan quickly sat on the first step, his leg bouncing nervously as his father approached from behind.

Dante seemed a bit more pleasant than the last time they were face to face, making the engagement seem less stern. "It's nice to see you, Deklan. You might want to get out of the sun before you burn up. It's a hot one today." Dante looked to the sky.

Deklan stood. "I suppose you're right."

182

Oakland hung tight in the shadow of the staircase, most likely listening. There was sincerity in Deklan's fathers' voice that probably hadn't been heard in a long while. It was gentle and from what Deklan had mentioned, wasn't what would have been expected.

Deklan shifted and said, "Pop?"

Dante ground his heels into the gravel and turned back around toward his son. "Yes Deklan?"

At a weird glance and hidden from his father, Deklan noticed Oakland had sunken deeper into the shadow of the staircase and stayed quiet.

"No matter what happens, please know that I love you and will respect your decision as you deem fit. I may not agree with all of them, but know that I won't let that get in the way of how I really feel about you and mother."

Dante hadn't said anything at first, but reached for Deklan and hugged him. Hugged him hard. Then, in a voice that had come softer than before, he whispered, "I just can't bear to see people hurting you. You are my child for God sake, and it's my job to take care of you and keep you protected. My Gawd, I love you, Deklan. The world is a cruel place. I need you to understand that, and sometimes it's necessary to do what we don't care to do, just to keep the peace and our safety. Not much in life is easy. You'll figure that out as you grow older."

"Thanks, Pop. I do understand," —Deklan grunted under the pressure of the hug—"I know you're looking out for me. But, I'm a grown man and should start taking care of myself. You need to allow me some space to figure my own way."

"Even so, you're still my little boy. To me. I used to change your filthy diaper for God sake. I still think of you as a snot-nosed whippersnapper that I still need to put over my knee and spank some sense into from time to time. Love comes in different forms, not always sunshine and rainbows." Dante kissed the side of Deklan's head as if he was still a young boy and about to be sent off to grade-school. He eventually let him go and then turned to walk away.

Oakland slowly rose from the bush, weeping like a small child and it hadn't seemed to have been because he was pricked by a rose. His voice quivered, "Are you alright?"

Deklan's voice cracked too. "I'm fine. Let's get inside."

Oakland commented, "I can see your father really loves you, and it seems he's only trying to look out for you the best way he knows how. This is all about keeping you from the wounds the world can inflict. I somewhat get it, but I still want you to be mine."

The two of them climbed the stairway that Oakland had once before climbed alone dressed in fabulous ball wear. He glanced around, his expression seemed to have remembered the other side, how elegant it was, and the image of that first greeting with his handsome Prince. It must all have become familiar to him again, however, the fear of the unexpected had to have been hanging over him, dousing him with anxiety with each step closer to where his love affair had begun. What was on the other side could also spin in reverse.

"Why are you trembling?" Deklan asked.

"I'm trembling?" Oakland asked. "I hadn't noticed," he fibbed.

"It'll be alright. My father is out of the house, and seemed calmer today than yesterday."

They'd taken each step together as if they were trained for a march.

Oakland had been led by Deklan through the doors that overlooked the grand hall before being taken down a short corridor to the left. That steered them to a long hallway off to the right where several doors were lined on both sides resembling an elegant hotel. The home was massive for a single family home and it seemed out of joint that anybody would need such a place.

When they reached the end, Deklan stopped and turned Oakland toward a door. It was like that of a castle. Deklan had sensed Oakland's anxiety, felt him perk up the instant he passed through the doorway of his bed chamber.

Deklan closed the door and clicked the lock into position. His heart was racing. The excitement and nervousness consumed him for having a man he loved in his bedroom for the very first time. Even though he'd been with Oakland before, the thought of having him in his own bed would surely have been unlike any other time.

The moment they entered, Oakland's gaze traveled around the room. There were mostly dark colors. Rusty brown tones, some greens and light shades of walnut. It was cozy the way a bedroom should have been. The fireplace along the wall to the left was mammoth—one that a tall man could have actually stood inside without head bumping the mantle.

As if the crackling fire had called to Oakland, he'd gone over and stood near the open flames.

Deklan followed and kissed him on the cheek, turned and confirmed, "This is it. My sleeping quarters. Around the corner over there is the water closet and sink basins."

"Quite nice," was all Oakland said, nodding his head and scanning the handsome room finely decorated for a striking chap like Deklan.

"The wardrobe is over there." Deklan pointed. "Inside is whatever you'd like to wear. Take your pick of anything. What's mine is yours."

Oakland smiled as if he was an invited guest who had been given a handout instead of a boyfriend being offered sanctuary.

The idea of Oakland being Deklan's boyfriend had a nice ring to it, but being his husband would have been more fitting. If only that was possible. Until that day would come and if ever, Deklan would dream. *"Sir, Oakland Royal."* That had a better ring.

Deklan was about two or three inches taller than Oakland, and with that bit of a difference, the pant length would have been the only issue with Oakland wearing his clothing.

There was something special about having Oakland dressed in his clothing. He knew having Oakland carrying his living sperm inside his body was one magnificent thing, but wearing part of his attire had added support to the claim he already had on him.

"How about we get changed so we can relax and enjoy the rest of the evening together?" Deklan opened up the wardrobe and had taken out a pair of gray woven pants that were hemmed just below the knee.

"For me?" Oakland asked.

Deklan pushed the hanger toward Oakland. "If you like them, they're yours."

As soon as Oakland had taken hold of the britches, Deklan reached for another pair quite similar to those he'd just given away, only brown. He disrobed completely, putting on the trousers, leaving his chest exposed.

Oakland on the other hand put on a white button down shirt, leaving several of the top buttons undone and rolling the sleeves back until they synched above his elbows.

"You are such a sexy man," Deklan confirmed, running a gentle finger down the deep center of Oakland's chest.

"As are you." Oakland said, then turned toward the looking glass with Deklan following his action. "Look at our reflection. Had you ever thought about how different we are from each other? Complete opposites in so many ways?"

"I hadn't, but I can see the differences on the outside."

"It's a good thing. Opposites seem to attract. That's probably why we are so connected to one another. I'm black and smooth, and you're white and perfectly hairy." Oakland lifted a hand and dragged the back of his knuckles over Deklan's chest. "So sexy," he said, still viewing their reflection in the mirror.

Deklan turned toward Oakland, "I love you just the way you are. Defects and all." He kissed Oakland. Gently.

Oakland sputtered, "Defects?"

Deklan grinned and gripped the front of Oakland's pants. "This here. This beautiful, beautiful bulge doesn't even fit in one of my hands. You said it yourself. Freakishly deformed."

"As are you." Oakland gripped back. "Whoa... and getting stiff."

"A sexy man can do that to me."

"Only me?"

"Only you."

Oakland released Deklan and stepped to the window, looking out at the place where he had been living. The bedroom was located inside the great big house, not too far from the carriage house where he stayed every night.

"It's funny isn't it?" Deklan crept up behind Oakland, pressing his warm body against his boyfriends back.

"What is?" Oakland leaned into him.

"That you've been living right outside my window all these years and I never noticed you."

"Well that tells me a lot about my character. But I'd always been known to blend in."

"I mean, I knew somebody was there, just never paid attention to who it was."

"That makes it much better."

"No, wait," Deklan choked. "I didn't mean that either. What I meant to say was I just never took notice of it being someone I'd be so attracted to."

"I see." Oakland grinned.

Deklan was only trying to be sincere and the way he was obliterating himself must have been the reason Oakland let out that quirky side winders smile.

"Forget it. I love you and you know it. You want some wine?" Deklan slyly changed the subject, hugging him from behind. His voice sounding demanding when he said, "Kiss me."

Spinning around, Oakland had given Deklan that kiss he'd come for, then shimmied around his side to collect the two metal goblets sitting on the table in front of the fireplace. "Would love some," Oakland said.

Deklan followed Oakland and pulled the cork from the glass bottle. He poured Oakland's before his own. It was red. Oakland's wine flavor of choice.

"I know it's predictable, but we can't drink our first carafe of wine together without making some kind of good cheer," Deklan proclaimed.

"Of course not," Oakland agreed while ogling Deklan's shirtless chest — as already known, the perfectly groomed hair had always gotten his attention, nearly causing a distraction from what was going on around him every time. As he'd mentioned before, he liked Deklan's chest and how good it felt against his smooth skin, especially the friction while Deklan made love on top of him.

"As outlandish as it might sound, let's toast to everlasting love between you and me." Deklan made the typical motion of raising his metal goblet.

Oakland lifted his and tapped it against the rim of Deklan's. The chime it made was magical, lingering a few seconds after the goblets clinked.

As soon as the chiming ended, they sipped. It was so good. Warm, fruitful and delicious.

"Good?" Deklan asked.

With a mouthful, Oakland replied, "Mhmm. I enjoy wine, but hadn't had it at my disposal that often. When I have the chance to drink it, I border line on indulgence because it's so good. I gotta watch that." He sipped slowly that time as if preventing an appearance as though he was a wine drinking lush. It seemed as though he waited for Deklan to sip from his goblet first before making a swan dive into his own.

Sneakily, Deklan had been tipping the carafe over Oakland's goblet every chance he could get, a sure sign Deklan was trying to get him tipsy on wine. The man was up to no good and Oakland was the target.

"I'm a little hungry. Are you?" Deklan asked.

"I could munch." Oakland had never eaten a meal in front of Deklan before except a pear or maybe a cracker crisp. The idea would have been strange, as if he really was about to eat with an honorably born Prince. Would his etiquette come out proper? It seemed he'd come to know soon enough.

"How about we sneak out of here to see if we can raid the kitchen without getting caught?" Deklan had acted like he was a young teenager on a sole assignment to rob the place. "There should be plenty of food in there tonight."

"No way. Somebody in the kitchen will recognize me." Oakland stood stiff, his eyes bulging.

"It'll be fun, like we're on a secret mission." Deklan grabbed Oakland's hand and started walking like a crouched tiger before they even left the bedroom.

Prowling already? What was that about?

Displaying a lighter tone, Oakland laughed at Deklan's

prowling technique.

Even though they were both in their twenties and should have been acting like adults, Deklan felt like a child and loved it, especially with Oakland holding his hand.

The two of them crept through the hallway like burglars, tiptoeing most of the way until they had come to a wall of bookshelves where they stopped. Deklan reached for a secret lever behind a book and tripped it forward. After a click, Deklan heaved the entire wall open like a huge door. They squeezed through the narrow opening where a back stairway had been hidden, a passage only the owners had known of. It was narrow as well as extremely dark, and whoever used it had to slink through in single file by touch alone.

Deklan stopped abruptly with a childlike chuckle and Oakland tripped down to the same step he was standing on, barely fitting all four feet.

Turning in the tight dark spot, Deklan kissed Oakland. Their tongues engaged while Deklan mumbled that he loved him again. He slid his hands downward along Oakland's abdomen until they reached the growing bulge in his pants. He squeezed and mumbled, "Had my kiss done that to you?"

"As a matter of fact, it had," Oakland confessed.

"Excellent. My dick is just as hard as yours right now. I've never wanted anybody as badly as I want you, Oakland." He pressed a palm to Oakland's erection, the head of his dick filling his hand.

Oakland's stiffened reaction indicated he might have let Deklan take whatever he wanted from him—might it have been his gripping black sex-hole? His wet mouth wrapped around his thick white dick? Just the kiss they had already been locked in? In the darkness, and even though their tongues had been tied, Oakland had still been able to fluently return his testament that he loved Deklan, too. They slowly separated and Deklan patted Oakland on the bottom before he'd given it a loving squeeze.

Deklan whispered, "Ready to move?"

Before Oakland had a moment to think about an answer, their mission was on again.

Reaching the stairwell bottom, Deklan pressed a hand and ear against the door. Hearing nothing on the other side, he pressed an eye to the small peep hole at the top of the door.

"I don't see anyone," Deklan whispered, turning back and kissing Oakland one more time. It was so dark, his mouth latched onto a facial feature other than Oakland's lips. He hoarsely whispered, "Was that your eye?"

Oakland replied, "Were those your lips?"

Deklan clicked the latch and slowly opened the door, peeked around the corner as if it would have made a difference if anybody was actually on the other side. He slinked through the small opening, propping the door open with a sack of potatoes.

Once inside, Oakland back stepped in Deklan's shadow, looking at the unit of shelves they had come through that were similar to the ones upstairs. He spun around and bumped into Deklan. They stood a moment in that small cupboard — the outside walls lined with more shelves, all stocked with odds and ends, books and items used for preparing meals.

Oakland commented, "Despite I'd been in the kitchen countless times before, I had no idea this room was here."

Deklan grabbed Oakland's hand and led him across the small pantry to the real door that would open up into the real kitchen. "You ready to conquer the place, my brave invader?"

"Unh... I guess so," Oakland warbled.

"Then, let's do it." Deklan's grin had spread out across his face, curling up his cheeks.

Suddenly, Deklan burst through the door like a barren soldier, ready to pull a blade on anybody who stood in the way of his only meal. He swiftly plucked a knife from the cutting block and stuffed it under the door as a prop to speed up the quick getaway. He looked heroic in a dangerous sort of way, a stud on a masculine rampage. His blood pumped faster.

Oakland mumbled, "Jeez, Dek. Excellent maneuvering. Your heroic beastliness had just given me another erection. Do we have time for...?"

Grinning, Deklan replied, "Then I'd say my mission has been accomplished. Keep it up. I'll be after that monster later."

They moved in like warriors of the wasteland. In and out. Fast and quick. Practically undetectable. Missed at a blink of an eye. The faster they moved, the blurrier they appeared.

Deklan had taken to the cupboards and Oakland charged the cooler. They were sleek and feline fast, like thieves in the night.

The few people prepping food or whatever they had been doing in the kitchen had probably been too shaken by the sudden outburst to have registered who had been doing the stealing.

Like a whirlwind gone unnoticed, Deklan and Oakland had flown in and out of the kitchen within a few seconds, that of which included the disengagement of doorstops by Deklan as they charged back through the pantry and up the secret stairway. The doors closed behind them with a bang and the delayed squawking out of somebody in the kitchen had Oakland and Deklan laughing at the late screamer.

Big houses with secret passages were made for kids.

They'd made it back to the second floor in record time, Oakland out of breath by the time they reached the bedroom.

After their full arms spilled food to the table near the wine they'd left behind, Deklan jogged back to the door and locked it.

"Omigawd, I was fitting out back there." Oakland breathed heavily as he dropped to the floor and laid face up in front of the fireplace. He looked miniscule lying next to the stone structure. It towered massively high as well as stretched across most of the entire wall.

Overhead of Oakland, Deklan crawled toward him across the floor on all fours. When he reached Oakland's head, he stopped and leaned down to kiss him from above. The sensation of an upside down kiss felt strange, but since it was Oakland who had kissed him back, it hadn't mattered how the kiss of love had been received.

"We did it," Deklan said, his lips lightly brushing Oakland's.

"You were a beast. I was completely aroused by your crafty maneuvers. Especially the way you burst through that door. Every muscle was bulging from the seams. I thought for sure that shirt of yours was going to shred and become an item of the past."

"You liked that, did you? I'll keep that in mind the next time I bring you down and take what's mine. Promise me you won't yell for help when I do."

Oakland put a hand over his stiffening dick. "Wouldn't happen."

"What wouldn't? Me bringing you down and taking what belongs to me or that I'd have to bust up your back door to do it?"

"Screaming for help wouldn't happen. Shucks, I'd gag-tie my own mouth shut if I knew it was you coming through that door to rough me up."

"No struggling, then?"

"Maybe a little. I need to see those bulging muscles having a go at me."

Deklan laughed, "I'm sure you'll see THE main muscle, and you'll feel every bit of it as I break through that back door with a massive bang."

Oakland's jaw dropping response to that was, "Ohmistars, my shuddering hole. Maybe we should first get to eating what we swiped." He rolled over onto his elbows and faced the food on the table top, groaning when his erection pressed against the wooden floor. He grinned and rubbed his hands together like a greedy banker would have done when touching money. He beamed a little bit.

A glint sparkled in Deklan's eye at Oakland's adoring response, which only made him want their last night together to upstage all that occurred in the past. Instead of wallowing in despair over what was to come about, there couldn't have been a better way to lift emotional melancholy than to reminisce about good times the two of them had so far. He dug into his memory and rekindled some finer moments he and Oakland shared, those that included laughter, kissing, holding hands, and thorough male affection. Like the time they unexpectedly stumbled into one another at the clover field, both unaware they were a few days shy from falling in love. Plus, the first time they traded glances in the grand hall on his birthday—their pivotal point in life. He couldn't leave out the time he politely asked Oakland if he could have a moonlight kiss that turned the event tenderly romantic and had made it a star lustrous moment Deklan would never forget.

Oakland had come back with a few eye-opening memories of his own, highlighting how much he enjoyed their first ballet in the Garden by the pool, even though he wasn't much of a dancer. A grin had creased Deklan's cheeks when Oakland mentioned how boundless the sensation felt the first time he accepted Deklan inside him, the man's expansive male erection unyielding, that of which included deposits of fertile semen. It was at that soul joining moment he'd known they'd always be together. Undeniably, there had been many good moments, a few eccentric, the one most memorable had been the shock he encountered the first time he witnessed a horse being given a thorough bath. But by far, their latest adventure through the kitchen taking food was the most adrenalin rushing instant and one that would truly remain a good memory of a synchronized duo.

After creating more good memories while sitting with his one true love in front of the fireplace drinking wine and eating stolen snacks, Deklan led Oakland straight to bed by the hand. They carried on the way they always had when they slept together—in and out of slumber, kissing, loving, and best of all, squirting semen on and inside one another.

During their nighttime sessions of affection, Deklan had ruled the dominant position on top, sliding his productive erection in and out of Oakland for hours, fully ejaculating at every instant, and doing it several times all over again. Deklan couldn't get enough, revering every one of those occasions he put himself inside Oakland, He could tell by Oakland's squirming body and verbal reactions, he equally enjoyed getting penetrated by the man he adored.

There had come a twist in destiny, and for the first time, Deklan had an irresistible urge to absorb Oakland's semen into his body and hold it there, to feel the man he loved becoming a part of him. That night, he released himself, taking Oakland so deeply, every bit of that man had reached his heart—the strongest sensation bursting his eternal soul wide open, accepting passion, receiving love. It was a moment in time he would forever cherish—never forget.

Fulfilled with Oakland's sperm inside him, Deklan

channeled his self-seeking desires and flipped their positions again, putting himself back on top of Oakland, his erection sliding right inside the man without exertion. At that moment, Oakland let out a whimper, one that sounded of pleasure exceeding delight. It turned from soft verbal pleading to loud vocal ordering, begging Deklan to flood his rectum with semen, that he needed to carry a part of him out of that room.

Without refuting, Deklan had given himself to Oakland several times throughout the night, satisfying him and making certain he kept his man's internal soul saturated with semen and love. There hadn't seemed to have been a better sensation than remaining snuggly tucked inside Oakland for those long lengths of time, ejaculating over and over again, keeping him filled until the daylight hour had come break them apart.

They shared their bodies one last time at about five o'clock that morning, and it was the most intimate they'd ever had. Deklan was convinced it was because it would be the last time they'd ever bond in the comfort of each other's arms without the need to sneak off into a dark corner.

After the final dynamic release that morning, Deklan remained submerged while holding Oakland tightly from behind. The desire to remain attached to the man he loved was stronger than it had ever been, and he knew why. How would he be able to pull himself away?

Chapter 30

The notorious wedding day had arrived, and the Royal Family's only son was about to get married. To a lady. With a vagina. Not a dick.

How perfect. For everybody except Deklan.

Oakland had woken, spotting Deklan sitting on the edge of the bed facing him with a hot cup of tea, a stirring spoon coated in candied sugar, and a few fancy fans of sliced strawberries arcing the edge of the plate.

That wedding was off balance. Would Oakland survive without the man he loved?

Oakland blinked away the bright window light and sat up, making more room for Deklan beside him. The blanket fell to Oakland's lap and Deklan reached out and rubbed his dark chest with the back of his hand. His gentle stroke felt good to Oakland—he liked his touch, hadn't been sure he'd have been able to live without the continued warmth and gentleness.

"I brought this for you, my sweetheart." Deklan set the tray on the edge of the bed next to Oakland.

Oakland hadn't much cared for putting his stomach through a workout so soon after he'd woken up, but he enjoyed a good cup of tea from time to time, and honestly told Deklan, "I don't usually eat straight out of bed in the morning, but thank you for what you've done. I could, however, start with this tea."

"We can share the strawberries later." Deklan pushed the cup of tea toward Oakland.

Oakland purred as he sipped its heated goodness.

"I'd like to tell you how much I'd enjoyed being with you these past few days," Deklan conveyed while he repositioned himself closer to Oakland. The saucer of strawberries clattered on the tray as it rocked between the two of them.

"I as well *loved* being with you. Every moment. But enough talk of that. It all sounds too final." Oakland sipped the hot tea carefully, his true emotions remained hidden. The scalding heat helped keep him from breaking down.

They both knew what would take place later that day and neither one of them liked it or wanted to think about it.

Oakland set the cup back down on the tray and reached for Deklan's hand. He sat quietly for a minute just looking into his boyfriend's eyes. He thought it before and it had come to him again. *"Omigawd, he's extremely beautiful. I'll miss him so much."*

As if he'd read Oakland's thoughts, Deklan gently placed his palm under Oakland's chin, moving it to his jaw, and softly repeated, "You are so precious and beautiful. I'm going to miss having you constantly at my side."

They'd only known one another for a very short time, but the strong fusion between them had practically allowed each other's thoughts to have been telepathically heard. With that, Oakland could sense Deklan's heart turned tortured and had known the Prince could identify his had too. All of it was unnecessary heartache and could easily have been prevented.

Deklan appeared strong, but Oakland knew the man was broken behind his smile.

There was a moment of silence before Oakland leaned over

196

the strawberry plate and had given Deklan the biggest hug he'd probably ever offered anybody, hanging on as long as he could, unable to let go. In time, he'd broken the bond, easing the situation by mentioning the tea was going to spill if they kept crowding the breakfast tray as they had been.

As though he agreed, Deklan pulled away.

Before too much time had passed, Oakland nudged the breakfast tray, making room to get out of bed.

"Allow me." Deklan lifted the shaking tray and carried it to the table near the fireplace. A bit of tea had spilled, but he hadn't cared.

Oakland lifted his trousers from the floor and started to put them on.

"Let me help you with those." Deklan walked toward him with watery eyes.

They carried on with minimal chatter as if they had just met for the very first time. Thinking about it, Oakland couldn't remember if Deklan had ever asked him what his role was at the Manor, so he answered the long overdue question with, "I feed the smaller livestock—the goats and chickens, mainly the ones who live with me in the carriage house. I also pick the vegetables, gather eggs and keep the kitchen stocked with whatever is needed for that day's meals. The same routine every day. That rarely changes." He strayed as far away from wedding talk as possible. In fact, he hadn't mentioned it at all. Likewise for Deklan.

Just as Oakland thought, Deklan refrained from bringing up the wedding blues too—that had been obvious by the joke Deklan made about how big and heavy Oakland's black dick was in the palm of his hand. He roared like an elephant while lifting it into his britches, tucking it neatly down Oakland's inner thigh and giving the monstrous member a gentle pat once finished playing with it.

"Where's your shirt?" Deklan shakily smiled.

"Over there." Oakland pointed to the chair by the fireplace.

Deklan had gone to get it and on his way back, held it against his face and inhaled deeply. His eyes closed as if embedding the memory of the stunning man who would soon walk away from him forever.

Oakland quietly told him to keep that one and asked, "Give me one of yours to wear."

"I'd like that." Deklan put Oakland's shirt on and went to the wardrobe to select one of his own. "I chose white because I like how it looks against your skin. This is my favorite one. I'll always think of you each time I search to put it on."

Oakland put on the shirt with a little bit of Deklan's help. The scent of his boyfriend covered him. It was as if Deklan's body was wrapped around his and having it so close had helped ease his splitting soul.

Deklan buttoned Oakland up in his quirky manner, from bottom to top, then laid his palms to Oakland's chest and brushed the fabric flat. "Good as gold," he quietly said. "You look nice. Like an angel who could never be missed."

Oakland kissed Deklan with his mouth closed, holding it for quite a while, not moving or expanding his jaw to take on his tongue in the usual battle. He just stood motionless, softly and quietly connecting with Deklan. Oakland's eyes closed and a tear found a way to break free. He couldn't hold it back any longer. He had crumbled and on the verge of bursting if the melancholy continued to mount inside him.

As hard as Oakland tried, he'd begun to fail at restraining the manifesting anger he felt toward Deklan's selfish parents. His insides trembled, as though every vein and vessel had pushed blood at the speed of a train. He had fallen apart, unable to stop the aching within him.

Deklan moved his hands to Oakland's shoulders, squeezed once, and then wrapped his arms tightly around him, hugging tighter than he'd ever done before. "I will always love you, Oakland," he said. "Nobody else. As long as I live."

With those few words, Oakland had broken down, hugging Deklan so hard they nearly had become a single person.

How could they take him away? It wasn't fair. It wasn't right.

Chapter 31

Deklan accompanied Oakland out the front door and down the steps as if he hadn't cared if anybody saw them together or not. Oakland hadn't been worried about it either, and held on tightly to express his disappointment in Deklan's family for ruining lives that were sure to have been good ones.

Regretfully, Oakland left Deklan at the bottom of the stairway, walked somberly to his small but cozy coop, turning back to look at Deklan so many times he might have made the entire trip walking backwards. The appearance on Deklan's face had let Oakland know there was true sadness there. The separation had left a tremendous gap between the two of them, physically as well as mentally.

Horse drawn carriages with more favors presumed to dress the wedding function had rudely taken over the front grounds, nearly running over Deklan where he stood. Memories of Oakland's mother returned and his blood boiled hot. Deklan was his soul binding beloved and when he hurt, Oakland hurt.

All alone, Oakland sat on the wooden bench at his tiny doorstep. He hadn't cared if the manor received the food it required or if the fat cook had been fed her grains on time. She could go to the pig trough and have at her own grains. Oakland hadn't felt up to providing for the people who hated him and Deklan for who they were. Instead, he sat still and watched the commotion at the Manor turn full swing without his assistance.

A covered wagon full of swans had pulled up next, that time nearly taking Wattsworth out along with the man standing next to him. He bumped into Deklan while hollering at the swan driver to take the birds around back.

During the harried upheaval, Deklan climbed a few steps, turning to Oakland before ascending the rest of the way.

At the moment Deklan disappeared through the massive doors at the top of the stairs, Oakland felt emptiness inside himself—the person he was missing had left a gaping hole of saddened right in the middle of his chest.

Oakland had gone inside his own tiny home, climbed the studded plank and fell face down onto his own bed. Tears burst free, finding a place in the pillow beneath his chin. His boyfriend had gone off to get married, to somebody else, and there wasn't anything he could have done to stop it.

"Sure there is." Oakland heard a voice. He ignored it at first, believing it was in his own head, but then sat and looked around the room, wondering if he'd find someone there.

Nobody.

Was madness settling in?

"Mirror Man?" Oakland called out. "Are you here?"

Chapter 32

Deklan passed everybody running around as though they were losing control of their own heads. The clock had gone on ticking and everything had to have been done before the first wedding guest rolled in. There counted eight hours left, but the way Deklan felt, seemed there were only a couple.

He returned to his bedroom and locked the door behind him, breaking down the instant the latch clicked into place. He crossed over to the bed where Oakland had slept the night before and fell forward against the pillow he'd laid his head on, breathing him in. He pressed his face deep into the pillow to muffle his uncontrollable sobbing, pounding the poof several times with clenched fists to relieve the fury that had caged itself inside him.

After all his angered sadness had been released at once, his exhausted body had suddenly gone quiet and he'd fallen asleep. Two hours had gone by before he'd broken out of dreamland, finding it unnerving that nobody had come looking for him or wondered where he'd gone off to.

Deklan had sluggishly come to life with the aid of cold water splashed across his face, glints of sparkle trickled off his chin, wetting the hair on his expanding chest as he breathed in and out. While standing with his head tilted forward to let the water from his hair drip into the basin, he spotted Oakland's ring sitting on the desk top next to the ewer.

Amazed the ring had come back to him that day, he picked it up and pushed it onto his middle finger. It felt comforting to have Oakland that close to him again. He spun it while bringing good moments of Oakland from his memory back.

After observing his drying reflection in the looking glass for several minutes, he peeled the shirt from his back and draped it over the one Oakland had worn the previous night during their kitchen robbery. He adjusted them on the hanger, secretly tucking the ring in the breast pocket and safely hung the shirts on a hook at the back of the wardrobe. His shirt holding Oakland's as if protecting the man he loved who wasn't actually in it.

Several more minutes had passed and he'd been pulled from his far away thoughts by an unexpected tap on the door. It wasn't intrusive, but more polite than a large man's fist — sounding like the knock had gentle intentions. He closed the wardrobe doors and answered, "Hello. Who is it?" Bare chested, he turned around, hands behind his back, pressing the wardrobe closed to hide what was inside.

"Deklan?" It was his mother.

Thankfully, it wasn't his father. He wasn't in the mood for that man.

He snatched a nightshirt from the bed post and quickly slipped it over his head. It dropped into place at the moment he unlocked and opened the bedroom door. "Hello, mother."

She looked at him with concern and asked, "Are you doing okay?"

"As good as can, I suppose." He closed the door and followed her to the chairs in front of the massive fireplace.

She sat down before Deklan had and said, "I can see you're

not doing well." She knew him. She was his mother. Probably even knew what he was thinking, but still asked, "Why don't you tell me what's on your mind?"

"I don't want to talk about it." He felt strange speaking to his mother about what he had in his head—love and intimacy with another man hadn't been a topic he wanted to share with his mother.

"Deklan, whatever you have to say isn't going to surprise me or make a difference as to how I feel about you." Both her eyebrows lifted and had gotten lost behind her strawberry blonde hair. "You met someone, haven't you?" She waited patiently for his answer, leaning forward, her delicate hands laid over her refined knee.

"I would just like to be alone right now. You can understand that, can't you, mother?"

"No you wouldn't," she replied. "It's about a gentleman friend, isn't it?" She was direct. Probably had known about Oakland.

He looked down and then up, giving a heavy eyed glance toward his mother who had been staring so hard he felt invisible. A good thing because what he'd been planning to say wouldn't have been easy. "It is, and I think I love him. No... not think. I do love him."

His heart sped up while he waited for her to react. He figured the response wouldn't have been the same way his father's would—with yelling, turning three shades of red, and throwing things across the room, including him. But, he prepared himself in case it had gotten ugly. He winced, pinched one eye tighter than the other and looked sideways at his mother.

She was calm and actually had a smile on her face. It was slim, but the smile was visible. Above her smile were those familiar green eyes that narrowed and displayed a hint of concern as well as sympathy.

Deklan had taken her expression as a positive sign, and since she was so sweet about everything all the time, he'd given in and leaked his secret.

He'd drawn a deep breath in and blew it out. Slowly. "His name is Oakland. The man that unexpectedly showed up to my birthday party dressed in ivory and silver. I know in my heart he is who I am to spend my life with. I'd never felt anything so strongly in my life."

She studied him and he could tell she knew all along it was about the boy and not the girl. "I noticed you hadn't been yourself since your birthday and I was certain it wasn't only because of the wedding that I would so very much want to call off."

"Then why don't you? It isn't right that I marry some girl I don't know." Deklan lowered the tone of his voice. "Mom? If I tell you something else, would you promise not to get upset at anybody but me?"

His mother looked him over with an expression of further concern.

Deklan dragged in a ragged breath and mumbled, "His name is Oakland and he works here at the Manor. He's living in the small feed barn out back by the kitchen and we have spent time together every chance we could get. Promise me, Mom. Please leave him alone, and whatever happens, let him stay and work here. He needs this place."

Her face had gone blank. She normally knew everything, but that bit of information seemed to have caught her by surprise. "You mean Miz Jennings' son? Little Junior? Why my stars, he's just a child."

Deklan laughed and corrected her. "Not anymore, mom. He's my age. Twenty-six and all grown up." He bowed his head. *"Very grown up if you saw what I'd seen."*

His mother clasped the pearls around her neck and rattled them. "Well, I hadn't seen him in such a while I suppose time had gotten away from me. I still picture him as a boy hanging on his mother's apron strings. Well, I'm glad he's doing well and survived the harsh times he'd been given. I never figured him to be" — she stopped, and then redirected what she almost said — "to be older than ten or eleven. My goodness how quickly time had gone by."

Deklan was glad she hadn't fainted to the floor or called the guards to have his boyfriend escorted off the property.

Returning her hands to her lap, she continued, "He looked so nice the other night. Very handsome and polished. Where did someone like him come across clothing of such expense?"

"I know it seemed strange he showed up to the party in such a costume, which I have yet to ask him about that, and if you're thinking it, he hadn't robbed or stolen them from anybody. He's not like that. In fact, even though the man is poor, he'd still give a starving person the food from his plate even if he was just as hungry."

She sat frozen. "I didn't mean to insinuate or make you understand that I had. It's just that your father doesn't pay his employees much more than a pauper's wage and to see a farmhand show up in dress wear like he had, just made me wonder is all. I'm sorry if I offended your judgment and the integrity of your new friend."

Sulking, Deklan sunk deeper into his chair. "I have such terrific times when I'm with him, and he makes me extremely happy. He's only been away from me for a short time, since this morning to be exact, and I can't stop thinking about him. I wonder what he's doing, where he's at, is he okay, is he thinking about me? When he isn't around, I miss him like crazy, and I seriously hate every passing minute I have to spend without him. It just doesn't seem fair. What is wrong with this damned world?"

His mother tilted her head, worry lines gracing her forehead. Her eyelids lowered, shadowing her bright green eyes.

Deklan pressed the heels of his hands into his closed eyelids as if that would stop him from choking up. He stifled his words as sadness swooped in and pecked at him. "When we're apart, I ache all over. Right now, I want him here with me. I should be holding him, making sure he's all right, because I'm sure he's feeling the same pain I am right now. He's mine, mother, and I am his. I'm dying inside and I don't think I can live without him."

A tear found a way to squeeze beneath his hand and roll down his left cheek. He sniffed and held his sleeve under his nose. Fighting back the tears trying to burst from within him, he shook his head and realized he said more than he intended. A part of him had become disturbed that he'd spoken so freely, yet another part of him had been glad he had. It'd all been locked up inside him for far too long. It was a lonely place, and right then he'd become happy to have shared his true feelings with his mother, who he'd known would somehow help him mend his breaking heart. He swallowed his emotions and forced a smile.

Deklan's mother handed him a napkin from the table in front of her. "Life is strange, Deklan. It throws us curves that we are supposed to live through so we can discover the good things that will happen because of them. Giving that, perhaps your Father's marriage idea to this young lady helped facilitate your search to find your soul mate. Think about the event and how it led you to him. To your friend, Oakland."

For a few seconds Deklan stared at his mother, totally shocked. "Do you think so? And, he's more than just a friend, Mom. I consider him my boyfriend, and would like you to call him that."

No holds barred, she actually smiled. "If this boyfriend is your soul mate. *The one.* Then you will eventually find your way back to him. I need you to hear an important story that led me to your father—*My* soul mate." She opened up to Deklan. "I am going to tell you about your uncle Joseph."

"I have an Uncle Joseph?" He never knew.

She scooted forward and balanced on the edge of her chair. "Joseph *was* your father's oldest brother. A handsome man, like you *and* like your father. They looked a lot alike. He was tall, but a bit shorter than your Poppa. Strong. He worked hard, you know." She added that last bit for some reason, her eyes looked dreamy.

Where was she going with this?

"Joseph and I were friends long before I knew your father. We would still be friends today if Joseph was still around." She lowered her head, crossed herself and then dropped her delicate hands back into her lacey lap, laying one on top of the other like a queen—palms up.

The story hadn't seemed to be heading in a positive direction by her tone.

She forced another smile. "That's how I met your father. Through Joseph. My friend."

"I never knew," Deklan's voice cracked.

"Well, this isn't something you normally share with your child. But you're an adult now, so it's okay that I tell you." She exhaled.

Had he really wanted to know?

"Your father and I met once during the latter days that Joseph and I were together. As friends," she emphasized. "We were never coupled romantically and in a few minutes I will tell you why. In those days and at my age, I thought the relationship we had together was real love, but as I found out when I met your father that one fine day, how affection really felt. From that day, I'd always known there was a missing connection between your uncle Joseph and me, and that I felt more tied to your father somehow. At the time, I wasn't sure what my feelings meant, but later on I discovered it. It was a soul mate incident. I tried my best to keep my distance from your father because I thought your uncle Joseph was supposed to be the love of my life. I tried many times to make your uncle show his affection toward me, but I quickly realized it was never going to happen. I could sense it."

"Mother! Nooo." Deklan winced. He wanted to stop her— afraid of what she'd tell him next. He wasn't sure he was up to hearing any more of her story about getting between the sheets with his uncle or his father.

"You see... your uncle Joseph was just like you."

"Like me, how?" He scooted to the edge of his seat.

"Infatuated with another lad instead of me, and the funny thing with my story here, the boy was a farmhand as well. Ironic, don't you think? Almost as though time is repeating itself." She seemed giddy about the similarities between him and Joseph.

"I started spending more and more time with your father because it seemed more natural for me to be with him instead of Joseph. I eventually noticed Joseph becoming more and more distant and I first thought it was because of your father, but as I suspected early on, it was because of the stable boy."

"Incredible." Deklan thought.

"Your father and I were together on their ranch one afternoon and innocently stumbled upon Joseph when we were bringing lemonade drinks into the barn for him and the workers. When we arrived, we found your uncle Joseph and his gentleman friend locked in an embrace more intimately than we ever expected. I'm not too sure which one of us was more shocked, him or us. I remember we all stood there for a few minutes before Joseph had taken off running out the backside of the barn. I admit I was hurt by what he did during the time we were still together, but at the same time a little relieved that I was no longer trying to confirm what I had suspected all along. A woman knows these things." She looked at Deklan, her eyes pinned on his gaping mouth.

"The one thing I know for sure through all this, and have always remembered, was that your father was the one who picked me up and healed my injured heart. He meant well then, and will always mean well, you know. So what I'm trying to tell you, Deklan. If two people are meant to be together, life will find a way. A good example is your father and me. Even though it didn't seem right at the time, I was led to your father, my soul mate, in a roundabout way."

Deklan stopped her. "You said *if* Joseph was still around. What did you mean when you said that? Where is my uncle?"

Her eyes glistened as she remembered the past. "Your uncle denied who he really was for a very long time and in the end it hurt him deep inside. He couldn't live with himself the way he was born, so one afternoon in the middle of a very bad thunderstorm, he ended his own life in the attic of the barn. Your father found him. It was a very bad day. Your uncle struggled too much with a lonely heart along with shame because he'd always been told there was something wrong with him. Back then, two men in love was unheard of. People didn't understand it and classified it as a terrible disease or a type of mental illness. Some still do—sadly. Many men were imprisoned and even hanged for being like Joseph."

Deklan was stunned. He couldn't believe what he was hearing.

She continued. "The reason your father hadn't wanted you to know about all this was because he's afraid you might follow in your uncle's footsteps."

"What?" Deklan barked. "I guess it didn't work now, did it? I still turned out just the way he didn't want me to."

"No Deklan, my Love. Not because you found affection for a young man, but because he's been afraid you would hurt yourself like your uncle Joseph had, or that somebody else would. If you didn't know the story, it wouldn't have entered your mind to end your life as Joseph had. All your father's doing is trying to keep you from getting hurt. He wants you safe."

"Well, he's hurting me in a completely different way," Deklan scowled.

"I'd been worried as well and also want you to be far away from harm, but I won't stand in your way because I know what it's like to be separated from the one you truly love. I'll protect you if I notice you're in any danger. It's just the way it is. I'm your mother. Your father is doing the same because that's what fathers do."

Priscilla crossed over and sat on the arm of Deklan's chair. Suddenly he felt like a child again as she rubbed his back like a supportive mother would have done to make all her child's troubles disappear. She added, "The two of you are bonded by a deep hearted connection and you will be together again. I can pretty much promise that."

A part of Deklan felt a little woozy when he heard his mother say he had a special bond with Oakland. "I hope so," he quietly muttered.

"There's plenty of room for hope." She stood up, rubbed his shoulders one last time before walking out the door.

Chapter 33

Oakland had taken note of the time, it had gotten late, and his anxiety about Deklan's wedding had caused his heart to race. In fact, he could feel it beating so hard it was pushing the booming into his head.

Feeling his soul mate drifting further away, Oakland had a difficult time sitting still and watching the timepiece on the kitchen table tick. He seemed certain the hands had been moving faster than normal, but in truth, it had ticked as it usually would have and had taken its sweet old time. Oakland turned it over, putting a stop to watching the big hand jump to the next hash mark and the smaller hand creeping close behind.

Oakland needed the time to stop ticking. Just for a while until he could figure out a solution to his and Deklan's messed up situation.

While standing in the doorway of the carriage house looking down the drive toward the activity taking place at the

Manor, Oakland felt his break down lift once that first guest carriage pulled up to the house. Following that one, another had arrived. Soon more lined up as though they all had come from town together — like a train without a caboose.

Oakland had never seen the bride-to-be arrive. He hadn't been too sure if she was already there or if she had been ordered to show up at the moment the wedding bells begun to chime.

From what he'd known about wedding superstitions, the bride dressed in her ceremonial gown should remain hidden from the groom until the chapel doors had opened. He and everybody else understood it would have been bad luck for the groom to lay eyes on the virgin in wedding day white before greeting at the pulpit. That irrational belief had given Oakland an idea, but it bordered on sinister. *"Push her in the street, Oakland. Push her in the street."*

Oakland had no choice but to have let the wedding go on as planned. But in his empty mind he begged for the Mirror Man fairy-person to show up and zap them all to their senses with a deluge of pixie dust. The ceremony had to stop, and stopped straightaway. Oakland was losing his man. To a female.

If there had been a time Oakland needed a little fairy magic, it would have been then. He looked around the small room in case the Mirror Man had heard his silent plea. No such luck, the place remained vacant. Even the animals had come up missing.

If it had been up to Oakland, he'd set the Manor under fire as way of smoking out the roaches and snakes that lived there. He figured the perfect time for that would have been while everybody was still on their feet and in a position to run. That would only have been fair. *"Light a sulfur stick, Oakland. Light a sulfur stick."*

Out of curiosity, he flipped the timepiece over to see how much time had passed.

"Holy, bollocks." He had somehow lost an hour. "Where had the time gone?" He looked at the front door as if time had actually gone out that way.

Oakland heard footsteps creeping up from behind and it startled him. He turned and shouted, "Holy, hairy bollocks." Those words had naturally fallen out of his mouth again.

It was Deklan. In his house. Oakland stared at him, and within a split second, Deklan gripped Oakland's wrists and crushed their lips together in an extremely tight bond.

Mumbling, Oakland's words had mashed together by the pressure of Deklan's mouth over top of his, "Wait. What the..? How did you get in here… er… what are you doing here?"

Deklan pulled back, his hands still gripping Oakland's wrists. "I came in through the back window. You left it open."

"I did?" Oakland knew he had. He'd always left it open during the day. It kept the place aired out as well as kept the animals cooled and had given them free rein in and out of the place.

Deklan begged, "I've gotta have you, Oakland. I need you right now. Make love to me. Please?"

Oakland's stability was off center at the moment and he'd been teetering on the edge of gloom because the man he should have been with for the rest of his life had a plan to get married to somebody other than him. Plus, the strange and unnatural thing about it was, that person was a female. "I don't know if your favorite parts on me are going to work the way you need them to, right now. I'm not in very good spirits at the moment."

"I'm not either, but we've gotta try. If I can't have you physically with me up on that platform tonight, then I need a part of you alive inside me." Deklan opened his shirt, exposing his stunning chest to Oakland. He kissed him again while grabbing hold of Oakland's soon to be stiff erection. "Come on Oakland, let loose inside me. I need you so badly right now."

Deklan walked Oakland backward until his heels bumped against the first rung on the board leading up to the bed. After another quick peck at Oakland's lips, Deklan had taken off up the plank like a bolt of lightning. He was beside Oakland one second and gone the next.

Oakland followed, unbuttoning his trousers as he climbed the plank, certain he wanted to have given Deklan what he'd come for. When he made it to the upper level, Deklan was looking exceptional on display across the bed completely undressed. He'd laid himself out on his back facing Oakland, his legs wide open— his hairy hole out there ready to accept Oakland's eleven inch erection.

Oakland looked straight between those masculine legs, finding that enticing point of entry where he'd inject the semen Deklan begged to carry. Nobody would have known it was there except Oakland and him. Oakland's dick expanded just looking at Deklan laid out like that. The man's hairy chest and stomach had gotten Oakland's attention—it never failed. The thick extension between his furry thighs had him, too—that cock perfectly erect, extended from those sagging nuts to the navel and beyond. Oakland couldn't resist that impressive white giant even if the day had been extremely bad. He'd been drawn to Deklan's body like a bear would go after honey.

Oakland finished stripping and lay down next to Deklan, kissing him roughly. Oakland's hand moved smoothly from Deklan's chest to his abdomen, bumping the head of his erection.

"Penetrate me, right now," Deklan begged. "Put that black cock inside me. Ejaculating. I need to take that part of you with me. I don't ever want to feel as far away from you as I had earlier at the house."

Enthusiasm spiked in Oakland as much as it had with Deklan, but he battled with his conscience as though he was about to commit some type of crime. If it hadn't been for Deklan heading off to holy matrimony with someone else, that argument with his own feelings wouldn't have been out of line.

Looking down, Oakland positioned himself between Deklan's legs, noticing his sex-hole had already been slickened with oil and there had been sphincter contractions in motion—true evidence the man was losing patience with having a black dick sliding into him. Oakland inched forward, giving his hips a slight push. Deklan's sphincter opened and closed tightly around the bulbous crown of Oakland's cock. It was happening. The head was in.

Deklan's rear end lifted with the tugging of his knees to his chest. He groaned, "Oh, Gawd. So good. Give me more-ohaaAH," his voice cracked. The exquisite internal pressure Oakland had known himself so well must have been what made Deklan's dick grow stiffer, lift and crash against his abdomen. Beading of clear ejaculate oozed from the tip—the glistening sheen had proven to

Oakland he'd hit that stimulating spot.

Oakland pulled his expansive dick out and pushed it back in, sliding deeper than before, giving Deklan a few more inches. Expressing pure pleasure, Deklan's face contorted with excessive moaning, and Oakland cried out, "So tight and hot in there." He wanted to bury himself all the way in, feel closer to Deklan.

"Shove it in, Oakland. I need you deep," Deklan whined. "No need to be gentle." He looked Oakland in the eyes more lustfully than he'd ever looked at him before.

When Oakland had given Deklan a few inches more, he noticed him breathing heavily as if trying to catch air. He asked, "Are you okay, Dek?"

Breathless but seemed sure, "Yes. Yes. Keep going, keep going, keep going. I can take you. All the way inside me. Ejaculating. Flood my hole, Oakland." Deklan sounded desperate. His expression had gone wilder than a hungry tiger.

Oakland knew damned well it wasn't easy to have been gentle with the dimensions of his cock. His excessive size when fully erect wouldn't allow him to jam it into a man's asshole without gut-wrenching results. The last thing he wanted to have done was bust Deklan up with a rip roaring ram in the ass with his rod, but he also wanted to satisfy the man he loved, give him the gift he'd begged for. Maybe Deklan could have taken eleven inches of hardened steel up his manhole all at once. After all, it hadn't been the first time Deklan had let Oakland stick his dick inside him, however, that previous time, he moved in gently, had taken more time, made certain he opened his rectum up with care.

To ease assault, Oakland grabbed Deklan's ankles and spread his legs farther apart. He watched his black dick going in, yet there was still a long way to go. He backed out, then gently sunk in even further than before, letting Deklan get used to how several more of his thick chocolate inches felt going in.

"Jeez, almighty. Go all the way," Deklan ordered. "I want to feel you pound those hips into me. Scrub that beautiful black dick hair against my sagging nuts."

Oakland had given his full dick as ordered, the great internal sensation might have been what caused Deklan to throw his head back and moan to the point of weeping.

Oakland slammed harder, burrowing all the way in to the fullest depth, thumping roughly like Deklan wanted. The black hair above his throbbing cock scrubbed against Deklan's taint and nuts like he wanted, sounding like crackling coals in a campfire pit. Oakland roared on every thump, his gritty growling had gotten louder.

As Oakland prodded, he changed his pace, moving inside Deklan nice and slow, massaging that magic spot that would make him squirm and squeal.

"Yeah. Right there. Give it to me. More." Deklan begged, his hips gyrating on Oakland's thick black cock.

"Oh my Gawd, Dek." Oakland could feel Deklan pulling him in, the man's asshole impatiently sucking his dick like it had a mind of its own.

"I love you, Oakland. I love you so much." Deklan moved his hands to the sides of Oakland's face, looking so deeply into his eyes there was a moment that Oakland thought Deklan wasn't even seeing him.

"Deklan, Ohmigawd. I love you too." Oakland dropped his chest against Deklan's, kissed him intensely while he power-ground his cocoa hips back and forth into Deklan's bottom. With each in and out probe, Oakland's back repetitively arced, compelling his rock hard abdomen to lift and crash against Deklan's. The heat building between them had gotten hotter.

They rhythmically rocked, Oakland switching from hard thumps to slow penetrating strokes. Oakland remained embedded, his entire length deep inside Deklan.

In an instant, it happened.

Oakland buried his face in the pocket of Deklan's neck and let go of a muffled roar. His passion had reached its peak and he could no longer hold back his restless release. His back bowed, punching his pelvis into Deklan's taint, forcing his eleven inches of thick black meat to its deepest depth.

Oakland's insides burned, he needed to let loose inside Deklan. His body had begun to quake. The intense vibration of a raging thunderstorm raced through his body. He hoarsely growled in sync with each sperm loaded blast he shot into the asshole of the man he was penetrating. Oakland's heart pounded while his erection continued breeding the man he loved, giving it to him the way he'd begged.

As Oakland ejaculated, he could feel Deklan's warm clutch squeezing his erection—his semen deprived body drawing in every spurt.

Deklan trembled and his shaky voice ordered Oakland to keep gliding in and out of him.

Before Oakland finished pumping spurts of pleasure into Deklan's sexy butthole, Deklan's erection perked up and stiffened. His groaning turned louder and his abdomen crunched inward. His body had gone firm and convulsed, that recognizable indication he was about to ejaculate.

While Oakland continued emptying his own sperm inside Deklan's body, he curled forward and had taken Deklan's expansive dick into his mouth. He'd gone down the entire length until he felt him deep in his throat and the hair above his thickened shaft scrubbed his upper lip. Exhilaration swept over Oakland as he'd taken in the aroma that fled from Deklan's hairy pelvis. It was intoxicating and the masculine scent had set him in motion to suck harder.

Oakland's gulping throat held out a couple more seconds before reversing the same path he'd taken going down his cock. He gently pulled off, toying with Deklan's stone hard erection, sucking the swollen head, circling the wedged crown with his tongue, anticipating the eruption about to burst into his mouth. He could hardly wait to swallow Deklan's white boy semen. He'd tasted it before and he wanted it again.

Deklan's body started to shake and jerk. His hips lifted, pushing his cock to the back of Oakland's throat. Deklan trembled. "I'm close, Oakland. Stay inside me." He'd gone tense and his upper body jolted forward. "Swallow me, Oakland. Take it all. I need you to swallow my sperm. Oh, Gawd, Oakland. Here it comes. Holee...eee..." His tone had gone gritty. His throat released a growl that surpassed the sound of rocky landslide. There was a bolstered moan, then a powerful upsurge of frothy semen.

A flare of heat showered over Oakland as Deklan pumped his first spicy stream against the back of his open throat. With each fruitful injection, Deklan's erect organ beat against Oakland's tongue, forcing his jaw to expand and throb.

Oakland backed off for a split second, taking in a full breath of oxygen as well as squeezed out a much needed, "Omigawd!" A shot of sperm splashed his chin.

Eager for more, Oakland immediately returned to where he'd left off. Head bobbing. Cheeks concaved from his powerful suction. The taste of Deklan's slick ejaculate was arousing as it repeatedly gushed in thick creamy streams across his tongue and down his throat. He hurriedly gulped, swallowing everything Deklan ejected, refusing to let him go, refusing to lose a single spurt, determined to suck his spitting erection clean.

Suddenly, Oakland pulled off Deklan's cock and groaned. He'd lost control as he felt his pubic hair sizzling.

"Jeez, Dek. I'm about to ejaculate again." He stiffened, freezing in a hip locking position, back arcing, muscles inflating to the max, Oakland fell against Deklan and growled. "I'm shooting. Omigawd." Deep grunts belted in time with each spurt of semen he blew into Deklan's gripping manhole. He was heaving savagely as he kissed him, letting Deklan taste his own unswallowed sperm. As they kissed, their fingers entwined around each other's and Oakland rotated them up and over Deklan's head. They stayed connected from top to bottom, quaking until the last spurt of semen had been pumped from his cock into Deklan's butthole.

"Don't give up on me." Deklan tightened his grip, holding Oakland's dick in place.

Oakland couldn't move. He just laid on top of Deklan, breathing heavily, listening to the words that had been whispered into his ear.

Deklan's legs had come around and locked at Oakland's waist, keeping him firmly in place.

Sexually satisfied but sad, Oakland lifted himself above Deklan with most of his weight balancing on the heels of my hands. He maintained his erection, keeping it deeply embedded inside Deklan's body. He looked down on Deklan who had been looking up at him—his gaze intense.

The look of fear had draped Deklan's face, causing Oakland

to weaken quickly. His shoulders had begun to shake and he started sobbing, not caring if Deklan had seen what was happening to him. He was no longer tough, or strong. He'd felt the loss of somebody he needed in his life. Somebody he wanted with him forever and ever.

Through the sheen of tears, Oakland glimpsed at Deklan's face. It had gone dismal with what appeared to have been sadness and fear.

Oakland's heart had grown sore from the ache he'd seen in Deklan's eyes. They had welled up with vapor, and when Deklan blinked, a lone tear trickled down his cheek and pooled in the network of his ear.

They lay fused for the longest time. Oakland on top of Deklan, joined as one soul the way they should have been.

Deklan softly whispered, "Having you sliding in and out of me so graciously was like the breeze caressing my skin. You felt incredible, Oakland, and I refuse to give you up."

Chapter 34

A short time before the arranged nuptial to Gretchen had gotten underway, Deklan removed the ring from the pocket of Oakland's shirt hanging under his and tucked the silver piece into the breast pocket of the formal jacket he had on.

He was dashingly handsome dressed in a crisp black coat and pressed white shirt, but none of that mattered if Oakland hadn't been there to share the union march with him. He lifted his hand to his chest, placing it over top of the ring that had instinctively merged with his heart. Knowing it'd be blessed during his counterfeit wedding was more important to him than the actual wedding to the lady bird.

He'd become exasperated from extreme sadness, unable to think about anybody other than having Oakland beside him on the wedding platform. That void had caused his heart to ache all over again. He really loved that man.

Cʒ ঙꝺ

Oakland heard the deep tone of wedding bells in the yard as though Christmas morning had come, indicating that dreadful moment was about to begin. He grabbed the time piece from the table where he'd left it earlier and stuffed it into his shirt pocket, having no idea why he needed it, but felt something old should have been with him on that day.

His anxiety had worsened, evidence revealed by his trembling hands and the tick of his lower lip. He retrieved the pendant from the bedside table, stringing it under his collar to keep it hidden. He flinched when the chill of the metal touched his bare chest.

He slipped on an old gray tweed jacket that once belonged to his father. It had a musky smell, but the dingy jacket seemed suitable for the event he'd planned to attend, going along with depression of watching his boyfriend marry somebody else.

The thought of losing Deklan was extraordinarily painful.

"Betty Lu, get back in the house," Oakland yelled at the chicken as he opened the door to leave. Silly bird must have thought she had a wedding invitation, too.

A funny thing happened when Oakland had spoken to the bird. Betty Lu looked at him, turned around and walked back into the house as if she understood exactly what he'd told her to do.

Oakland patted his tightly trimmed hair, pressed the shirt that was loosely hanging down his front and pushed most of the fabric into the waistband at his backside. He held his head up, tugged the lapels on his jacket and walked to the Manor where he'd quietly enter as a guest.

The homobirduals, Razzle and Dazzle, as he'd named them, scampered in front of him as if passing reminder that it was okay for two chaps to live as companions.

Oakland reached the top of the Manor's stairway outside. He'd become more tense. He couldn't budge. His feet remained frozen in place.

This was craziness.

He stood outside for a couple of minutes, contemplating if it was better to run back home or head inside. His body had become restless with notion to hightail it out of there, but his mind was itching to bust through the door and find a seat inside that fabricated chapel.

By dumb luck, there hadn't been anybody at the entry once he'd become brave enough to open the door. He stepped inside and immediately looked around. Gleaming gray and white had covered the room, gushing from every corner. Glints of light flashed, bouncing jewel tones from one wall to the other.

Since Oakland was a hired hand at the Manor and still one even though dressed as a guest, he couldn't find comfort in taking the front stairway. Preferring to remain unseen, he forced himself to come up with a different plan and revisit the secret passageway Deklan had taken him down before.

He thought back to the kitchen raid and mapped out the halls in his head all over again. It wasn't difficult to reimagine, and since the second level appeared vacant, he'd been able to creep to the left along the wall unnoticed. He passed Deklan's room, fighting the urge to stop, kick the door in, and take claim to his man who probably wasn't in there. Shutting down that thought, he'd taken another left until he reached the stairway behind the bogus bookshelf at the end of the hall.

His anxieties slightly settled once he safely tucked himself behind the secret doorway, and like before, the narrow tunnel was extremely dark, but eventually had found a hint of light at the last step. Before creeping through that storage room door, he centered an eye to the peep hole and looked through. It appeared empty on the other side, persuading him to make his move.

The door to the kitchen was straight ahead, his attention captured by the bright light coming through the small window at the top.

Maximizing caution, he slowly pushed a hand against that door.

"Bollocks!"

Somebody was coming.

Letting the door close, he scurried off to hide behind a large trunk set in the back corner of the room. He hung there for a few moments, waiting for the area to become clear.

He'd gone for the door again, giving it a slight push.

"*Bollocks!*" Not again. Maybe sneaking behind the walls hadn't been the best idea.

Another person had scurried into the kitchen and Oakland's intuition convinced him the visitors weren't stopping. He rushed behind the bookshelf he'd come through and waited. After a few minutes he returned to the store room and like a stalker who had a deviant mission, peeked through the lower corner of the small window, watching Wattsworth glance around while counting on his fingers.

What was he doing?

The lanterns in the kitchen dimmed and Oakland saw Wattsworth leaving. But, the moment Oakland started pushing the door open again, he caught a glimpse of light flickering outside the kitchens main entryway.

"*Bollocks! What now? Who is it this time? Wattsworh?*"

If Oakland hadn't gotten out of that closet soon, he'd miss the sketchy nuptials. He released the door and it bumped his toe with a thud. He winced. Not because it hurt, but because he feared whoever had been lurking on the other side would have heard the thump.

The light he'd seen from the incoming lantern flashed across the far wall. It ended up being Wattsworth again, returning to the kitchen for another reason. Oakland stayed quiet, keeping an open eye pressed to the windows corner, waiting for the man to leave.

Finally, Wattsworth had moved out of the kitchen.

Solitude.

Maybe?

Oakland grabbed a broomstick and a dust collection tray from the closet he'd been hanging out in for the past ten minutes, disguising himself as part of the cleaning crew. He tiptoed quietly through the kitchen and out into the hallway.

The layout of the corridor was the same as it was upstairs, aiding Oakland with keeping his bearings while wandering the part of the big house he wasn't too familiar with. He noticed several doors along the inside wall and presumed they opened up to the great room where the wedding was about to take place.

Oakland cracked the first door he'd come to and peeked in, recognizing the front of the chapel. Somebody was on a platform lighting candles and he'd seen rows of forward facing chairs. He kept moving.

Before opening the last door he'd come to, he'd hidden the broom and dust collector behind a drape in the hallway. His nerve endings had about burst through his skin and the booming in his chest continued increasing. His anxiety had gotten the best of him.

He'd taken a deep breath before daringly heading through the doorway, finding noisy whispers resonating from every chair. He selected a seat toward the back and waited patiently like everybody else—his hand instinctively clutching the pendant beneath his shirt, making sure the jewel hadn't mysteriously disappeared.

Soon after he'd arrived, the hum of musical cellos had begun playing, followed by the crowded room politely turning quiet. The low volume in the room elevated the noise of rustling fabrics as everybody shifted to face the back doors where the wedding couple would traditionally arrive through.

Then it had occurred, the man Oakland had come to see had appeared, putting an ache in his heart so damaging, he found it difficult to breathe. Nothing he had been witnessing seemed right, even though he'd done his best to prepare for it. All of it, totally out of sync.

Deklan stood in the back doorway to Oakland's right, the side he'd always occupied when the two of them were together—standing, walking, and in bed. The man was elegantly dressed, looking downright stunning. There were no other words that could have properly described the way he looked. The white shirt, black and gray diagonally striped tie, and the neatly pressed black pinstriped suit turned Deklan into one of the most handsome men Oakland had ever seen. He was crisp and clean, strong and dignified. So striking—inside and out.

Occupying the spot at Oakland's far left where he should have been standing was the damsel in pure white silk and frilly lace—her face covered with a fine netted veil, leaving her features barely visible. The wedding couple had been standing at their own entrance, divided by nearly twenty chairs situated along the back row, and Oakland wished the separation between the two would stay that way forever.

Oakland resorted to holding his breath, choking back sadness and hiding tears behind a sniffle and a cough. He was the only one in the room who'd taken a seat before the wedding march had gotten started. It might have been a sign of insolence, but he couldn't stand a minute longer while watching what belonged to him get taken away. It was utter insanity. All wrong for all the wrong reasons. Oakland's quivering chin had made it impossible to keep his sadness confined to only himself. He was breaking into pieces and his reaction had surely become visible to those around him.

Nearly every eye had been pinned on the bride except for one person a couple rows ahead of Oakland, who seemed to have been aware he'd taken a seat before he should have. The tall thin chap must have been concerned, since he hadn't looked away from Oakland for a single moment, not even as much as to glance at the bride or the groom.

The man who had an eye on Oakland left his seat and reassigned himself to a chair next to him. "You're Oakland, aren't you?" he asked.

"H-how... how'd you know?" Oakland stammered.

"I'm Jedidiah. Deklan's friend. He told me about you, and from the look on your face and the way you had been observing him, I was pretty certain you were his secret." Jedidiah kept his tone low and breathy.

Had Oakland stood out that obviously?

Oakland cracked a smile, looking at Jedidiah crossways beneath a lowered brow. His subconscious mind had flashed an image of the Mirror Man sitting there instead of Jedidiah. Was it a disguised message telling Oakland to go after his boyfriend? He doubted that thought and decided to stay seated.

Trading the bizarre hallucination for an even more inexplicable demonstration, he'd heard a voice next. Oakland figured that could have possibly been another message from the Mirror Man, telling him to go after the man he loved. First an image, then the voice. It had to have been subliminal communications from The Mirror Man. He'd sworn it was him.

He'd recognized his familiar voice, and presumed Jedidiah might have been an exaggerated form for him to believe in.

Oakland turned toward Deklan and watched him, noticing he was swaying in a manner that displayed a nervous disorder.

"It'll be all right." Jedidiah pressed his shoulder against Oakland's.

Oakland was thrilled to hear those words from Jedidiah. A part of him needed assurance from somebody other than himself. It somehow set the truth he'd been seeking into motion.

The progression of the nuptials started moving on both sides of the room. Deklan walked one side while the bride toe-tipped some strange skip and a hop on the other side, appearing to be tripping with every step.

"*That should be me,*" Oakland thought. He watched the man he loved very closely, couldn't take his eyes off of him. Deklan looked so elegant, so regal, and all Oakland wanted to do was holler with anger. He was breaking apart—on the verge of falling to pieces. It felt as though he'd been stabbed in the chest over and over again with the dullest knife in the land.

Noticeably depressed, Deklan walked toward the front of the room where the mountain of candles had been flickering brightly. His hand lifted and rested over his lapel as if he'd been pledging allegiance to the Nations flag.

At the same moment Deklan's shirt gleamed beneath his hand, Oakland felt the pendant vibrate against his chest. Remembering the Mirror Man had mentioned the ring and the necklace were linked, had surely meant the shimmering within Deklan's pocket must have been that ring.

With his hand pressed to his chest, gripping tightly, Oakland noticed Deklan glancing around the room as if looking for someone—perhaps the man he truly loved.

A few moments passed, and once eye contact locked, Oakland instantly recognized Deklan's slanted smile he'd always found charming. But little by little, over the next few seconds, the hum, the glow, and the tether between the two metal pieces had begun to weaken. The further away from Oakland Deklan marched, the fainter the jeweled connection had become.

Was he losing him? Was that a sign of which separation had begun?

This couldn't be happening.

There had come an ache in Oakland's chest that tightened the further away Deklan had gotten from him.

During most nuptials, Oakland recalled an awkward pause when the master of ceremonies would ask if anybody objected to the marriage. Even though he and Deklan might have been cast away by many of the people in that room, the last chance to have spoken would have been then. But, how would he approach his disapproval of the marriage without being stoned, or causing embarrassment to the Royal family when publicly pointing out their only heir was in love with another man instead of the lady standing next to him at the pulpit?

The clock piece in his pocket seemed to have been ticking louder than the ceremony verbiage, reminding him time was no longer on his side, and that notable pause would soon come up. Oakland's hands were sweating and his bleeding heart had been racing at top speed — any faster, his entire being would explode from the inside out.

"*Omigawd,*" Oakland muttered a whispered tone. His nerves had spiked and his skin felt as though he'd been covered beneath a thousand ants.

"All will turn out as it should," Jedidiah had calmly spoken, as if he seemed to have sensed Oakland's tension.

Who was that man beside Oakland and how could he foresee the future?

In the back of Oakland's mind, Jedidiah had to have been another version of The Mirror Man. He appeared much differently from the last time he'd met the fairy visitor in the small carriage house, but to Oakland's understanding, a mystical character might have been able to change forms on convenience.

Was he going mad in the head?

The words of confidence Oakland heard from Jedidiah had already been spoken by his fairy godfather, and since stranger occurrences had happened related to The Mirror Man, that only justified his thoughts to have been believable. He was sure the two life forms were the same spirit. He sensed it.

Oakland had been able to see Deklan was exceedingly distracted. He might have been standing on the platform with the bride-to-be, but Oakland could identify Deklan's whole heart and soul wasn't there.

Then, as if time had warped, that awkward moment had come.

"Omigawd." A stomach sickly feeling had instantly come over Oakland. His tongue felt thick and his face lit up as if burning.

"Ladies and gentlemen" — Parishioner Parson looked out into the large crowd — "Does anybody have reason to believe these two should not be wed. If so, please stand and speak, or hold your thoughts well into eternity."

Gretchen had kept her intent focus on Deklan while his head turned toward the guests. After observing the room, his gaze had stopped on Oakland.

Oakland swallowed, taking the lump in his throat further into his chest.

Deklan glanced at his mother and then back at Oakland, smiling at Jedidiah as his gaze traveled by him.

Oakland had begun to stand, but before he'd made it too far, Deklan signaled for him to stay seated, governing a nod that appeared he'd carry out what Oakland had thought of doing. At the same moment, Jedidiah tugged on Oakland's coat tail, bringing him back to his chair.

Deklan combed his hands through his hair, stopped the wedding and attested to the marriage he'd been forced into, insisting it should not proceed. "I'm sorry. I am truly, truly Sorry," he repeated. "We cannot go through with this wedding. It's a mistake." He couldn't have spoken more clearly.

In the front row, Deklan's father had risen from his chair, scowled at his son and then looked back toward everybody seated, giving a phony smile, a nod, and a wave that appeared he was trying to let everybody know everything would move along as planned.

Oakland was beaming, his smile bright, and when he looked at Deklan's mother, she was smiling too.

Since a shield hadn't mattered anymore, Deklan lifted the lacey veil from in front of the brides face. She was a pretty little thing, but not the right type for Deklan as he and Oakland had both known.

Oakland sensed an explanation coming.

Deklan looked at the bride as if she was the only one in the whole place, and that pleasant voice Oakland heard several times before had softly spoken, "Gretchen,"—he'd gotten her name correct that time—"You and I have known of each other for only a few days. I'm far from comfortable moving forward with this wedding, neither of which can I imagine you being content with the arrangement set for us."

She nodded as an unspoken gesture that she agreed with him.

He placed her hand into his. "It's important to me that I'm truthful with myself and to you. I wish I had been strong enough to bring up my concern before this moment, but because I feared hurting the people closest to me and not looking out for myself, I allowed it to get this far. What I'm trying to say is—I need to step away from this wedding. I cannot marry you like this."

Gretchen's eyes had gone soft, almost appearing as if she was relieved. She whispered, "It's okay, Mister Deklan. I'm glad you said something before the ring was placed on my finger. It's for the best, and I know it too."

Deklan smiled at her and quietly said, "You're a beautiful person from what little I know, but I have to be true to myself and be with the one I truly love."

Gretchen's hand rested on Deklan's cheek before she turned and walked away.

Chapter 35

Deklan's Father stood with a glare in his eyes that could have started a fire in a wet forest. His mind had to have been raging, *"What have you done?"* His mouth stayed shut. A good idea.

In the meantime, Gretchen's parents shuffled into the aisle and chased their child out the exit door. They scowled at Deklan as they passed by him.

Everybody involved should have known the wedding wouldn't have ended well, had it been announced that day, or soon into the future following the nuptials. Deklan had been attempting to explain that since the first day the idea of marriage had come up.

On the other hand, Oakland was happy to have seen Gretchen flee from the scene. His plan hadn't meant to have been cruel, but the act Deklan finally pulled off was the moral proposal to have done, and as heart wrenching as it might have been for everybody else, it was overall for the best. Oakland sat quietly in the chair next to Jedidiah, or could he have been The Mirror Man as he'd thought, and waited for Deklan to make his next positive move.

Without further delay, Deklan turned toward all his parents' friends sitting in the chairs and said nothing, only stared, appearing as though he was looking at an empty hall. A low tortured sigh had come out of him as he ascended from the platform and walked the same aisle he'd come down on the way in. He actually seemed happier that very moment.

Oakland stood up and Jedidiah mimicked his action. They were the only two standing with the exception of Deklan's angry father who stood with fisted hands and what looked like flames shooting out of his ears. His face beet red. Everyone else remained seated, stunned and gasping at what had just taken place.

When Deklan had come to the row where Oakland and Jedidiah had been seated, he stopped, rolled a hand inward, charming them to follow him the rest of the way out the door to wherever it was he planned on going.

Excusing themselves, Oakland and Jedidiah squeezed by the people sitting in the way, joining Deklan in the vacant aisle.

Holding back any further explanation to the people staring at them, Deklan grabbed Oakland's hand and threw an arm over the back of Jedidiah's shoulder. Together, they walked toward the door without looking back.

Oakland felt like a spectacle in a circus for freaks, and he was sure the many faces watching exhibited curious expressions as to what was going on between the three of them. He chuckled to himself, figuring Deklan's father could add clarity to the story since he'd been the one who created the show. Oakland had a slight urge to sneak a peek back at their audience, but decided he could have cared less about what they all thought.

Jedidiah seemed as though he'd cared less, and Deklan's face had told its own story—a definite, "I don't care what anybody else thinks anymore," expression.

Jedidiah ended up being a hero that day, pushing Deklan and Oakland out the door and ordering them to take off without him. He stood back and let the doors close behind him while watching the two lovesick gentlemen skip down the steps two at a time.

As recommended by Jedidiah, Deklan and Oakland left him behind in pursuit of high-jacked the wedding carriage meant for Deklan and his brand new female bride.

The best thing about the revised setting was that Oakland had dreamt a carriage would someday take him and Deklan to paradise one day, however, a race with a clean getaway hadn't been part in that dreamy sequence he'd imagined. Yet, it was thrilling in a nerve rattling sort of way, similar to the night they hit the kitchen up for an evening snack.

Deklan hurriedly pushed Oakland into the seat and hopped in, kissing him quickly before snapping the reigns. The horse stomped the ground and had taken off running. Where to? Who knew? Getting away from the Manor fast was the ultimate goal. Dust lifted behind the carriage wheels, and every bump and dip jostled Oakland closer to Deklan's side.

It was a jarring ride for a few minutes until Deklan unexpectedly tugged the reigns to the left and turned the horse toward the barn.

Oakland looked at him.

"Chadwick," was all Deklan said.

Oakland was quick to respond to Deklan's idea, scooting toward the carriage's exit, ready to hop out and help Deklan round up his favorite Clydesdale.

Before the carriage had come to a stop, Oakland pushed himself from the seat, hitting the ground with a choppy stumble. As though rehearsed, he rose to his feet, ran to the barn door and lifted the crossbar from the cradle.

Beyond the opening barn door, Chadwick was there waiting, prancing in circles and bobbing his nose as if ready to take flight at the front of Santa's sleigh. The big animal seemed to have known they were coming, and without a doubt, seemed telepathically linked to Deklan as if they were of one mind.

"Chad, come," Deklan hollered, rolling his hands over and over toward his chest.

Suddenly, as if it all happened in slow motion, Chadwick

backed up, pawed the ground and had taken a flying leap over the rail of his pen. Oakland crouched to the ground, watching the great big animal soar above his head with a solid landing only a few paces outside the doors. Stunned at least, several moments had passed before Oakland had a chance to catch his breath.

While Deklan tossed the horse saddle into the back of the buggy, Chadwick trotted proudly, circling Deklan and nipping at locks of wavy hair on the top of his head.

Deklan laughed as Chadwick tugged.

"Let's go, Chad," Deklan said, patting his rubbery nose and pointing toward the clover field the horse had known so well.

As told, Chadwick cantered ahead of the carriage, but stopped, looking back as if thinking, *"Are you coming or what?"*

The two climbed into the marriage carriage, and Deklan snapped the reigns. The further away from the Manor they'd ridden, Deklan slowed the buggy. The ride had become peaceful, and the mellow bounce turned as relaxing as rocking in a baby's cradle.

Oakland scooted closer to Deklan's side and held his hand across his lap.

A smile from Deklan had come with it. "Now this is how it should be. You next to me. Holding my hand, in a, *"Just Married,"* wedding carriage."

"Wish that scenario was true." Glancing to his right, Oakland found Chadwick walking beside the carriage as if he'd been tethered to it, the entire time keeping an eye on him and Deklan. There hadn't been a moment noticed where Chadwick looked away, and to find a horse passing no judgement on two men falling in love had Oakland wondering why the human race couldn't see life the same way a pet had. Animal's, supposedly classified as the lower life form, had no issues with who hung with whom, and Chadwick valued Deklan no matter that he loved a man.

They'd arrived at their hideaway, and before getting out of the carriage, stared out across the lake for a few quiet minutes. The place was peaceful and the stars above reflected off the surface like tiny sparks begging for attention.

Deklan left his seat first, and like a gentleman, held out a hand to help Oakland down.

As if Chadwick had a plan, he head bumped Deklan from behind, and since the horse's sneaky matchmaker plan had come as a surprise, Deklan tripped forward and fell into Oakland.

Chadwick snorted before casually trotting away for a drink of water from the lake. It was interesting how a horse could change its thoughts within seconds. One moment the animal might have been frightened, and the next, it was content and eating grass.

Deklan pinned Oakland against the carriage and whispered he loved him three times in a row. Immediately after, as if he couldn't wait another moment, lunged into Oakland and kissed him long and hard, grinding at his cocoa mug with a rotating jaw.

Oakland had kissed back, unwilling to let him go—his Prince's warm breath had filled his lungs. He held Deklan at the waist, both hands pulling him closer. He whispered, "I love you more than anything, Deklan. I never want anything like that to ever come between us again. I almost hadn't lived through this one."

"It won't, my love."

Oakland backed away, one eyebrow lifted, and said, "Promise?"

Addressing a permanent promise with body language, Deklan gripped the back of Oakland's skull and pressed their lips together so tightly he hadn't left any room for his man to breathe.

Chapter 36

Other than Chadwick and the horse that pulled the carriage, Oakland and Deklan were the only two who seemed to have been left on earth. Even the lake appeared untouched, the smooth glassy finish reflecting the moon from above.

Lying on the ground together beneath a sky full of stars, Deklan commented, "You seem deep in thought. What's on that mind of yours, my handsome Prince?"

Oakland rolled onto his side to face Deklan and released a few fasteners on his boyfriend's shirt. He laid a hand against his exposed chest, petting the silken hair. His tone was but a whisper, "I can't believe what had just taken place—that you put a stop to your own wedding for me. Right in the middle of the ceremony. That's unheard of."

Deklan's hand moved to Oakland's cheek as he shifted to his elbow. "I couldn't help myself. It's you I'm in love with. You I need to be with. I reached that nerve constricting point where I would have self-combusted if I'd gone one more second into that arranged marriage. That pivotal moment opened up the opportunity to put a stop to the well-known madness, and if everybody had plans to hold their peace, it wasn't going to be me who remained tongue tied. I could tell you were about to speak up, too, and I couldn't let you take on that burden my father created and I let go on. I couldn't go through with the sham any longer, Oakland, nor was I going to let another day go by without you permanently in my life, holding you in my arms, kissing you, feeling every part of you, putting and holding myself inside you. Sharing everything I have. I love you, Oakland. Not anybody else."

There was a film of mist that had glazed Oakland's eyes the moment Deklan mentioned he couldn't live without him. He realized several days earlier he'd have died without him too, and had the same reaction of living a tortured life if he'd gone another moment watching the man he loved move on with someone else. He muttered, "As you noticed, I had that same idea in my head, and if you hadn't spoken up, I was seconds away from full disclosure, myself. I'd been fighting with my own anger watching the two of you together, Deklan. It was terrifying and unnatural to witness. I despised the fact you were getting away from me, and I was breaking apart knowing somebody else was taking what had become a part of me. The love I have for you is so strong it's unexplainable. I feel like half a man if you're not next to me. I'm sure you understand."

"Completely, I do, Oakland."

"What made you decide to speak at that moment instead of days earlier?" Oakland asked.

"Because I was trying to make my parents happy, doing what I thought was right by what I'd been told and made to believe was the proper way to live. I know deep down, their way of life isn't for everybody. I fully realized that during my march down the aisle and when the ring in my pocket had begun to buzz, reminding me of you, shifting my gaze toward you. That there was the slap in the face I needed and the true sign from above telling me not to pay any mind to the voices around me, but to follow my heart. The closer I'd gotten to the phrase, 'I thee wed' part of the ceremony, the fist grip on my chest had gotten tighter. I could hardly breathe and I knew there was only one way to fix my aching heart. I had to confess. Confess my love for you, and I hadn't cared how it affected those who wouldn't agree. I had to be happy, Oakland. I was tired of feeling so miserable and disconnected all the time. I had to be me, and if being who I am and with the man I love, then everyone else would have to deal with the misery they are putting upon themselves. It's their misguided issue, not mine. It makes me sad to know I'll never have my parents' full acceptance, or ever hear them tell me they are happy with my love life. If my family can't receive me as I was born, then I suppose I never belonged there in the first place. Life is challenging enough without having family on the hate wagon, too. But I suppose I sort of have them to thank for how this all turned out. If they hadn't come up with such a silly plan for me to find a little woman as my wife, I probably wouldn't be with you today, holding your hand as my boyfriend. I'm with you now, Oakland, and that's all that matters. I'm ready to put the crazy past behind me. Starting, right now."

Although what Deklan had said was truth, Oakland refused to hear his gloom or allow it to continue. He needed to cheer him up, help him forget about the despair of life he'd almost fallen into. After all, they were a God selected unit, and nobody could divide them anymore.

Oakland removed his clothes and helped Deklan take his off too.

"What's going on here? You have a plan I'm not apposed of." Deklan grinned.

After removing the final article of clothing from Deklan's body, Oakland crawled into a comforting position with half his body lying over one side of Deklan's. He heard a sigh of relief come out of his boyfriend, the man's contentment of a closer bond.

Fascinated with everything masculine about Deklan, Oakland skimmed his hand across Deklan's chest, down his defined abdomen, stroking his fingers through the warm hair above his dick, and on to the hot spot between his legs. He massaged Deklan's sagging scrotum, rolling the heavy nuts in the palm of one hand, lifting the low hanging sac to expose Deklan's inviting sphincter.

Deklan lifted his knees that spread his legs further apart.

Recognizing Deklan's gratifying moans, Oakland slid his hand further between his boyfriend's legs and gently inserted two fingers into his warm hole, steadily sliding them in and out, feeling the wet semen he'd ejaculated into him before the ceremony. Holding his hand still, he asked, "Is that my..?"

"Sperm?" Deklan finished his sentence, then answered, "It is. I'm still carrying you with me. It was my reminder of who I really wanted walking that aisle with me today. I wasn't doing it alone. Plus, knowing it was there, helped drive my confidence."

Starting up again, Oakland inserted a third finger, massaging and pressing upward against the hot spot they'd learned was sensitive to sexual stimulation. Hearing Deklan's agreeable whimpering while keeping watch on his responsive body had made Oakland want to keep the rhythm going. Understanding his own internal sensations, he knew how to apply the pressure to intensify the emission of semen. The technique seemed to have been working. The harder Oakland stroked, the louder Deklan's whimpering had become. His sex-hole flexed, sucking his fingers in.

Deklan inhaled, tossed his head back and let out a pleasured cry, "Omigawd, your fingers are incredible. Jeez. I'm gonna ejaculate all over you if you keep that going." His dick throbbed, lifting and dropping against his abdomen in time with Oakland's pumping hand.

Oakland leaned into Deklan, feeling his deep breathing against his lips. He whispered, "Not yet, sexy man." He sluggishly pulled his fingers all the way out, laid back in the cool grass next to Deklan and gazed up at the twinkling stars.

"Jeez, Oakland. How could you leave me like this?"

Oakland's mood had shifted from what it was earlier and he chuckled. "Trust me, Dek, I know what I'm up to. You're dick is rock hard, ready to let the semen go, and my ass is irritably prepared to suck it out of you."

"Clever man." Deklan rolled over, comfortably positioning himself on top of Oakland, kissing him roughly. He dropped between Oakland's legs, hard cock pointed straight at his active hole, the head sneaking in. "I can't wait another second, Oakland. I need to impale you." Tightening his abdomen, Deklan's pelvis pushed forward.

Oakland lost his breath. It wasn't from forced shock to his system, but from thorough mind blowing pleasure of Deklan's dick trying to get in. His boyfriend's stiff cock had felt incredible burrowing in before, and at that moment, Oakland wanted it again, Deklan's full erection filling him completely, not to waver until the head of his meaty dick had reached his chest. He spread his legs wider, submitting to the man he desired.

Over top, Deklan looked down on Oakland, held still a moment before pushing his dick into his black hole. He added spit, but Oakland's resistant sex-hole wouldn't let him beyond his sphincter. His cockhead remained half exposed, the tip only hidden away. He laughed beneath a scowl.

"What's so funny?" Oakland stared weirdly at Deklan.

"Your hole is too dry and tight. I can't get my dick in." He gripped his cock, added more spit and wiggled it forward with additional pressure. "Jeez, I like it tight, but this...?"

"Hold onto that eager beast. I have an idea." Oakland gripped his erect dick and started stroking, slowly at first but soon turned into a speed demon. Deklan watched, stroking himself as well, but keeping the rhythm sustainably slower.

Oakland's face had begun to change, then he whined, followed by a raspy groan. His stroking hand stopped. His body stiffened, followed by a pleasured whimper. He held his breath deep in his lungs and tugged on his tightening nuts. Soon after, a single spurt of semen sluggishly oozed from the slit of his dick and pooled in the gutter below his sternum. He shuddered and then lay relaxed, let out a sigh and said, "There you go. Self-drawn lubricant. But, there's more where that came from, and is your job to pump it out of me, now."

"That was brilliant and pleasing to watch," Deklan seemed thrilled with the idea, reached for Oakland's semen and slathered the head of his dick. "Okay. I'm so ready for this. Spread those legs."

Without sparing a second, Oakland's legs had gone wide

open and he felt Deklan's dick slipping in. He grittily groaned, "Omi-gawd."

"I agree. Oh. My. Gawd. What you just came up with was incredibly sexy. Using your semen as butt butter has me about ready to ejaculate. I better move in slow or this will be over at a single finger snap." Deklan bowed his back, forcing his cock into Oakland's rectum. "Yeah. Looking good. The head is in. You're nice and slippery now. How does your own sperm feel being pushed into your butthole?"

"Incredible. Who would have thought? Keep going. I want you to add yours."

"For certain. You're getting it. Right up the butt." Hip grinding, Deklan moved his erection in and out of Oakland with slow lasting strokes, popping the sperm slickened head out and back in again. He groaned and huffed, "Omigawd... your asshole feels splendid. Jeez. Here comes the sperm you want. Already. Omigawd. So intense." Deklan growled, jamming his pelvis into Oakland's backend. He collapsed on top of him, his body immediately going rigid — every muscle bunched and swelled. His face contorted and turned beet red. He roared, "I'm... shooting... in your hole." He yelled profanity with each thrust. His thrashing body pumped sperm into Oakland like a shotgun going off. One forceful blast after the other.

"Give it to me, Dek. Unload inside me." Oakland cried for it, stroking his thick black dick, jerking in time with Deklan's cocky jabs, feeling every prod.

Semen oozed out of Oakland's butthole, spitting noisily around Deklan's sunken dick.

Deklan muttered, "So much sperm. Very slippery now. Omigawd!" He warned, "I'm going all the way in again. Brace yourself." Deklan plunged his slickened cock deep — his fleecy pelvis scrubbing against Oakland's taint. He moaned.

Jolted, Oakland cried out, "Ga-yaaaah. Yeah. Give me that hard steel. All of it. Saturate my hole with your sperm." The overwhelming sensation caused Oakland's toes to curl, and the feeling intensified when Deklan's hand roamed over his chest. A twist of the nipple shot pleasured sparks to Oakland's cock. It throbbed in his grasp. He hollered, "Oh Gawd. Don't stop.

Hammer me. Fill my black hole."

Rolling his hips, Deklan forced his cock further. "I love you so much, Oakland. I want to go as deep and stay there forever," he'd spoken honestly.

Taking every bit of Deklan, the punishing pleasure had Oakland panting, virtually losing his breath. He whimpered, "I love you too, Deklan." He cried for more dick, couldn't hold back what he wanted and needed from his man. He hooked a hand at the nape of Deklan's neck, pulling him down into a ravaging kiss.

Deklan's rhythmic thrusts clasped hold of Oakland with rousing excitement, pushing him to that place of desired chaos, turning him sexually wild. Oakland yelled for more, demanding deep dick penetration and a butt flooded with his boyfriend's semen. His entire body had suddenly stiffened, every muscle inflated to solid rock. He'd lost control. His eyes clamped shut and he growled a gritty groan as his dick squirted semen between their torsos, the creamy eruption painting Deklan's chest and dripping down onto his in goopy gobs. He trembled from the intense orgasm, his prostate aggressively pulsing from the profuse beating it'd taken from Deklan's prodding dick. In time, Oakland eventually finished ejaculating and settled down.

Still partially inserted, Deklan gently lay down on top of Oakland, commenting with warm breath filling his ear, "Once again that gorgeous body of yours made me ejaculate too soon. I need to get that under control, but the tight grasp you had on my dick felt so incredible. As soon as I sunk inside you, the flood gates burst open. I couldn't hold it back. That beautiful black hole felt so damned good sucking on me so flawlessly."

"We have lots of time to perfect that skill. I'm all in at trying again, and again, and again, and again, and again." Oakland hugged Deklan tightly, and with a softer tone, whispered, "Deklan? Marry me?"

Lifting his head from Oakland's ear, Deklan looked at him as if trying to absorb his every thought. Following a caring kiss, Deklan smiled and said, "Yes, my beautiful, beautiful Prince, I'd love to marry you. Our secret."

Deklan removed the ring from the jacket pocket and slipped it onto Oakland's finger where it always belonged. It shimmered as he spoke, "With this ring and in front of our creator above, who I'm certain made us for one another. I... Wed... Thee." His finger traced the shell of Oakland's ear. "I love you, Oakland, and never plan to stop."

Accepting the ring, Oakland hugged the man who put it there.

Even with no ordained minister, or human witnesses present, their private marriage under the apple tree was real to them — official beyond anyone's imagination because they were truly in love.

Deklan held Oakland, kissed him with more passion than he'd ever kissed him before.

ణ ಐ

The carriage seat cushions weren't fastened permanently, which provided ample bedding on the ground for the night. The clothing worn would hopefully keep them warm until morning.

They lay snuggling on their sides, Deklan's body tightly clinging to Oakland's back, his arms wrapped tightly around his chest. The closeness, pure.

There was no going back to the way it had been. The two of them separated — unable to touch one another. If Deklan's father wouldn't accept his son sharing a communion with the lad next door, then Deklan would find a life outside The Manor. Oakland was too important, a major part of him — his close personal family.

"Stay." Oakland scooted into Deklan, feeling the warmth of his body pressing snuggly at his back side.

"I'm still right here." Deklan adjusted himself, inching his entire body tighter against Oakland, hugging and pulling him closer than he already was.

Chapter 37

The sun seemed to have taken its sweet time coming up, but from what Oakland had been able to see through weary eyes, it had just clipped the horizon and he knew the roosters would crow at any moment.

He'd eventually come fully awake, still feeling Deklan clinging behind with an arm snuggly pinned across his chest and the pressure of his dick head digging at his manhole. He shifted to rouse Deklan, overhearing him moan when his body trembled into a stretch—the forward momentum of his vibrating hips burrowed his erect cock right up inside Oakland's used rear end.

The internal pressure bearing down on Oakland's prostate had provoked his dick to grow stiffer and ooze pre-ejaculate into the grass in front of him. He whispered to himself, "*Jeez, my man's dick is so damned good.*" He arched his back, helping Deklan's cock sink deeper.

Making use of the slick semen loaded into Oakland the

previous night, Deklan slid his man sized dick in and out of his butthole. The rhythm had been kept slow, almost at a standstill. Deklan growled as his body moved in smooth waves, his hips bumping into Oakland's rear end, the hair above his erection scrubbing his butt cheeks. He rumbled, "Gah. Get ready. Oh Gawd. I'm..." he hadn't finished. His face contorted, then warped into clenched eyes and gritting teeth. His body had gone stiff, pushing hard against Oakland from behind. He trembled and jerked, hips grinding forward in time with each vocal grunt.

Opening himself further, Oakland lifted one leg and pushed back against Deklan, letting go of an unrestrained howl. The pleasure had come at him too great and increased, moment by moment. With each thump against his back end, he felt his Prince's erection expanding and contracting inside him—surely from spurting semen into his chute with flooding effects to his rectum. Much of the injected semen soaked his butt crack and inner thigh as it squirted back out around Deklan's dick. Oakland's pleasured vocal thundering had come from deep down, "Ohmigawd, I need every inch of that amazing dick. Give me every spurt. Breed me, Deklan. Please breed me."

"Yeah, baby. You're getting bred," Deklan rumbled, sounding dominant. His hips forcefully pressed to Oakland's rear end. Generously ejaculating. It seemed never ending.

Even after five, six or maybe seven massive sperm injections into Oakland throughout the night, Deklan had dumped another supercharged load into his begging man's butt that morning. He was fertile, for sure, and if possible, Oakland would have been with child.

Matching every one of Deklan's releases, Oakland's dick had spit gobs of his own sperm clear across the grassy knoll and onto his and Deklan's body. Both had felt reckless. Sexually stimulated. There had come a thrill with connecting out in an open field—a sense of freedom neither had ever felt before.

Regretfully, reality was rearing and the time had come to face the events that had taken place the previous day. With that dreadful thought, Oakland loosened the cock locked grip he had on Deklan, letting him snake his meaty dick out of his used up sex-hole. The exit had taken a while, but eventually once

Oakland's push and Deklan's pull decided to work together, the cock head popped free.

They'd taken off for the lake to rinse the night away. The water was cool, but seemed warmer than the air.

Deklan circled his hand over Oakland's chest and mentioned, "I wasn't much of a stud back there was I? I acted like a teen aged boy who'd gotten his dick sucked for the very first time. I ejaculated way too soon. Again. I couldn't help it though, Oakland. You are so damned sexy, and feel so amazing in my arms and wrapped around my dick. That ass of yours is divine. I don't know how I'd ever gotten along without its sweet grip."

"Every bit of you was a stud, back there. I counted six, or was that seven times you ejaculated in a single night. That there is anything but unstudly." Oakland felt Deklan's hands move upward to his shoulders.

"I just couldn't get enough of you or your magnificent body. I turn crazy if I'm not touching you. I'm so in love, Oakland. You're all I think about. I need to be close to you, wrapped around you, inside you, so I can be a part of you."

"After last night, and how much of you I have inside me right now, I'd say you are a permanent part of me and always will be." Oakland imagined how settling it would have been to live day to day with Deklan, each night and every morning. The idea of going to bed and waking in each other's arms would have been the perfect happy ever after. "Since you seem to be quite fertile, I'd say I'll never find myself deprived of having a part of you with me."

"You're probably correct, and I'll make sure you never go hungry."

Oakland added, "In fact, your semen is still spilling out of me. I can't possibly hold it all in." The cushion under him was even wet.

"Sorry about that, but you are to blame for sucking it out of me. Totally your fault. By the way, you had shot off a few hefty rounds yourself. Look at my chest." Deklan ravenously smiled, rubbing the sperm deposits into the hair.

"That happened because how good you felt inside me." Oakland greedily smiled back.

"Yeah. About that. Who knew we had a hot spot inside our assholes that could make us ejaculate so powerfully when nudged. I wonder how many other men know about that semen inducing button hidden away inside their asshole? When you hit mine, I thought I was going to go blind. Seriously. I don't think I ever ejaculated so hard."

Oakland hadn't been surprised to have heard Deklan mention that pressure point since he himself knew the pleasures it added to ejaculating, but wondered the same thing Deklan had — who else knew about it and what a dick thumping could do to their sexual sanity. Since Deklan noticeably liked the feeling as well, meant Oakland might have to give up his favored place in the relationship and put his black eleven-incher inside Deklan a whole lot more. He wasn't opposed to being on top once in a while, but the bottom was where he belonged and felt most comfortable.

Deklan huffed. "Wish we could stay right here forever, never go back to where we'd come from."

"That would be heaven, for sure," Oakland replied.

They air dried and dressed, and as far as Oakland could tell, it appeared they were left undisturbed throughout the night. It had, however, troubled him to discover nobody had come looking for Deklan, making sure he was all right.

"Deklan?" — Oakland had spoken while buttoning his shirt — "You okay with going back to the house?" He thought a part of Deklan had already rubbed off on him since he caught himself fastening the buttons on his shirt from bottom to top, the same quirky way Deklan does.

"I'm good, Oakland. We can go back together and if the doors are locked, we have this place we can call home." While lacing his boots, Deklan whistled for Chadwick. The massive Clydesdale had come running almost instantaneously.

Oakland walked over to Deklan to fix his jacket. Even though a little crumpled, Deklan still looked good to him. He brushed his hands down the front of Deklan's chest, flattening the lapels. "You look very handsome," Oakland told him before lightly kissing his lips.

Deklan looked Oakland in the eyes, held his jaw in both

hands and returned the kiss. Oakland felt it was more passionate than ever before—the depth of the kiss had gone straight to the heart and spiraled around his head like a halo of stars.

He was in love.

Chapter 38

Father Dante had been standing in the gateway of Chadwick's empty stall, appearing irritated while waiting for Deklan and who he knew as the stable boy to have returned from wherever it was they had run off to for the night. Where they had gone hadn't mattered to him, as long as they arrived home safely. That was all he ever really wanted for his child — safety.

Since he understood they'd been with Chadwick, the horse that would trample anyone who lifted a stick to Deklan, he figured the boys would have been okay.

Being separated from Deklan had given Dante the time he needed to digest what it would have been like without his son, serving him the truth about Deklan and what was meant to be and was unchangeable. He'd lived the same situation with his brother Joseph, identified the struggles and suffering he'd gone through for being his true self. It had frightened Dante to think Deklan could end up in the same situation his brother had, hanging dead someplace to enable himself an escape from such a cruel world that couldn't relate to or accept him for who he was. It had struck Dante into understanding he had been included in that part of the world driving his son further away.

It was unlike Dante to pick up a whiskbroom and use one, but he reached for a weed claw anyway and raked Chadwick's stall as though he'd been hired as a farmhand. He no longer had a hand in hard labor, but his mind required a distraction from the horrifying thoughts of what could have or might have happened to Deklan. Raking horse droppings and dirty hay was exactly what he needed to get his mind off the worst scenario.

While cleaning the barn floor, aged memories from his younger days had come rushing back to him—those where he shared responsibilities of household chores with his late brother Joseph. He'd almost broken down at what could have been a repeat occurrence, but the hung man would have been his son, instead. To block it out, he raked faster.

Dante was a strong man and wouldn't allow anybody to see his weak side. He of all people knew he had one, but it was never out in the open or even detectible by anybody but himself. He'd always remained hard as steel and made sure everybody around had seen only that side of him, giving the impression he'd been born without a heart. The only person who seemed to have known he had a soft side to his thumper, and who'd ever seen it blossom was Deklan's mother, Priscilla.

As Dante raked the trampled straw from Chadwick's stall to a pile in the middle of the barn, he visualized the day he walked in on his brother hanging from the barn rafters by a rope.

That wasn't a good day, for anybody.

The picture in his head had come as clear to him as the day it happened, and just then, his nerves combusted when he envisioned Deklan in place of Joseph. "Oh God, this can't happen again. Not twice. Not in my family."

He let the claw go and it hit the ground with a triple handled bounce. He trudged to the outside door of the barn to look out, hopeful the bright light from the sun would burn away the frightening images in his head. He worked like mad to channel his thoughts to a better place as he prayed Deklan was okay. His only son. The son he loved.

"Please come home, Deklan. Please come home," he pleaded, squinting into the sun that was as painful as the image in his head.

His heart sped up the more he tried to get Joseph out of his mind and a possible scenario that could have been his son, Deklan. Dante, the strong man who'd built the plantation from the ground up with his bare hands resorted to trembling and for the first time had fallen to his knees, repelled by his own actions for what he'd put his pure hearted son through. Again, he bowed his head and pleaded, "Please come home, Deklan. Please... come home."

As if the sun reached out and lifted his chin, Dante spotted a speck coming over the hilltop in front of rising dust. It had grown larger and looked like Chadwick alongside the horse carriage he remembered taking off into oncoming dusk the night before. As the speck moved closer, he knew it was Deklan. Invisible to anyone if they had been watching, he crossed himself and clasped his hands together in another silent prayer. Pleading, and that time, thanking.

He stepped from the barns shadows and shielded the bright sun with an arm above his brow.

Dante scorned himself for what he'd put Deklan through and promised at that very moment he wouldn't allow their differences to come between them ever again. He hadn't fully understood Deklan's attraction toward men because he wasn't living in his boots. The image Deklan had given him about separating from Priscilla had also put him in a different state of mind. That difficult consequence had never left his thoughts since the day Deklan painted that picture for him.

Smart kid.

It had, however, helped him make sense of pure love and how it cannot be interrupted. The vision he had in the barn was also a message he needed put out there in front of him, as though it was coming from above, telling him to leave a perfected creation the way it was supposed to be.

C3 ∞ 80

Deklan and Oakland glanced at each other during the carriage ride down the rocky hillside with Chadwick leading them home. The horse seemed to know the way as though a trail of carrots had been laid out for him to follow.

Oakland sensed Deklan was anxious by how tightly he had gripped the reigns. His knuckles had gone white as he squeezed the leather straps. Lately, his father had pricked an angry streak in him each time the two had come within eyeshot from one another. That particular incident, however, might have been the worst.

"I'm not ready for this." Deklan twisted the reigns together in both hands, grinding them as if trying to wring water from fabric.

To Oakland, Deklan's father hadn't appeared too outraged, and if he'd been correct about that, the man seemed more concerned than upset. Oakland glanced over at Deklan and kept his mouth shut, only patting a hand on his knee and giving it a loving squeeze.

Even though Oakland had known his touch would have normally been appreciated by Deklan, he'd felt at that moment, Deklan's reaction was distant, might have been triggered by the shattered contact he had with his father. That connection seemed to have left Deklan tunnel locked as though he was trying to figure out what his father had been thinking before he reached him.

The carriage had finally arrived at the barn where Dante had been standing, and by the way the air hung heavy around them, Oakland sensed a bitter moment was coming.

With a more cheerful voice than expected, Deklan asked Chadwick to go to his room, and without argument or a stomping hoof, the horse had done what had been asked. Deklan tugged on the carriage reigns, pulling the leader horse to a stop.

The clanging of the bridle sounded pretty and Oakland was hoping it would lighten the mood a little bit.

"Father." Deklan formally addressed his hello, adding a head nod. If he'd been wearing a rancher's sunhat, he'd have gripped the brim.

Dante walked around to the side of the carriage where Deklan had been sitting and rested a hand on the large front wheel. The carriage rocked as Deklan and Oakland climbed out.

During the stifling engagement, Oakland was as nervous as a worm on a hook below sea level. He hadn't felt acquainted enough to mention his observation, but from what he'd witnessed, Dante had changed for the better, overnight.

"Where's mother?" Deklan asked, appearing to break the ice between him and his father. The frozen wall had shown signs of melting, a little bit, but needed some heat to get it started.

For some reason, Dante hadn't spoken. If hard core love had served its purpose, Oakland would have guessed the man was happy to have seen his son.

Could it be? A heart was making its appearance.

Dante stepped toward Deklan and pulled him into a hug so hard it appeared to have been an unconditional embrace. What had happened to that man overnight?

Oakland wasn't certain where the display of affection had come from or where it was headed, and he wondered what the outcome of that family hug was going to bring. He stood impassive, since a father and a son moment wasn't heard of or seen very often, if ever at all.

Men showing affection? What would the world think?

Dante let go of Deklan and had finally spoken a few words, "I'm happy to see you. Are you doing okay?"

Deklan stepped back, showing off a stunned appearance across his face. "Yes... father. I'm well."

"Are you sure?" Dante asked again, looking him over as if he was secretly questioning his heart and mind, not his physical being.

"I'm quite sure, Father."

"Okay. Good. That's good to hear. Are you and your friend hungry?" Dante asked, gripping Deklan's shoulders at full arm's length, giving him a subtle shake, that of which a buddy would have given.

Wait a minute. What just happened?

Had Oakland heard correctly? Was Deklan's father concerned for him, too? Oakland couldn't move. He wanted to, but he couldn't. He stood on his own side of the carriage and stared.

Deklan glanced at his boyfriend and nodded, apparently meaning Oakland was supposed to go with the flow if he was hungry or not. "Yes, Pop, we could eat something."

Deklan's father smiled. "I like it when you call me Pop."

Deklan grinned. "I thought? Never mind."

Oakland left the two of them to walk together while he lingered a few steps behind. He kept a steady pace that allowed the two gentlemen to bond the way they should have done a while ago. It was important that he remained distant, keeping clear of the noticeable baby steps Deklan and his father had been taking. Whatever happened during the night to Deklan's father ended up being a good thing. A turn for the better.

While the three of them walked, Oakland overheard most of the conversation.

"Deklan?" Dante started.

"Yes, Fa—,"—he stopped—"Pop." Deklan had taken off his jacket and flipped it over his shoulder.

"I love you, son." Dante turned Deklan toward him with a grip to his shoulder. "I'd do anything in the world to make sure you knew that, even if a mistake had been made that seemed as though I didn't love you."

"I know, Pop."

"No, I'm not crying. Darn those pesky gnats." Oakland claimed he had a bug in his eye, not a joyful tear. "We really need to invent a way to kill these damned bugs. Something that'll zap them right out of thin air." He swatted into empty space around his head.

Dante looked over at Oakland who had been rubbing his eyes. He nodded at Oakland as if telling him it was alright for him to overhear what he was about to say. "Deklan, please understand what I'm going to tell you."

Oakland detected something good coming next.

Shedding a bit of humor on the sensitive situation, Dante

mentioned, "Your mother made me sleep on the floor last night. She told me if I didn't come to my senses and put an end to all the hard headed nonsense I had put you through, then it would be a permanent place for me along with having to make my own meals if I wanted to eat. She mumbled something about the barn, too. You know there aren't many people who are able to intimidate me. But... your mother? Now that lady has one heck of a hold on me by her littlest finger alone. Don't tell her I told you, but she scares me, you know."

Both, Deklan and Oakland laughed. Dante's mention of his punishment had come as comical, however, he truly deserved to have slept on the floor after what he'd done.

Moms know best and she's the real boss in the relationship.

Dante had flat lined the humor with a more serious tone. "Just know that parents do things they think is best for their children. The decisions might not always be good ones, but we try. We make sacrifices so you don't have the same worries or problems that we had. Do you understand?"

"Mm-hmm," Deklan hummed.

"I was only trying to protect you from what is outside our home. People don't take a shining to what you have with the stable boy. I mean, stable man." Dante pointed at Deklan's boyfriend.

"His name is Oakland," Deklan added.

Oakland waved, suddenly feeling ridiculous once he'd done that.

A wave? Really?

Deklan grinned, and the look in his eyes indicated to Oakland the man wanted to kiss him for being so cute and corny.

"Nice to meet you, Master Oakland." Dante smiled at him.

"Likewise, Sir," Oakland answered, and waved again.

Apparently he hadn't learned how senseless the wave was the first time.

Dante turned back toward Deklan and told him, "Your mother mentioned the conversation you had with her the other day in your bedroom and I wouldn't be able to live if that same thing happened to you."

"You mean, Uncle Joseph?" Deklan clarified, raising a brow.

"Who?" Oakland mumbled.

"Yes, Deklan. Your uncle Joseph. My brother," Dante confirmed. "I'd thought about it all night long, so I spent most of the night out here in the barn to make sure there was no repeat performance of what had happened years ago to my brother. I'd die right along with you, Deklan. I can damned near promise you that."

"Dear lord, Father. I mean, Pop. No... I'd never."

"What I want more than anything right now is for you to be safe, as well as happy, and I'm extremely remorseful for making you feel as though I hated you for being the person you were born to be. I thought I knew best. Being a father isn't easy, Deklan. I'm learning every step of the way, and every decision I make, hopeful it's the right one." Dante had made it clear that if Deklan had gotten injured by another hand or meeting death because of who he was had made him quickly understand the treasure he would lose if such a thing had happened to his child.

They finished the walk into the kitchen where Deklan's mother was helping the servants prepare breakfast. She'd done that from time to time since cooking was a passion of hers, and on the days she needed some nostalgic home therapy.

"Priscilla, dear. Look who I found?" Dante announced their arrival.

Priscilla spun around and flounced toward Deklan, pulling him into a motherly hug. "Deklan, dear. I'm so happy to see you. Thank goodness you're well."

"I'm good mom. I... or we just needed some space for the night."

She let him go.

"Mom, this is my... Oakland," he almost said boyfriend.

"Hello, Oakland. Breakfast?" her invitation was subtle—her smile even more welcoming.

"I'd like that. Haven't eaten since yesterday afternoon, and that was a pear."

"A whole pear? Then you will join us. No doubt about that," Dante firmly professed.

The thought had run through Oakland's mind that the wedding should still go on, but the exchanging of rings would have been with him and Deklan instead of a female virgin bride. If only that fantastic idea was possible, but the truth of the matter was, two men wedding one another would never happen in his lifetime. As it was, Deklan and Oakland would have to keep their private ceremony at the lake to themselves, a personal gift between the two of them. Perhaps the world would someday come round and accept all love as equal and acknowledge two men holding hands and kissing in a public place to be other than a sinful crime.

As soon as breakfast had come to a close, Dante requested a private moment with Oakland, telling him there would always be a place for him under his roof as long as he continued making Deklan as happy as he has been. In another breath, Dante mentioned how good of a person Deklan was and thankful his son had grown into a man unlike himself.

That last part struck a sour chord with Oakland and he had no idea how to respond to what he'd heard. He noticed a decent side to Deklan's father that morning and would make sure he kept Deklan happy as long as he was alive. He wasn't sure Dante was ready to hear how he truly felt about his son, but Oakland still told him he'd never loved anyone like he loves Deklan. He hoped he understood.

Dante's face had gone a bit angular at the mention of love Oakland had for his child, but from what Oakland had witnessed, the man had gotten over it almost as quickly as he'd said it. Dante must have been preparing for that moment for quite some time. A parent knows.

Before the servants had a chance to clear the table, Oakland and Deklan had gone outside to visit with Chadwick. That smart horse seemed to know they were coming—identified by the way he pranced around the stall like he always had whenever Deklan showed up. That horse was addicted to that man, and now Oakland was too.

Chapter 39

It'd taken a while, but trivial freedom had found Deklan and Oakland. It wasn't full blown, but it was something and better than it had been. Baby steps.

Oakland smiled, kissed the love of his life before helping him hoist the saddle onto Chadwick's back. The plan was to ride horseback to their private place under the pear tree. It was the first place they had met by accident. It was the same place they always seemed to run into each other whenever either of them thought they were out alone. It was the place Deklan and Oakland sat during the more troublesome days. It turned out to be the place their souls had actually collided, and from that day on, was the place they'd always returned to.

As had been done in the past, Deklan climbed aboard Chadwick first, followed by the reach of a heroic hand to swing Oakland into place behind him. He was getting good at that one handed scoop and the weight of Oakland seemed to have made

Deklan stronger.

Deklan snapped the reigns and Chadwick had taken off running. He mentioned the clover field to the horse and just like that, away he'd gone.

To Oakland, he'd never come across a horse that knew the English language like that one had, but harpin' horny toads, that Clydesdale caught every word and knew what was being asked of him.

The wind Chadwick created while running felt good against Oakland's face and the rolling gallop seemed much smoother than the buggy ride they'd taken earlier. The way the horse ran felt as though his feet had never touched the ground. The sensation of floating above clouds had come to mind when running that field on horseback.

Deklan and Oakland made it to the pear tree where they were finally alone and their secret love for one another could go on. It seemed that each strange chapter in their life had something to do with that tree.

Before they'd gotten down off Chadwick's back, Oakland pressed his body against Deklan's back and had given him one of the biggest and tightest hugs he'd ever given him, or anybody had for that matter. His hand slipped under Deklan's shirt, feeling flesh and the silken hair he liked so much.

Deklan turned his head back and nipped Oakland lightly on the lip. "Omigawd, I Love you, Oakland." His hand rested over Oakland's, giving it a gentle squeeze.

Shifting, Deklan slid off Chadwick first and then progressed to help Oakland down, trapping him backside against the horse for that expected dismounting kiss. It happened every time. If Oakland wasn't crazy, he believed Chadwick had been in on the ritual kiss and made sure not to move until he was lip locked with Deklan. The damned horse had even turned his head back and watched the two of them carry out the passionate deed.

"Who do you love?" Deklan blurted out.

"You, of course," Oakland answered honestly.

"Will you love me forever?"

"Without a doubt. Now give me that mouth."

When the kiss finally ended, Chadwick moved away.

Deklan grabbed Oakland's hand and led him under the tree, plucking a pear from the nearest branch along the way. He tossed it to Chadwick and reached for another for the two of them to split.

Deklan shared the crunchy pear with Oakland, kissing him between bites. One bite. One kiss. Another bite, another kiss.

Oakland had taken the last bite before tossing the core someplace behind them. The same way he devoured the pear, he'd gone for Deklan. One lip nip and one kiss at a time until it led to something more, going for his core. Soon, lying unclothed beneath the pear tree.

Funny how that works.

Oakland lay on his side, facing Deklan, completely in love with him without a doubt. Deklan's physical form was a genuine bonus and the fact that Deklan expressed his love for Oakland's body just as much, had made the two of them insanely compatible.

Deklan ran his hand over Oakland's chest. "Man, I love your skin," he said. "It's like brown silk and you know exactly what happens to me when I touch you." He continued downward, taking hold of Oakland's growing erection with both hands. It was hard and in position up the center of his rolling abdomen.

After receiving a moment of cock thickening exhilaration, Oakland kissed Deklan's beautiful hairy chest that smelled of lavender oil and forest wood spices. That seemed to be his signature scent. Always clung to him. He moved his kisses to Deklan's lips, pecking him lightly. "I have a thought," He mentioned, pulling his lips away slowly.

"And that would be?" Deklan whispered as he rolled on top of Oakland.

Oakland grunted from the weight of his private husband, but wouldn't have wanted his pinned situation to have been any different. "I know it's light out and anybody passing by could see us, but let's be daring and make love, right here under this tree where we first met. It will complete the circle and tie the knot."

"Let's do it. Right now. You know how much I like being

inside you." Deklan seemed eager by the way he'd spoken and dived for Oakland's mouth to kiss him. His breathing turned sharp and his hair fell forward, swishing across Oakland's face, brushing his cheeks from each mouth rotating movement.

Oakland's hands pressed against Deklan's chest, the hair pleasing his palms. He let out a gratifying moan when he felt Deklan growing harder, his dick had instantly gotten bigger.

Deklan rocked his body, rolling his hips into Oakland, their erections gliding side by side. He unexpectedly broke their embrace and retrieved a small square of butter from his shirt pocket he sneakily stole from the breakfast table. Oakland watched Deklan move into position between his open legs while masterfully coating his erection with the oily pat. The excitement of what was about to come had turned his dick even stiffer.

Deklan was a vision to Oakland, coming on strong, looking overly masculine while propped on his knees with his hand stroking his nine inch cock, gliding from bulbous head to hairy pelvis. Every muscle flexed and bunched.

A slight gasp and a body quake had come out of Oakland when Deklan's oily hand brushed over his puckered manhole. The wait that would lead to penetration had become long and difficult. The need to feel his boyfriend slipping in was great. He pulled his knees to his chest and lifted his black nuts away from Deklan's way in. His actions to be punctured by his boyfriend's cock had come on strong — proven obvious he needed dick.

Noticeable it must have been since Deklan hadn't asked if Oakland was ready to have been penetrated. He just pushed forward until every large inch was so far inside him, his nuts had practically sunken in, too. "Jeez, almighty. Again, that slick rectum of yours feels incredible," Deklan confessed, watching his thick white cock disappear into that gorgeous black hole.

Deklan was gentle when he needed to be, but that time, Oakland's sex-hole had invited a dick with blunt power. After a few sharp thrusts of his hips, Deklan dropped down and passionately kissed Oakland, keeping his rhythm smooth, moving amiably in and out of Oakland's buttered butthole. The throaty moans coming out of Oakland upon each stiff plunge had proven the man was in a total enchanted position. His hard dick leaking pre-ejaculate was another bit of proof.

Oakland had become so in love with Deklan that his emotions had tipped to a level that made him soften. Every time Oakland was with Deklan, it was unbelievable. Every time Deklan moved inside him, it felt incredible.

Deklan moaned as the man he had put a ring on drew him in. It was peculiar in a perfect way how Oakland's body desired his cock so much that his sex-hole actually pulled Deklan deeper inside, literally sucking on his rock hard erection.

They moved together perfectly. Friction instigating orgasms.

Lying on top of Oakland while kissing him, Deklan muttered broken words into his ear, "You feel fantastic, Oakland." — he gasped — "you... ready" — he huffed, driving his hips into Oakland's rear — "oh gawd" — he groaned — "for me... Oakland." His face changed to a pleased knot. He pulled out and pushed back in again.

Deklan had felt so good to Oakland that he struggled with his answer, "Yes... Dek." Then he fought to keep control of his orgasm. He growled, "Here it comes. I... Gaaaah." An extraordinary buzz dominated him as he sprayed stream after stream of hot semen between their chests.

A few spurts lashed Deklan's tongue as he looked down and watched Oakland ejaculate. He swallowed, and as if that had pushed him to the limit, his entire body had gone tense and every muscle swelled. He released a grating roar as he pumped his sperm into Oakland. He collapsed, lying over top of Oakland, clearly sensitive, body surging along with his trembling. Their mouths met, bodies convulsing, kissing until their passion turned tender and the tremors ended.

Before they reached orgasmic aftershock, Oakland started laughing. He hadn't meant to, but it had just come out.

"What did I miss? What's with the snickering? Was it my face when I ejaculated? My weird body spasms? I know I can appear crazed when I'm shooting semen into you. Perhaps I had reached a funny bone up in there?" Deklan laughed back, still moving his hips, but slowing down.

"I'm Sorry. I just love you so much that my emotions had gotten the best of me. I'm extremely happy right now. I can't believe this is happening. You and me." Oakland's rectum squeezed Deklan tighter, pulling him in.

"That's a relief. Laughter wasn't quite the reaction I had expected. I thought perhaps my enthusiastic rhythm had become a gag to you." Deklan dropped back down onto Oakland, pinning him to the ground.

"Quite the opposite," Oakland grunted. "After all this time, I'm finally in a place I want to be and I feel relaxed enough to really enjoy a moment to smile about it." He couldn't believe what they'd gone through to get to where they were. First they'd convinced the family, next project, the world.

Deklan pushed his hips forward, burying his cock deeper.

"Gaah!" Oakland's head rolled back from the incredible sensation Deklan had given him with his erection.

"Let's trade places." Deklan's voice was deep and sexy, but a grunt followed when he grabbed Oakland's shoulders and rolled him over.

Oakland was still wearing the necklace around his neck as well as the ring Deklan had placed on his finger. Both shone bright like a diamond.

"This belongs to you." Oakland removed the chain linked piece and transferred it to Deklan, over his head and around his neck. The medallion looked attractive lying against his hairy chest and the shimmer from the two trinkets when separated let it be known the two pieces should never have been pulled apart.

Oakland looked into Deklan's eyes and every thought he had about being exiled had vanished.

It was a magical moment consisting of a ring, a necklace, and undeniable love.

Connected.

Together.

Forever.

Happily ever after.

Epilogue

Truth be told, my time spent with Deklan had been life changing as well as extraordinary. To speak of it lightly.

It's still difficult for me to believe how it all started. The affair between us on the plantation had been initiated when the mystical Mirror Man appeared and sent me to find a companion I might not have found if he hadn't come along. I never knew what happened to him after that night – where he'd gone, or if he really existed. For all I knew, it started as a dream that turned into some fairytale reality when I'd woken up. That perfect birthday evening was so short lived and magical, I found myself challenging the memories of it actually being real.

The only possessions from that night I'd been left with were the necklace and the ring. Everything else had vanished into thin air. How? I don't know, but they had. It still remains a mystery to me why the jewels hadn't disappeared, too, since they seemed to have been more magical than the rest of the items from that night. Those two gifted trinkets, however, were convincing enough to have proven the night or the magical man wasn't just a figment of my imagination, and since Deklan had seen me in those striking textiles, only added truth to The Mirror Man's existence, and the fabulous event that started it all. If the clothing, ring and the necklace existed, that fairy man must have too.

Deklan and I hadn't talked about that enchanted night much, but the bits we had spoken of, helped us believe that angels, spirits, and transcendent fairies quietly guide us through our lives in mysterious ways. Some visible. Others not so prominent. Most walk in and out of our lives without us even knowing it. I, however, had been lucky enough to have met one of my guardian fairies face to face. Apart from my own sentinel, I believed Deklan's friend Jedidiah was his personal messenger. It seemed that way since Jedidiah had also disappeared after holding back a sullen mob behind those chapel doors on that memorable wedding day I'd liked to have forgotten.

We are two men in love, but the sad part of our relationship resides with keeping it a secret from those who'd rather witness us hanged than see us holding hands. Those so called Christians and extremists are so far off the beaten path with what the meaning of true love is, they can't see the one most valuable lesson of life. Sadly for them, they might find a dreadful surprise waiting for them in eternity for having so much unnecessary hatred in their hearts. Love goes way beyond the human form, and living as flesh and bone is just a stepping stone to educate us for what's in store for the souls we keep. These are my thoughts, and I'm sticking with them. Love is love. Let it be.

I have a difficult time understanding the animosity many people have toward something they can't find ease with. I'm not able to explain why I'm attracted to men, or why I don't find any female sexually appealing. I just know deep in my heart and my mind, it's the way I'd been born and there's no changing the way I'm supposed to be living. I like men. Find them attractive, and that's all there is to it. Period.

Mine and Deklan's happily ever after had begun on that mysterious night, and once the piece I needed to make me a complete person was introduced before midnight, I couldn't have been happier the man my soul was connected to was Deklan Royal, The Prince of Almond Manor. Even though that evening was Deklan's birthday, it had been me who received the true gift. He'd given me him.

In my mind, I believe I'd been put on that plantation long ago for this very reason—as a child, to grow into my life and meet my one true soul mate. If not then, I would have been led there sooner or later to find him. I also accepted as the truth that Deklan had been put there as well by our higher power. Our ultimate connection had been set afoot well before either of us realized it.

I'll never forget that enchanted night as long as I live and I don't think Deklan will either.

Chadwick still seems to enjoy taking Deklan and me everywhere we need to go when it's a place off of the Manor's property, including trips to our most memorable spot—that perfect pear tree secluded in the middle of an overgrown field of tall grass and cloves. We still continue to share our admiration for each other from time to time under that tree. In a crazy way, I believe our unguided sexual releases that spilled across the ground might have helped that tree grow so fruitful. It has become the most lavish one in the pasture, producing luscious fruit every blossoming season. We had both noticed the change since we'd ejaculated under it so frequently. It seems as though it's one of the best trees there, and hadn't produced a single bad pear yet. I swear. The fruit juices sooth my throat as much as Deklan's semen does, rather tastes like him too. I swear, again.

There was a day under that pear tree I won't ever forget. That time as we sat in the nude tenderly kissing, something had gotten into Deklan. He'd become carefree and expressive in a manner that indicated he'd gone a little bit uninhabited. He spun on his knees and pulled his butt crack open with a clawed hand, presenting his asshole to me in a way I hadn't seen him do before. There was an eagerness that seemed he wanted me to plunge more than just my dick into him. Undoubtedly, I was enjoying the view as my thoughts ran wild, imagining what I was going to do with his tight hole and those low hanging nuts that banged against his inner thighs when he shifted.

It was a delightful shock to my system when he spread himself open like that in broad daylight, however, I wasn't objecting his action and it made me want him more.

"I need you to use me, Oakland. Any way you'd like," he'd sort of given an order, passing on a look in his eyes that was deviant, made me think he was up for anything no good, even if I'd done something surprisingly unusual.

I wasn't sure what he was really up to. I could have asked, but I felt like surprising him as much as he had caught me off guard with his open butt crack in my face.

I reached out and put a hand to his deeply dimpled butt cheek and caressed it, pushing it apart from the other so I could see his starry knot in the center. His hairy bum felt as it always had, yet that time seemed brand new. He lowered his chest to the ground as if he was submitting to me, giving me the power to do whatever I wanted with him. Take his body. Use it to join his soul all over again. Any way I wanted.

Hesitating hadn't entered my thoughts, so I advanced with what he might have been looking for. My heart beat faster and if my flesh weren't so dark, he'd have seen the blush of red rushing to my anxious face.

He pulled a bit harder at his butt cheek, spreading himself open a little bit more. Understanding he wanted me to explore, I went for his manhole faster than a hummingbird flits to a hibiscus flower dripping sweet sugary nectar.

I dragged my fingers across his ass, rubbing my palm along the inside of his crack, massaging the globes of his butt, parting his cheeks and exposing the hole hidden there. I played, enjoying the softness of his sphincter combined with the coarseness of the dark hair surrounding it. He was all man and I liked it. The feeling was masculine and all I wanted to do was go to town on that ass. Fingers, dick and tongue. Whatever. I just wanted in.

Since he'd already had the pleasure of feeling my entire dick crammed inside him, a snap idea had come to me — something I'd never done before and one that just might blow Deklan's mind to bits. I wanted to give him a new experience as well as to myself, show I'd do anything to please him, and see if I could work him into such a sexual frenzy, he'd ejaculate without a single stroke to his cock.

He followed my direction by getting on his feet and leaning into the tree as if he were hugging it. He looked at me over his shoulder with smiling eyes and asked, "What am I in for?"

I moved in behind him, spread his crack open again and pressed my thumb against his starry knot, working through that gorgeous course hair I liked so much, but abstained from entering him. He pushed back. I resisted, still.

He whined a little bit, "Oh, Gawd. Use my hole. What's the hold up?"

It was clear what he wanted, but I continued teasing him with massaging hands—no penetration of fingers or dick. The foreplay was keeping him hard as well as arousing me.

He was shaking as he cried out again, "Omigawd. Don't leave me empty like this. Put something in my hole. Go after that hot spot you helped me discover. Please, use me." His dick was dripping semen—a clear thin rope dithered in the breeze.

I decided the time had come to give it to him. I dropped to my knees and pushed my face between his butt cheeks, digging my tongue into his asshole like I was going for the nectar in the center of that hibiscus flower. The lavender and spice tang tickled my taste buds, and it surprised me I was enjoying it so much. I heard him moaning as he pushed his ass against my face. My tongue naturally burrowed in and out of him and the sexual act was turning my own dick hard as wood. I kept going, even though my jaw had begun to ache.

I eventually snaked my tongue from his slickened sphincter and flicked it down along the hairy trail to his large nuts that hung low like two ripe peaches, quite responsive by the assault of my lapping tongue. I sucked one in and tried like mad to take in both.

"Jeez, Oakland. That feels amazing." Deklan squirmed, legs spreading wider, his hands flat against the tree trunk in front of him. His ass out, back arched perfectly so I could easily access everything, especially his spit lubed pucker.

At the same time I twisted my shoulders through his open legs, licking my way up his nut sac to his hard mushroom headed dick, I jammed a few fingers into his butthole, sinking in to the last knuckle. He thrust his ass back down onto my hand, expelling growls and moans that sounded like total pleasure. He seemed eager for more, as if he wanted my entire fist inside his rectum. Unhesitant, I'd given it to him, plunging my fingers in and out with twisting momentum, stretching his chute, keeping the rhythm going until he was good and ready to take eleven inches of my throbbing cock inside that gorgeous sex-hole. After a few minutes of minimal ass play, I had jammed four fingers inside him, practically opening him up with my entire hand. I pumped my fist, kneading his pulsing hot spot with four hooked fingers.

The concentrated jolt seemed to have caused his entire body to tremble as well as push pre-ejaculate out the end of his dick. I immediately dove in and sucked on the bulbous head, impatient to extract the dripping semen from his heavy nuts. There was no chance I'd let his tasty essence go to waste on the surfs of the headwinds.

The harder I sucked, the louder Deklan groaned. He dragged his words, "O-oh, Gaw-aawd. Doe-oen't stop. Jeeeez." He quaked as if he was about to collapse—his heavy nuts swung and struck my chin. Was his sperm about to coat my throat? I hoped, because I wanted it. But—

Before he ejaculated, I spit out his cock and rotated to my feet behind him. Without delay, I rammed my erection straight into his tongue lubed chute, deep dicking him to the point of pushing my nuts in, too. I felt his asshole squeeze my black meat, the sensation of sucking it overwhelming, making my erection expand to its maximum dimensions. Thicker as well as longer. He consumed me like a master bottom man would, taking it all without flinching.

As I cock hammered like I was busting stone with my dick, I reached under and clutched his nipples, pinching and tugging the same way I liked done to me, hoping to send orgasmic flashes to his rock hard cock.

It seemed to have worked.

I could feel his asshole clamping down on me, enthusiastically sucking my erection like a fish was taking in water. His entire body quivered so intensely that his internal pulsations charged clear to my bones, all while his powerful rectal suction worked my dick until it felt as though my black swinging nuts were being yanked through my body and into his. I was stuck to him, no way of pulling out. His body seemed determined to hang on, as if breeding was the goal and there was no chance of backing out until the seeds had been sowed.

The longer I nailed him, the more I wanted to flood his hole.

Instinctively, I spanked him, sounding bossy when I told him to get down on his hands and knees. I hadn't cared, and neither had he since he dropped like a heavy rock to all fours within an instant. Jeez, my man was ready for more.

Back into position behind him, I spanked his muscled rear end again as I rammed my dick back into his snug hole, each time I smacked him, the grip around my cock had tightened beyond tight. It was so good. So intense. A glorious sensation as I tried pulling out and pushing back in. I was so close to ejaculating. My pelvis buzzed, and the sparks of my rising orgasm shot circles around my asshole, damn near catching the course hair surrounding it on fire. I ripped my dick out of him, smeared pre-ejaculate around his sex-hole and quickly shoved my black rod back in. I was so aroused at that point, I resorted to shaking. If there had been a blasphemous word I could have shouted that expressed how incredible I felt, I would have verbally ground it into Deklan's ears.

He cried out, "Shoot me with your love. I gotta have it."

That whimpering order had done me in. The thought of filling his rectal chute had set my sperm to full speed ahead. My entire crotch stung and my cock thickened.

That's when I cried out, "Oh, Gawd. Here it comes." I squeezed my butt, deep dimples formed in my ass cheeks, forcing my pelvis forward — my flat pubic zone pressed so tightly against his ass, we appeared conjoined. If it weren't for the color separation of our skin tones, it would have looked as though we were. I hollered again, "Ohmigawd. It's coming."

Mind boggled, I'd fallen against his back and grunted. My spine bowed, pushing my stiff dick even deeper. I felt the rush of semen, the spreading sparks strangling my asshole. My cock expanded and contracted as I ejaculated into his slick sex-hole. I jerked, heaved, and spurted — emptying load after load after load into his butt like he wanted. Like I wanted.

I viciously yelled, "Sweet ass cock sucker, take my sperm." I had gone wild. Misplaced my mind. Lost control of every bodily function except for the crotch muscle pumping sperm into my boyfriend's ass end. I couldn't hold back my surging semen or any of the words I blurted out. He had me so sexually aroused. His beautiful body. His cries of pleasure. The ass grip he had on my dick. All of it combined had pushed me over the edge.

I was hardly finished, but his turn had come. I could feel the tension in his asshole gripping hold of me. The pulse inside him pushing and pulling, stroking my cock. As I skewered him from behind, he thrust backward onto my dick, hollering for me to dig deeper, thrashing erratically as if his body was about to implode. I had him bursting apart as I continued power spitting one load after another inside him, feeling like I'd never be done.

As if my seed had shot right through him, he pumped several spurts of semen clear beyond his chest, hitting the pear tree trunk in front of us. Thick gobs oozed lazily down the bark like the tree was expelling sap. His head flipped back so sharply, I'd sworn he nearly snapped his neck. As Deklan ejaculated, his rear end continually slammed into my hips, pulling my hard cock into his spasmodic sex-hole in a starving manner. He trembled, shook, and gasped—using my stiff dick until he was done. His grizzly roars turned to heavy breathing, then wheezing whimpers that changed to quieter puffs. He appeared ass whipped. Unable to hold himself up.

Once our twitching bodies settled down, we dropped to the ground in a body locked lump—kissing again, caressing, and expressing tender love as if the rebellious encounter hadn't just taken place.

I was physically worn—exhausted beyond comprehension. My topping abilities exceeded my potential since I was used to being the one lying on my back with Deklan on top of me. One thing I knew for sure, my penetrating skills had pleased Deklan beyond what he might have expected. His enthusiastic reaction indicated that. All his spilled semen had proven it, too.

It turned out Deklan was one exceptional bottom man that day, seemed to love taking my dick and everything else I stuffed up his ass. He probably hadn't realized how enjoyable a wet tongue and a hard dick could feel going in the butt, one right after the other.

Before I pulled my erection out of him, I heard him say, "That was the most incredible sensation I'd ever felt."

My reply to that was, "I aim to please. You really liked all of it, didn't you?"

"For starters, the surprise tongue invasion was sensational, and of course when your dick went in, that there sent me right into space, as it had done before, but this time it felt amazingly different switching from a tongue to a huge dick. Where on earth had you come up with kissing my asshole?"

I laughed out loud at his astonished expression. "It just came to me on the fly, figuring a wet tongue might have been better than a big dry dick."

"Meh, I'll have to argue that. I like that big black dick of yours. Wet or dry."

I glanced at him, having a chuckle. "Ya wanna know a secret?"

Deklan looked intently at me. "Sure. Shoot."

"I might have enjoyed doing that as much as you seemed to like having it done. Did you?"

Deklan had a huge smile on his face when he admitted, "I loved every bit of it. I can't even explain how fabulous that was. When I do it to you, you'll understand what I mean."

That sounded like a conversation we'd had the first time Deklan put his erect dick in me, but it had been *me* telling him how great *he'd* felt. I lifted my head with a surprised appearance on my face, eager to get ass-tongued by Deklan, but first commented on his choice of word, "Fabulous? Never heard that from the mouth of a man before. I'm going to use that. Hope it sticks. And, I'm gonna hold you to that ass kissing. Since I love your dick so much, I'm certain I'm gonna like your tongue."

"You can count on it. I want to see how you react." He kissed me, and we both dropped to our backs, looking up at the sky.

After a short pause, Deklan casually mentioned, "You know, there was something you growled when you were about to ejaculate, and I think a play on words with what you said would add a little bit of orogeny when we put our dicks into each other. We should make it a permanent part of our lascivious sexual behavior."

"Growled?" I chuckled. "What did I Growl? I wasn't exactly paying attention to what I had come out of my mouth at that body crashing moment," I'd made known.

"Ha! Body crashing. I get that. When you were about to empty your sperm into me, you hollered, it's coming, and I thought you yelled, I'm coming. At first I thought it was off track since I'd never heard that before, but then thought the cutting outburst seemed to relate well if ejaculating more intensely. Plus it seemed to perfectly describe the warm musky semen that comes out of our ejaculating dicks. We can call it cum instead of semen. Hollering, Oh, Gawd, I'm gonna cum, or I'm cumming, is sexually grittier than saying, Oh, gawd, I'm ejaculating—don't you think? I like the sound of growling the phrase when reaching such an extreme moment where such valiant words are better at describing what's happening."

"It is more gut punching, for sure. The hard 'C' when grunting, Cumming, forces the abdomen to tighten, helping push the semen out. You might have something here."

"I think I do. Let's give it a try. Watch my face and body, then tell me if it expresses a more aggressive gunfire of semen charging into your butthole." Deklan climbed between my legs, looking Sooo... Damned... Good... positioned there—majestically propped and in control, spreading and pushing my knees to my chest that lifted my butt for penetration. I thought he was actually going to put himself inside me. God knows I was ready and willing. He grittily rumbled, "Oh, Yeah. Take my big dick. Oh, gawd. Oh, Gawd! I'm, I'm, I'm... cumming. Holy hairy COCKS, I'm CUMMING!"

Did he? Had I just been bred by that stunning man?

Hearing him robustly hollering like that, I found his performance accurately convincing, which added much more thrill to the sexual act. "Oh, damn. You were right, a huge improvement. Everything about that had gotten me hard as stone. Definitely sounds better than... Oh, dear, I'm, I'm... ejaculating." I laughed at how weakly homeopathic my version sounded and that stout announcement had given me the idea to pair it with a new word for having sexual intercourse. It didn't seem right to use something so medicinal when there was such an impulse to just cram his dick in my ass. It needed to say something more stout, so I mentioned, "That raises good reason to come up with a word for the extreme urge to put our dicks into each other— should be something more butt hammering—a gunshot-strong word with shocking gusto. Something like, Pow, Bang, Chock,

Puck, Huck, or oooo, how about FUCK. That has a bold, profane, and nasty punch to it. Fires off the fact. Point blank."

"Now, you might have something gut punching here. I like, Fuck. It feels sexually dirty and even sounds like what it means. Hear me out—I'm gonna FUCK you so hard it's gonna make you CUM harder. Oooo, that's good. Savagely dirty. I could actually fuck you right now." Deklan seemed determined to endorse the word was perfectly selected.

"My fuck hole is all yours." I liked that. "Even saying it to describe your point of entry has a banging ring to it."

"Multi useful. FUCK!" Deklan yelled.

"FUCK!" so had I.

Deklan confessed, "That dirty word makes me hard. You?"

"Yep. Stiff as wood right now. Maybe you should get off me before you accidentally fuck my hole and really make me cum." I laughed.

Saying it as a disapproving expression, Deklan groaned, "Fuck." He kissed my mouth and rolled off me, landing on his back at my side.

As for the lakeside property, Deklan and I have been slowly clearing a place for our new home. Chadwick has been a big help when it came to sowing the field and lugging the heavy timber and stone. His intelligence is quite elevated for a horse, making me wonder if The Mirror Man found a place within him too, just so he could keep an eye on both of us. He was a spiritual fairy after all. That man popped into my thoughts from time to time, leaving me wondering what had happened to him. Maybe someday he'll reappear in a recognizable form, and speak so I know it's him.

Regarding the progression of our home on the lake, it has been taking some time, but slowly and surely we are getting closer to finishing its construction.

My dream house with Deklan is going to be a cozy home, with a porch we can enjoy with a dog and a cat, while overlooking the lake out in front of us. The stacked stone fireplace on the inside will be a nice perk for when those cold winter nights crept up on us and cuddling with my handsome man would require a little bit more heat.

Deklan's father has plans to hand over the plantation to him and me, for which someday we would own and manage the almond growing business. He mentioned two strong men would be better than one, but truthfully, the two of us would prefer to make a home of our own. Until that bequeathing day comes, we are proceeding to build the house of our dreams on that secret lake while living together in the upper wing at the Manor.

We'd become so close, it's rare we are ever apart. I love that I'm next to Deklan more than I am away from him. There's so much enjoyment living with him, sharing my body with him, kissing him, and holding him every day and every night. As far as we're both concerned, we are the perfect match, fit together like the wind and sky.

Times seem to be changing, but unfortunately not fast enough. We still have to kiss and hug when nobody's looking. That part of our affair is quite trying and I find it strange that people see us as doing something immoral. Other people's thoughts pertaining to same gender affection isn't going to stop me from loving Deklan. He belongs to me and I'll do whatever it takes to keep him by my side.

I'd love to marry that man, my soul mate, the love of my life, my friend—let the world see how much I love him, but society and the written constitution won't allow me to take a husband. From what I could tell, if that would ever happen, neither I nor Deklan would see the day. It seems too far out there. I suppose since slavery had been abolished, perhaps equal gender love would too.

Giving in to what the world dictates, we lay low and keep to ourselves, however, secretly considering the two of us married, calling each other husband, and letting the outside world go their own way. If our love and affection troubles them, then the problem should be theirs, not ours.

Deklan and I can't keep our hands off each other, or hold ourselves back from sexual activity that involves penetration and semen exchanges. It's an addiction we both can't quit, and if I couldn't have Deklan, I'd curl up and die. I need him that badly. All the time. There is no denying that.

My pulse always speeds up whenever Deklan is near me. It's an uncontrollable reaction. I love him so much that whenever he is out of my sight, my heart hurts and the ring on my finger actually buzzes. That proves to me the magic of our undeniable love is alive and real—no matter if most of the world seems to believe it is wrong.

WE WERE BORN THIS WAY. Meant to love. Plain and simple. And I'll never, ever, ever, understand why much of the human race can't understand that.

Deklan is mine. I am his. And we are going to live happily ever after.

Forever and beyond.

THANK YOU

Thank you for reading THE PRINCE OF ALMOND MANOR. If you enjoyed Deklan and Oakland's story, please consider leaving a review. They help immensely at getting the story out to more people.

Be the first to know about upcoming releases and special events when you subscribe to my webpage at:
gregoryjonathanscott.com

Also, be sure to connect with me on Instagram, Twitter, and Facebook.

ABOUT THE AUTHOR

Gregory Jonathan Scott was raised in the small town of Belmont, Michigan, survived the city of Grand Rapids, before relocating to South Florida with his longtime companion, Scott.

Growing up with a creative imagination and the artistic ability to sculpt and color another world was what prompted his goals to be a writer, which ignited the desire to captivate readers with short columns in magazines pertaining to art and leisure. From there, it continued. Finding the joy of writing, along with an artistic hand, had given Gregory Jonathan Scott the inspiration to design and write M/M romance & erotic Novels.

Gregory Jonathan Scott is currently enjoying air conditioned living with Scott and their pets in a scorching village off the coast of South Florida.

OTHER WORK BY
Gregory Jonathan Scott

TAKE TO THE SKY TRILOGY
INTO THE HEADWINDS – 2ND BOOK
TAKE TO THE SKY – 1ST BOOK

STAND ALONES
SHAKEDOWN
INTENSE ATTRACTION
ENCOURAGED BY SPARKS
CRASHING INTO LOVE
THE PRINCE OF ALMOND MANOR
(PREVIOUS VERSION; THE PLANTATION AFFAIR)
HEARTBREAK BEAT